THE SHIP'S CARPENTER

THE SHIP'S CARPENTER

'TWEEN SEA AND SHORE SERIES

BOOK I

D. E. Stockman

PENMORE

www.penmorepress.com

The Ship's Carpenter
By David E. Stockman
Copyright © 2021, 2025 David E. Stockman

ISBN-13: 978-1-957851-88-4(Paperback)
ISBN-13:978-1-957851-87-7(e-book)

BISAC Subject Headings:
FIC014000FICTION / Historical
FIC032000FICTION / War & Military
FIC047000FICTION / Sea Stories

Editor: Chris Wozney
Front Cover and Back Cover Illustration by
EMILIJA RAKIĆ

First edition published 2021 by Fireship Press, Tucson, AZ
Second edition published 2025 by Penmore Press, Tucson, A

Address all correspondence to:
Penmore Press LLC
920 N Javelina Pl
Tucson AZ 85748

Visit our website at: www.penmorepress.com
Visit the author's website at: www.stockmanbooks.com

DEDICATION

For my precious ladies—Valerie, Lorien, and Krista.

*"It is going down into the abyss that
we recover the treasures of life.
Where you stumble, there lies the treasure."*
—Joseph Campbell

ACKNOWLEDGMENTS

Books are written with the encouragement and help of family, friends, and publishing professionals. To all of them, I extend my deepest gratitude. I especially must acknowledge my indebtedness to my consulting editor, Sue Schumer, whose kind words over dinners, advice, and superb editing skills on my manuscript brought this work to fruition.

—D.E.S.

A Note to the Reader

This is the first of the *Tween Sea & Shore Series* of historical nautical novels that follow the lives of fictional and historical characters in the mid-1700s. French pronunciation, a main character list, and nautical term definitions are included in the List of Terms and Glossary at the end of the book to help facilitate the reader.

Many of the characters mentioned in this book can also be found in Book 2: *Captains of the Renown,* and Book 3: *On Waves of Glory.*

CHAPTER ONE

The Feast

By mid-1742, the war between Great Britain and Spain waned. As warship production slowed, so did the chances Abraham, a shipwright, might find permanent work. The Royal Naval Dockyard in Woolwich had terminated his employment after he crushed his hand. Now healed, he had neither steady pay nor the certificate to protect him from impressment—an increasing risk to replace whose sailors who deserted or died. Settling for any carpentry jobs to survive, he often scoured London's dockyards for repairs.

In his small room, after a day without finding work, he mulled over the problem. Somewhere from his jumbled memories of childhood, his mother's adage echoed, *"Deux ancres sont bons au navire,"* or "Two anchors are better for a ship." It reminded him he had an option since France was at war with Austria. If he crossed the Channel, he might find work at French shipyards where jobs were plentiful. The next day, he left for Brest.

THE SHIP'S CARPENTER

On a slate-clouded morning, Abraham rushed along Brest's rain-puddled docks. The harbor resonated with the sounds of commerce as workers bustled at their trades in a chain of workshops, offices, slips, and warehouses along the banks of the Penfeld River. Near the citadel, warships crowded the docks, their sails and spars hiding the sky. The leather bag hanging from Abraham's shoulder carried documents to prove his abilities. Even so, the scarred left hand shoved in a coat pocket handicapped his chances of gaining a position at the navy shipyard.

Abraham entered the three-storied building and an attendant showed him into an office with four busy bookkeepers at desks.

"If you please, monsieur." The farthest clerk motioned with a raised arm, his attention on his inky paperwork.

"Good day, my name is Abraham Robinson." Tension strained his voice. "I have just arrived from England seeking shipbuilding work."

"You've come at the right time. I am Mael, the carpenter procurement officer. Sit here. Tell me about your shipwright experience." He gestured for Abraham to take a chair.

"It's been over a year since my last job at the naval yard at Woolwich," Abraham admitted. "Posts became scarce when the fighting stopped. As a guild journeyman, I did framing and joinery. I've constructed and repaired various ratings, everything from sloops-of-war to ships of the line."

"Excellent...a naval shipyard? We need skilled shipbuilders, particularly if they've worked on rated ships. Carpenters turn up here from everywhere but few built large warships. If you qualify, a master will decide whether to engage you. Your French, however, is superb for an Englishman. That and your guild membership will help sway the master shipwright."

Abraham's mother had taught him French. To marry his father, she had moved to Britain from Paris. In a way, he was honoring her by returning to her native land and its customs. Still, he hesitated for a moment at what he had to divulge next.

"That's encouraging, but I must admit one slight nuisance before we go further. I lost my previous position after injuring my hand. Although it's healed, my fingers are not as dexterous." Perspiration had gathered inside his collar and panic grew as he revealed the disfigurement.

"My, how unfortunate." The lumpy red flesh and twisted fingers took the clerk off-guard. Two tips were missing and ended in stubs. "Can you use those?" Mael asked, tipping his head in doubt.

"They're fine for gripping and holding wood and tools, yet not as nimble as my right ones."

"Your grip may improve after a while. But I don't think you'd be suitable for framing work. The master shipwright will see there's not enough strength." He stared out the window in thought, frowning.

"Yes, I understand." Abraham's expression melted. "Thank you for letting..."

"Just a moment." Mael sat straight in his chair. With so many shortages of reliable workers, he might fill a hole with this impaired one. "There is another opening which doesn't demand the same heavy lifting and grasping. Do you carve well?"

"Carving wasn't part of my training, I must be honest." Abraham didn't want to waste anyone's time.

"There's a shop needing a joiner to attach ornaments and carvings. However, I believe you could manage such without much sculpting background."

Although Abraham often saw the carvers work, he'd never possessed artistic skills. "Yes, I suppose so."

"Then I'll introduce you to the master carver, Caffieri." Mael reached back to a peg on the wall, put on his coat and hat, and led Abraham to a large carpentry workshop two blocks away. It was an old structure, a huge brick cavern with heavy beams and cranes, just as in Woolwich, except Abraham heard the repetitive tapping of mallets on chisels and the whirring of a lathe, not the hammer's loud crack or a saw's raspy grunt.

While building hulls required strict procedures and geometric precision, everything was undisciplined in decorative carving—curves and flowing shapes guided by only instinct and a rough drawing. When repairing battle-worn vessels, Abraham had always left the fancy work to those with the talents for it.

A short man strode toward them. "Mael, good morning, what brings you here?" The master sculptor had a heavy Breton accent.

"Charles-Philippe, I've brought someone to meet you. A skilled Englishman who constructed warships. You mentioned a need for a joiner. This is Abraham Robinson."

Abraham stepped forward and bowed, saying in French, "The honor is mine, monsieur."

"So, you've come for a position in Brest." Caffieri spoke in English, assuming Abraham likely knew little French. "Many of our yardmen are foreigners these days but few have warship experience."

Abraham replied in French to prove his ability, and explained his qualifications, then lifted the flap of his leather bag to present his certificates.

"We need a sculptural joiner. You're a carver?" Caffieri asked, ignoring the documents.

Abraham hesitated.

"Charles-Philippe, he is inexperienced in carving," Mael interjected. "Regardless, he makes up for that with excellent skills and a deep commitment. His abilities will complement your crews. He has overcome hardships coming to France. Show him your hand."

Surprised, Abraham offered it, expecting a look of disgust.

Without hesitation, Caffieri placed it in his own. "Squeeze hard," he ordered.

Abraham had performed the same test in earlier interviews; just after the accident, his fingers had gripped too weakly to force a pip from a lemon. He squeezed now as much as his mangled, weakened muscles allowed.

"Strength of a boy." Caffieri added, "That's enough for the task, though. But now show us your English-style mastery."

Abraham followed him to a sea-worn carved panel with an acanthus leaf design. Caffieri grabbed four treenails and pounded the round stakes into the old openings. "Let's see what you can do without messing up the carving." He and Mael left to discuss schedules.

Abraham took care, sawed away the ends, and chiseled the stumps so they blended in with the decoration. The results made him rethink his artistic doubts. After he finished, Caffieri returned and inspected the panel.

"We shall make a French sculptor out of you someday," Caffieri said and smiled. "Bring your tools tomorrow to start work at daybreak."

Abraham's spirit soared as Caffieri explained the salary and hours. The pay was less than in Woolwich yet it was adequate, and there were more holidays for local saints.

"Watch Anton the rest of the day. He'll show you what we do and how we do it."

Over the next few weeks, Abraham joined completed work to hulls and sanded panels for the carvers. The others didn't mind that he was English, and most welcomed him to their cadre. One late fall day, Caffieri relieved him of his usual tasks. "Abraham, go with Anton and take the finished decor over to Recouvrance. Help him attach it to *le Royal Louis.*"

The first-rate ships of the line, armed with three-and-a-half decks of 124 guns, dwarfed the ships he'd worked on in England. As they approached, Anton looked up in pride at the craft. "She'll launch as the largest French warship afloat, ruling the Atlantic. The navy has never built a vessel as expensive and with such advanced features."

"What a glorious monster. Such power and beauty." Abraham was overwhelmed by the size and dominance—it was a giant wooden Poseidon in all his glory and brawn.

For three days, he and Anton took the carved sections across the Penfeld to the slip. They rigged them for hoisting and attached them to the hull. On the last day, a caulker showed them the immense hold, cabins, and gun decks. Nothing at sea compared to her: she was a waterborne fortress and a gallery of exquisite craftsmanship nearly finished.

Yet a few weeks later, all of Brest woke to the blare of ringing bells, alarming shouts, and blowing horns. Hordes ran to the streets overlooking the river. A glow lit up the sky and surrounding hills as an orange and red conflagration engulfed a two-decker that had anchored for repairs, as well as *le Royal Louis*. Hundreds of men passed water buckets while others doused cinders drifting onto the dry timber stacks. Fire pumps squirted thin streams into the inferno.

A joiners shop blazed; a warehouse and other smaller sheds collapsed. The flames grew more intense with each passing minute and at last, the searing heat forced the rescuers to withdraw. After six hours the great *le Royal Louis* sank into a sea of burning timbers. Nothing could prevent the greatest warship France had ever created from becoming a morale-shattering disaster. Her destruction had wasted thousands of trees and spars from far-off Scandinavia and Prussia. The undertaking had lasted years; wood had been dried, shaped, and wedded into place, then diminished to ash in a single night. Everyone dwelt on the catastrophe. "How did it start?" "Was it set?" Rumors of English spies, Protestant arsonists, and worker carelessness circulated for days. After rejecting every lead, navy officials uncovered only suspicions and turned to searching for scapegoats. They declared the fire was sabotage and more investigations were to follow.

* * *

Just before Christmas, Anton approached him. Abraham liked the cheerful man: he was thirty years older and a fourth-generation shipwright.

"Where are you eating the Noël feast?"

"With the other tenants, I suppose." Abraham's usual sunny tone hid his loneliness. He had moved into a cheap room at a boardinghouse soon after beginning work; occasional card games in its parlor became the sole distraction of his cheerless social life.

"No," Anton insisted, "you must be with friends to celebrate the holy day."

"Holidays don't bother me. I've made a few friends where I live." In truth, it was just one old, Dutch salesman.

"Because of the grandchildren, we'll be having our feast on Christmas Day. You must come! Besides, I've already told my wife and daughter you'll be coming." Anton smiled slyly. "So it's arranged and we'll expect you at one o'clock."

Abraham accepted the forced invitation despite its ulterior motive, a suitor for Yvette, Anton's unmarried, twenty-one-year-old daughter. The next day after work, he rushed to a goods shop and purchased gifts for his hosts: two inexpensive ox-horn combs for the ladies and a bottle of monks' beer for Anton.

On Christmas Day, he found Anton's place amidst clustered stone houses. Anton welcomed him. Festive green wreaths and garland hung from ceiling beams. His eyes caught sight of a large red bow above the fireplace and a nativity scene on a table near the door. Cooked meat and spicy foods added a savory aroma to the home.

Dishes clattered in the kitchen and Anton called, "Louise, Abraham's arrived!"

"I'm coming!" Anton's wife popped into the room. Bright gray-blue eyes on a round, wide face topped her heavy pear-shaped body. Around her neck, an ivory crucifix on a thin gold chain bounced upon her bosoms, giving Jesus a bumpy ride.

"Here's a small offering of appreciation for inviting me." Abraham grinned, handing Anton the bottle and offering Louise the wrapped comb.

"Sit here by the warm fireplace." Anton uncorked the beer as he fetched mugs. "You'd better have a taste too, or Louise won't let me have any."

"Tsk—sacred wine at holy mass and mortal beer at the holy feast." She laughed and toddled back to the kitchen and her boiling pots.

As he settled into a cushioned chair near the fireplace, Abraham noticed an engraving of a port scene on a wall. He rose and examined it. "This is unexpected." It was old and yellowed from tobacco pipe smoke and uncountable winter fires.

"Oh, that." Anton handed him a mug. "I bought it because I thought it was Brest. But the buildings aren't right. Maybe it's La Rochelle or someplace."

"No, this port is in England. It's Woolwich, where I apprenticed and worked. Here's where I stayed, behind this building, and I kept my tools in that one. There's the slipway where I injured my hand." The image jogged loose a flood of memories. It surprised Abraham that a picture of the shipyard had found its way to France, especially to a house in which he, a former resident of Woolwich, would find it.

"How interesting," said Anton. "The print disappointed me when I realized it wasn't Brest. I should have known since the château isn't visible and the hills are lower."

Anton watched Abraham inspect each building and spire. Happy to see the engraving meant more to Abraham than anyone else, he took it off the wall. "Take it to remind you of home. And if you bring me another bottle next year, I'll find another picture for you. Beer is my delight, and Yvette's, too.

She's still up in her room fixing herself...and fixing...and fixing. My son André's family should come soon, too." He sat and poured beer into their mugs. "Here, let us toast the day."

"To a happy Christmas." The beer had more carbonation than most. "Quite bubbly."

"I'll pour a mug for Yvette. She'll enjoy it."

Just as Anton spoke the words, footsteps tapped their way down the stairs.

"Abraham, my daughter, Yvette." Anton hoped Abraham had attended Christmas Mass. Yvette resembled Saint Agnes in devotion, and religious commitment was a prerequisite for courting her.

She was short like Anton and had his slim build. Her eyes were a sparkling light blue and hooded. Her dark brown hair matched Abraham's, and she wore it pulled back into a simple bun. Yvette curtsied and moved to the remaining chair near them.

Abraham handed her the last present. "Joyous Christmas to you, Yvette. Thank you for allowing me to join you."

"How kind." Yvette smiled; she was alluring. "I've been looking forward to meeting you. Father has told me good things about you and how well you know your craft."

"And he has solved a mystery: the nameless port is Woolwich in England. He is from there." Anton pointed to the engraving now sitting upright on the mantle.

"Aha! You've put to rest a family puzzlement. Father felt guilty for buying that picture for years."

She smiled, the remarkable coincidence not going unnoticed. A sign to prove heaven works in strange ways, she reflected. As her father left to check on her mother's progress in the kitchen,

Yvette said to Abraham, "André should be here soon. He's coming from Recouvrance, across the river. As a pilot, he needs to be near the docks in the bay. He received his certificate three years ago and hasn't lost a ship yet." Yvette laughed, though she often worried and prayed for him. Now she needed to assess Abraham. "Do you think you'll stay in Brest or are you planning to return to Woolwich someday?"

"Prospects in English shipyards are few. I'm enjoying my duties and I'd live in Brest forever if things go well."

"Father says you're a good builder. I'm sure you'd stay if they promoted you," she said, probing his ambition.

Before Abraham could answer, a commotion announced André and his wife, Gaëlle, followed by their two children. Anton carried away cloaks, hats, and scarves as the youngsters ran to their grandmother.

"Fine. Everyone is here, so let's begin." Anton, now satisfied, clapped as Louise carried in a platter of meat. After a blessing, they started on the roast mutton glazed with honey and spices, then the puddings and pastries. Every course was tasty and generous.

It had been a fine feast; Abraham had missed them over the years. His self-made, skimpy meals at the boarding house tasted foul compared to this sumptuous banquet. "André," he said sociably, "your sister told me you received your pilot license a number of years ago. No doubt you've had frightening incidents."

"Ha! There's nothing but danger. The coast is treacherous here. To enter the Road of Brest takes luck as much as skill."

"I can name every part of a ship's hull and explain the design and use. To sail a ship, however, is another bird," Abraham admitted. Yvette, he noticed, had leaned closer to hear his answers. "I know nothing of winds and currents or sailing at sea."

"You must understand, then, that Brest lies at the mouth of the Penfeld River, which empties into the great bay, the Road of Brest, which is separated from the ocean by the Goulet strait." André arranged the plates and cups to form a makeshift map. He continued, describing the geographic specifics. "To cross the Goulet takes exact timing. Most ships anchor outside in Bertheaume or Camaret Bay and wait for the next tide to get through the Goulet to anchor at Brest."

"To arrive or leave, the wind must be favorable and blow constantly without changing direction. When you come to Brest, you take the prevailing southwesterly. To depart, you need a northern or eastern wind." André paused but, hearing no questions, added, "Most often I pilot from one of the outer bays through the narrows and up the Penfeld."

"My God, Brest has such precarious channels surrounding it." Abraham put his hand to his brow.

The mild oath drew Yvette's attention. She disapproved of profanity; it was the first flaw she found in Abraham.

"Well, the hazards are our protection." André again pointed to his map. "The tides are the key and enemy admirals can't risk part of their fleet at sea while the rest enter the bay. The tides and winds are our greatest defense from attack."

"And the fortifications around the city and along the coast protect Brest from land invasion," added Anton. "The old château will keep enemy ships out of the river even if they sail into the bay."

"God blessed us with unsafe passages to protect Brest," chimed in Louise.

"It appears to be invulnerable," Abraham replied.

"Indeed, for over a thousand years." Anton stood, rubbing his hands in anticipation. "Enough of the work talk. Let's have music and dance; I'll get my violin. Move the table for room."

Everyone cleared the dishes, and they carried the furniture to the side. Anton tuned his violin and played a simple folk tune.

"Father, play something so Abraham can join us," suggested Yvette. "Come, Abraham, dance with me. Are you familiar with the quadrille?"

"I tried it in Woolwich this summer. I hope I can remember how the steps go." He hesitated, and then confidently stepped to the melody.

As Anton fiddled, the group danced the quadrille, rigaudon, and a few contredanses, forming parallel lines that even included the children. As they chatted, Yvette sensed Abraham's openness and by evening's close, she uncovered only honest intentions. In addition, she found him attractive, despite his injured hand.

"If you wish, open your gifts now instead of waiting until New Year's," Abraham said. "Anton opened his the moment I gave it to him." He chuckled, raising a finger toward the half-empty beer bottle.

"Thank you, we will!" Louise left to fetch the gift.

Yvette nimbly untied the string, unfolded the paper, and smiled. "Abraham, it's darling. How delicate and attractive!"

The little ox-bone comb awoke memories of her deceased sister who had a similar comb. Yvette considered whether it was another sign.

An hour later, an epidemic of yawning convinced everyone that Christmas Day had ended. André and his family bade good night and left, the children too sleepy to walk. Anton and Louise cleaned up the house while Abraham and Yvette sat by the fire, trading childhood histories and memories.

"My, it's been years since I've had such a fine time. When I apprenticed, I hadn't time for the holidays," Abraham remarked.

"On Father's birthday, the house is so full one must stand!" Still flush with the evening's delights, Yvette was smiling and talking with her hands. "Papa so enjoys his birthday and will be fifty-six next month. I have some ideas for a present, though I'm not sure where I can get them."

Abraham was intrigued by Yvette's contrast, a coy bearing undercut by deep-centered conviction; it bordered on rebellion. So he gladly offered, "Perhaps I might help you decide what he needs since I see him every day." His heart pounded faster. "We can meet on Saint-Sylvestre Day. I get half the day off work."

"That's a marvelous idea."

"Monday at noon then? We could take a stroll to that café nearby for a dessert."

"That will be fine, Mother will chaperone."

"Well, I regret it is time to go." Abraham did not wish to overstay as the last guest. With a smile, Yvette fetched his hat and he bade the family goodbye.

All night, Abraham's thoughts centered around the merriment and warmth of Yvette.

"We enjoyed having you yesterday," Anton told him at work. "My daughter and wife appreciated your gifts, and you and André seemed to enjoy one another's company."

"He's interesting and loves his profession. Although I'd never work at sea. Beyond being dangerous, I get seasick with the first wave. Yvette highlighted the afternoon for me with her wonderful dancing. She is quite talented."

"The beer highlighted my afternoon." Anton beamed.

The next Monday on Saint-Sylvestre Day, Abraham finished work, rushed to his room to clean up, and hurried to Yvette's house. Yvette and her mother were standing in front of a neighbor's door talking.

Abraham bowed with a flourish. "Ladies, I am at your service."

At the café, they all ordered pudding and beverages and debated which present would be best for Anton. "He needs the tobacco pipe," Abraham said with finality. "The clay ones he uses break too easily. He must be buying a new one every month!" Abraham had noticed the parade of new pipes since starting work there. "And I shall find him a replacement for the etching of Woolwich he gave me."

"The pipe I want to give Papa is so expensive in the shops," Yvette sighed.

"Maybe we can find one elsewhere for less," Louise suggested. "There are cheaper deals at the stalls by the dock."

"Yes, and there are cutthroats, purse-snatchers, smugglers, and lots of police." Yvette threw her hands up to the sides of her head in mock fear. Then she smiled and added, "Although, if you're along, Abraham, we'll have a brave guard to protect us."

"Well, the stalls are still open. We can go now," Abraham suggested. He wasn't quite ready for their time together to end.

"I didn't bring enough money. But I can go home and meet you at two o'clock by Rue de Mer. We want no suspicion aroused and must keep it secret." Yvette put a finger to her lips. "Thank you, Abraham, I hadn't planned on solving my problem in one day." His heart lifted at her praise.

The ladies left homeward and Abraham, spellbound by Yvette, didn't detect the silhouette of a man watching from a shadowed doorway. He strolled the streets, resolved to find a print of Brest for Anton's birthday. For almost an hour, he asked in various shops without luck as he continued to Rue de Mer.

The crowd at the dock jostled one another while eyeing the wares. Abraham looked for Yvette and Louise in both directions among the little two- and four-wheeled handcarts. Vendors barked their wares, enticing shoppers with ridiculous banter under their canvas awnings. In less than fifteen minutes, he saw Yvette, alone.

"So, I see you made it without an escort! You're a brave woman." His brows lifted in surprise. "Your mother didn't come with you?"

"Mother noticed you leaning here and left to do errands. And besides, it's daytime in a public market." She wanted to be alone with Abraham and had slyly cajoled her mother to leave her.

"Then let us begin our grand tour of the stalls!" Abraham held his arm out for her, his pulse quickening.

She slid her arm onto his and they began. "Onward and remember—meerschaum pipes."

After an hour of walking and talking from handcart to handcart, they had covered most of the way, but not one pipe vendor or picture of Brest turned up amid the multitude of items. Yvette then spied a leather vendor with a new meerschaum pipe in his hand.

"Excuse me, sir, did you buy that here or from a tobacco shop?"

"Here at the market. If you're hunting for one, there's often a stall at the other end that sells them." The man pointed down the dock.

"Thank you, we'll try to find him." They retraced their steps and, when they approached the end, sighted the cart with smoking materials.

"I see you're admiring my pipes." The dark-skinned man had round, deep brown eyes reflecting a sunny glint.

"The meerschaum pipes. How much are they?" Yvette asked.

"That depends on the pipe, madam." The peddler reached for boxes to show her. "Still, I will not sell one to you. Madam might appear silly smoking it." The man grinned, laughed, and dug beneath his cart to retrieve more samples.

"Is that so? Might I look silly smoking your most expensive piece?" Yvette spread an enchanting smile and sorted through the pipes. She examined one and put it back, pretending frustration with the assortment. Most had a geometric-shaped bowl or were carved like the turbaned head of an Ottoman.

"My most expensive pipe will make anyone appear grand smoking it." The pipe vendor hunted for more, afraid she might leave.

"By grand do you mean large? I don't want to appear fat, monsieur," she teased.

"No, you're just right, neither lacking nor 'grand'."

"Well then, somewhere between. What do you have between lacking and grand? Show me one of those."

At last he brought out a handsome pipe with a black ebony stem. The white meerschaum stone formed the shape of a horse's head in fine detail. Yvette liked it at once, and the vendor began his outrageous pitch.

"For ten years Sultan Mahmud's private artisans sculpted this one in Constantinople's Topkapi Palace. The Grand Vizier's own galley carried it here guarded by fifty Ottoman Janissaries. It is beyond priceless and I should charge three times as much—but for you, my dear, only half an écu."

"Pish. Offer a better price even if the Sultan himself carved the little horsey pipe. I shall give you two livres and not a sou more."

"This exotic piece should be in a prince's palace. Never. My poor children would starve tonight." He stuck his nose in the air.

"Outrageous! Goodbye." Yvette turned away. Then she spun around with a more reasonable bid. "Two livres and ten deniers and we will part as friends."

"Very well...my friend." With a sigh of hopelessness, he tied a ribbon around the little wood box. Yvette fished the coins from her bag and paid him.

"Please, do not come to me anymore. I shall soon be a beggar if you do." He made a mock sad face, then chuckled and waved his hand.

"There! And done at a good price." Yvette put her arm around Abraham's.

"One stands little chance when you set your mind to something. I thought he wouldn't budge from his price. You've not only the looks to enthrall men but the wits, too," he said.

The pair walked to the end of the crowded market and continued along the quay. Even in cool weather, one could enjoy the walk along the ship-filled river with the great château catching the last rays of the low afternoon sun. Within the picturesque seascape, they both spotted the remaining blackened timbers of the burned *le Royal Louis*. The charred giant fingers poked out of mounds of gray ash, a ghoul reaching up from a nightmarish underworld. The grotesque reminder marred the perfect scene, and they left the river for pleasanter views.

On the climb, they stopped to explore the seascape and Abraham decided it was time to express his feelings. He put both hands on her waist, lowered his head, and kissed her ever-smiling lips. Yvette didn't protest and caressed his cheek. When Abraham moved to kiss again, she placed her fingertips on his lips. "Enough for now." He understood, hugged her, and held her hand as they moved up the street in silence. The sunlight was fading when they reached her house.

* * *

Though entranced by Yvette, Abraham had one concern: that her religious inclinations might bias her against him. Reared Anglican and raised with a Catholic mother, his young, science-oriented mind sought answers neither religion could satisfy, but Yvette's beliefs did not bother him.

At work the next day, he sought out Anton. "Anton," he greeted. "I just wanted to thank you for introducing me to Yvette. She is lovely, and I would appreciate your official blessing to court her."

Anton was amused at Abraham's formality. "Of course, Abraham. I wouldn't have introduced you if I didn't think you could make a good match." He paused, then added, "Though, a word of caution: Yvette has a habit of torturing her beaus. She is exacting, and quite picky."

Abraham only laughed. "That's one of the things I like about her. To be honest, though, my future holds somewhat of a risk. I don't know if I can commit to staying permanently in Brest."

"Good lord, Abraham! No one can predict what will happen even tomorrow. A risk? If you knew the rascals who sought to court Yvette. I found out one young ship's officer had a *placée* in the West Indies. Today people accept *plaçage,* but having a wife in one country and another somewhere else is not right. You're more than decent enough. Put your fears aside if you think I'm opposed to you courting my daughter."

"Well, my intentions are honorable ones, Anton."

"I'm familiar with you by now. You have my permission." His mind was still reliving Yvette's painful breakup with the officer. To Anton, Abraham was a saint in comparison.

A week later, Abraham arrived at Yvette's house after work for their customary stroll. Her companionship was now paramount to him.

"Abraham, on Christmas Day you mentioned you attended a service at Saint-Sulpice in Paris." Yvette probed now for insight into her most fundamental issue: religion. His answer would be the deciding factor whether she should continue their relationship.

"My mother had me baptized there. And later I attended mass with her. But since I don't consider myself a Catholic I never went to any others. My father and I worshipped in Anglican churches in England when he was still alive. When they died, regardless of whom I prayed to, I stopped going."

"Oh, I assumed you were Catholic since your mother was. Well, did you ever consider turning Catholic now that you live in France?" A cold shadow passed over her hopes.

Abraham knew it boiled down to two responses: either he'd lie and say he didn't mind becoming a Catholic, or he'd tell her the truth that religion didn't play a role in his life. The first would compromise his honesty and make her happy; the second, although the truth, might destroy their relationship.

He chose the practical lie. "Well, if I stay I'll become Catholic of course."

"That is well-reasoned if you intend to live here." Blinded by the illusions of love, she accepted his reply without question.

Once home again, her anxieties over his religious beliefs put to rest, she divulged to her mother the new revelation. "Abraham was an Anglican, but he won't mind converting to Catholicism."

"Oh, I see." Louise, stunned, continued to crochet; she felt she'd made a mistake. "Well, I hate to shake you from your reverie, my dear, but men lie to avoid problems, even Abraham. He's fine enough a gentleman but do you believe being a Catholic in name is being a Catholic in heart, such as you or I? Abraham's an Anglican, a Protestant. What does that mean if he switches to please you?"

Yvette stood horrified, having never detected doubt in her mother concerning Abraham before. Now she tossed out her hopes as if they were dirty soap water. "Mother," she hissed, "If you felt he isn't right for me, why didn't you say so instead of letting me go on seeing him?"

His conversion, she knew deep down, must be absolute or not at all. But now she doubted a spiritual change possible if he had not yet attended church after so much time in France. Abraham's fealty to religion might be no different than to a pair of stockings. She let out a slight, sad gasp.

"Now, now." Louise gently patted Yvette's hand. "Don't give in to melancholy. But I've seen how men change skins like snakes when they want a woman." Yvette bowed her head, accepting her mother's wisdom. Her heart ached from the realization she had been wrong about him.

Before light, Abraham rose and prepared for work. As he left, two uniformed policemen approached in the darkness.

"Monsieur Robinson, the commissioner-general of police has ordered you in to answer a few questions. Please come with us and cause no trouble."

"Why, of course." Abraham's jaw dropped.

"The inquiry won't take long," the officer promised and snatched the leather bag from his shoulder. With a man on each side grasping his arms, they led him to the prefect's stone-block station. Its door of thick wood planks had black iron braces and creaked harshly when opened.

Abraham was left in a cramped room smelling of sweat, where he sat before a small, dirty table set against a blood-splattered wall. A swarthy officer entered carrying a brown card cover of papers.

"My name is Pierre LaBrouche." The man stood over Abraham, thumbing the documents. "You're a foreigner, Monsieur Robinson." His thin hawk-like expression scowled. "English—ill winds blow from the northwest. It is best to be truthful and answer without hesitation. We will keep you here until we find you guiltless."

"Please, I don't understand what I've done! I'll tell you whatever you want to know."

"What is your intent in coming to Brest?"

"My job. I'm a shipwright."

"Yes, you work at the shipyard in the sculpture shop. My question was what your intent is here."

"I don't understand. My purpose is to work, nothing more."

"Of late, others have overheard you asking to buy maps of Brest. Tell me why you need maps of Brest."

"It was to be a gift to replace one given to me."

"So, you've been exchanging maps of ports."

"No! What I mean is I received a picture of Woolwich. So, I wanted to return the favor to Anton."

"Monsieur Façonneur, a colleague, supplied you with a plan of Woolwich. And you tried to supply him with one of Brest."

"No, a picture of Woolwich. Since I couldn't find a picture of the dockyards, I searched for a map of Brest." Abraham's mouth was going dry.

"A witness overhead you discussing a secret meeting near the docks and a money exchange. Mademoiselle Façonneur used words such as 'mission' and 'secret.' Others observed the two of you near the château, a military fortification. Just what mission, what secret, and who sent you? Your picture story is falling apart, monsieur!"

"Mission? There is no mission. No one exchanged money by the docks. Yvette and I take walks, often by the château. For God's sake, I'm a carpenter, not a spy!"

"Spy? I haven't accused you of being a spy. Strange you should use that term." He pulled out another paper. "You've worked on *le Royal Louis,* I see."

"Yes, I attached its carvings." Abraham suddenly realized the reason for the interrogation. "I didn't burn the ships!"

"We'll see, monsieur. Why did you and Mademoiselle Façonneur go to the dock stalls? Whom did you meet there?"

"Yvette wanted to purchase her father a gift. We met no one."

"After the holidays you are buying more gifts. Isn't this excuse running a little thin?"

"It was a gift for her father's birthday; a meerschaum pipe. If you doubt me, I can take you to the vendor."

"Of course, I'm sure he'd protect you. What is his name?"

"Name? The peddler has a cart with pipes and tobacco; he's a dark-skinned man and speaks with a foreign accent, maybe a Moor." Abraham was squirming.

"Where was your prior employment?"

"The English navy at the royal dockyard in Woolwich. Then I had an accident on my hand, and that ended my employment. Ship projects slowed, so I came to France."

"Why France? Why not Ireland, Scotland, or the colonies? Wouldn't you be more at home in English-speaking countries?" LaBrouche loomed over him.

"Is my French that poor? I've spoken it my entire life. My mother was French and I've been to France many times. I'm as at home here as I am in England."

"Where were you when *le Royal Louis* burned in December?"

"I saw it burn from a street above the Penfeld." Although a weak alibi, it was the best he could offer.

"Who can verify that? Should I take your word for it?"

"I was alone in the crowd," he admitted.

"That's what I expected you to say. Are you a friend of André Façonneur, a ship pilot? One familiar with ship movements and the Penfeld. It's convenient, isn't it? The pieces are coming together."

"André? We've spoken twice, once at Christmas and once on New Year's Day. Don't involve him in this!" Abraham's voice bounced off the walls.

At the sound of his shouting one of the other policemen entered the room and stood by the closed door.

"Involve him in what? To what involvements are you referring that you didn't tell me?"

"No, I mean this investigation. André and I had conversations on shipbuilding and piloting." He could see the inspector's evidence mounting against him even as he spoke.

"Ah, so he's been informing you how to sail into Brest? See how your words ensnare you? You had direct access and knowledge of *le Royal Louis;* you sought information on piloting the channels; you are English and worked for their navy; you asked for maps of the harbor; you consorted with others, including an African foreigner; and you used suspicious terms and exchanged money in secret. No suspect in France, let alone Brest, has this much evidence implicating him. Yet you want me to believe it resulted from shopping for presents? Enough!" He slammed his hand on the small desk. "Monsieur, your answers are suspicious. We have more to ask you, and we now consider you a risk to France."

"What did I do? Nothing! You distrust me because of being English," Abraham pleaded. "I've told you everything you wanted. I'm not the saboteur."

"Perhaps you are innocent as you say and the evidence is coincidental. Or it may be the evidence is proof you are not innocent. Time will reveal the truth. Monsieur, I must inform you that you are under arrest, a suspect in the sabotage of *le Royal Louis.* Until we straighten this out, you'll remain here in jail." The inspector moved toward the door to leave.

"Wait! Is there a way you can tell my employer I'm being detained? This will jeopardize my position if I don't show up for work."

"You have far greater things to lose. If we free you, you can take care of it." LaBrouche scowled and walked out.

The uniformed officer came and escorted Abraham from the room through a corridor lined with dark heavy doors. After opening an iron gate with a large key, the guard pulled him along a dim tunnel that led to the main cell house. A horrendous odor of urine and sour, rotting vegetables emanated from the big room. Smaller cells, empty or holding three or four men, lined the hall. The jailer shoved Abraham into one occupied already by two men and clanged the door shut.

One inmate nodded hello. Abraham returned the gesture, asking, "Have you been here long?"

"Two weeks. My name is Jacques."

"And I'm Jacques, too." The other prisoner added.

Great, thought Abraham, Jacques One, and Jacques Two—more confusion. "My name is Abraham."

Jacques One admitted his crime without hesitation. "The police arrested me for smuggling a pound of spice off a merchant ship. I couldn't pay the tax. As soon as my brother gets the fine paid they say I can go. And your crime?"

"They're holding me because I'm English. The inspector thinks I burned *le Royal Louis*. It'll be cleared up soon, I hope."

Jacques Two laughed. "So do the others. There are a bunch of men they think burned the ship. Just how many of you set the fire?"

"Others?" Abraham's hopes of a brief stay vanished like a winter's breath.

"Four or five." Jacques Two pointed to the opposite cell.

"They're Frenchmen, not English. One is from southern France though."

"How long have they been here?"

"Oh, a long while. The southerner has been in jail for weeks, arrested soon after the fire. One of his thumbs is broken now; we always can tell when he's being interrogated. I've been here for four months awaiting my trial. They say I robbed a man at an inn."

"Jacques, you *did* rob the man," Jacques One pointed out.

"But they don't know that. There's no evidence." Jacques Two rose a finger in the manner of an attorney. Both laughed and settled into staring at the floor again.

Abraham had never felt so hopeless and things had never felt so out of control; he would have to rely on fate to free him.

Hours dragged by and prisoners in the cell across the way played a word game. Abraham wished he had the book in his leather bag to help him soothe his fears.

When night came, he crawled up on the wooden bed to sleep under a filthy blanket. Because of the constant coughing and other bodily noises of the prisoners, he couldn't sleep more than an hour or two in a row.

At sunrise, a policeman released everyone into the central room for a head count and marched them outside to stretch and use a latrine. After an hour the guard herded his cattle back inside for gruel.

Abraham lay on the plank bed to nap and dream of better things, slipping into a deep, troubled sleep.

"Hey, wake up!" Jacques Two was shaking him. "They're here to question you, or maybe you'll get out." Jacques One laughed at the sarcasm.

The policeman placed Abraham in the same horrible interrogation room and the same hawk-beaked officer entered. "Do you want to change your story? Or do you still stick to the gifts tale?" he grunted.

"Monsieur, I'm just a shipwright. I won't admit to what I didn't do."

"Humph—you're English and we'll watch you as long as you're in Brest—every minute. If you caused the fire, I'll find out." LaBrouche frowned and left.

A moment later a uniformed guard gave Abraham his leather bag and remarked he was free to go. Although relieved, he felt whip-lash from the shock of imprisonment one moment and freedom the next.

When he walked outside, a navy officer was waiting for him at the door. "Master Sculptor Caffieri regrets he didn't hear of your arrest until today. He's vouched for you with the intendant of the navy who ordered your release."

The exhausting ordeal had caused Abraham to miss a day and a half of work, so after thanking the lieutenant, he hurried to the shop, arriving just as the men were returning after their noon break.

Anton spotted him. "You're all right? How was it?"

"I'm fine. How did you find out?"

"When you didn't show up at the shop I asked around, and no one had seen you. So, I rushed to your boardinghouse after work but you weren't there. I suspected something amiss and checked at the police station. They said they were holding you as a suspect for burning *le Royal Louis*. Well, that sounded foolish. So I told Master Caffieri in the morning and he sent word to the intendant."

"I have a new respect for freedom." Abraham wagged his head. He later found Caffieri sitting at his desk on a tall stool. "Thank you, Master Caffieri. I'm indebted to you. While under arrest I worried over losing my job."

"Don't make a habit of it by burning any more ships. And don't think I did it out of preferential treatment. I need a strong body for a hard job." A half-hidden grin undercut his gruffness.

"May I work late to replace the hours I missed?" Caffieri agreed to allow him to work an extra hour every day. Abraham hurried to the slip but his exhaustion kept him from doing a good job.

When he arrived at the boardinghouse, he collapsed on his soft bed and slept without stirring until sunrise.

The next evening he went to visit Yvette. She was waiting, her cloak in her arms, and on his first knock, she opened the door and rushed out. "Abraham, I was so worried! Tell me everything. I felt so sorry for you that I cried the whole day!"

Abraham related the episode, beginning with the police. By the time he finished, they had reached the café. Yvette came to a sudden halt.

"When I heard they'd arrested you, I wanted to run to the station, but my father said they'd release you soon. I realized my affection for you outweighs the beliefs I earlier held as important. Sometimes we must reorder our lives; prerequisites once thought vital can take on a different value...Abraham, I love you." Yvette pulled him to her, kissing him passionately.

He didn't understand what Yvette meant about their relationship, but he assumed her revelation was a good sign.

CHAPTER TWO

The Letter

François always loved the view of the low hills of Crozon Peninsula from Camaret Bay. Putting the spyglass to his eye, he watched the sun lift the morning mist and reveal a pilot's boat making its way through the waves.

"Excellent. Lieutenant, prepare to receive the pilot. Bring him to my quarters when he boards."

François left the quarterdeck for his cabin. *La Naïade*, a corvette, was compact and cramped. Still, he enjoyed sailing her. She was only 22 guns but fast. Despite his family's contributions to the French monarchy and navy, François had earned his ship command. His brother, René, was likely to become a commander as well, especially now that Great Britain threatened war against France.

"Sir, here's Monsieur Façonneur," said the lieutenant.

"Come in, Monsieur Façonneur. Look at the chart and show me the route."

"Thank you, Captain Saint-Alouarn." Briefly, André wondered if the captain recognized his last name before pointing out their route. "We'll take a more southern passage through the Goulet today due to the wind. The tide will run in less than an hour. I see you're riding a windward anchor."

"Yes." To the lieutenant, François said, "Purchase and weigh on the tide and set topsails." To André, he added, "Façonneur—that name sounds familiar."

"I believe your brother courted my sister, Yvette, two years ago."

"René? Ah, Yvette." François recalled the affair. "He thought much of her."

"And she of him, but it wasn't meant to be. Shall I assume my post at the helm, sir?" André didn't wish to make issues of the past.

"Yes, I'll join you in a few minutes." François blushed, remembering the predicament. René had no right to court below his station in a doomed romance with a commoner. No damage to the family name had resulted, but he hadn't learned and still dashed from one pretty face to another.

On deck, sailors hoisted and hung the anchor from the cathead. A steady wind carried them, with André in command at the wheel, and the ship sailed over the dangerous shoals that guarded the opening to the bay up the Penfeld.

After giving instructions to his first lieutenant, François took a boat to shore and submitted his reports, finishing in the afternoon. As he relaxed for the rest of the day, he thought about home and wondered if Marie, his twenty-eight-year-old wife of nine years, ever got bored while he, ten years her senior, sailed the seas, although taking care of the children and the estate must keep her busy enough.

He spent the bulk of the next day en route, arriving at his manor house late in the day to cheerful shouts of servants, alerting Marie and the children of his return. The pounding of small feet on floorboards and a click of the door latch greeted him. François laughed and allowed his son, Louis, to jump into his outstretched arms. Marie appeared at the entrance and watched François hug the boy to his chest.

"Papa, Papa, you're home!" The five-year-old laid his curly brown-haired head on François's shoulder.

"Louis, you've taken good care of the manor while I was away."

Setting Louis down, François approached Marie, kissed her in the doorway, and picked up his older daughter, Marie Josèphe, as they walked to the lavishly decorated salon. Though François controlled the purse strings, Marie managed everything he considered home: the farm, forests, livestock, and the manor itself. Her sincerity and glowing warmth were the harbor he voyaged toward the moment he departed Brest, and her unwavering love was his true ship.

"When will you leave next?" she asked.

"My ship sails in five days. I know it's not much time, but someday the sea will tire of me and cast me ashore. Then I'll be yours forever." He kissed her again.

"Did you see René in Brest on the way home?" Marie had few kind things to say concerning her brother-in-law.

"No. However, I did meet André Façonneur, Yvette's brother. He piloted *la Naïade*."

"Lucky he didn't run you aground just for spite."

"André's an intelligent man; he understands I had little to do with their love affair. René couldn't have wed Yvette. By spreading the story that René had married a *placée* in the West Indies, I ended their romance soon enough."

"Poor girl. Your brother can be so cavalier, and then you create a lie to save him from himself."

"Marie, he wasn't insincere. René did love her and has loved no one since. I hope it hasn't ruined his prospects to marry; hopefully, he will change, if first he doesn't get killed by someone's husband."

Later that evening, alone in the salon after dinner, François confided in Marie: "I'm afraid that the British will soon be at war with us. Reports say they've moved troops onto the continent."

Marie held her breath. "I hope the Admiralty prepared for it."

"Well, we've waged most of our Austrian war on land. That gives us an advantage over the English who have fought with Spain at sea; their army has less experience." Though Marie seemed worried, François felt a more optimistic excitement at the prospect.

Marie shook her head. "Right now our enemies have no threatening navies and our fleet has been dominant against them. However, the British fleet is experienced, large, and close. If Great Britain enters the fighting, you'll be facing formidable warships." The thought of it shattered her nerves.

"Don't worry my dear," François said, noticing her unease. "I shall always return to you. I sense I'll never come to harm at sea." He reached over and took her hand. "It's hard to explain, the ocean is a comfort, a second home. I've always felt good being on water, and I can't imagine myself being killed there."

The word *killed* was a poor choice. Tears flowed until they wet her face from eye to chin. Nothing François said stopped her from weeping. After a time she regained her usual spirits and wiped her face dry. Marie pulled him close and rested her head against his chest.

"I don't know how I'd live if you didn't come back through that door." Her voice barely reached his ear.

François relished each remaining day before leaving for the harsh seas, imperiled by nature and enemy ships. He couldn't tell Marie even half of the blood-curdling incidents he suffered or she'd never trust in his return again. Nevertheless, despite the pains and danger, the honor, adventure, camaraderie, and accomplishments beckoned him to sea.

Back in Brest, François entered the Admiralty office and stepped up to the clerk positioned before the large, ornate double doors. "Captain Saint-Alouarn reporting for orders."

"You are expected. Please sit until I call you to go in, sir."

François joined two other officers waiting on straight-backed chairs beside the entrance. The three frigate captains chatted about the prospects of war with Britain. Du Guay, Commandant of the Navy at Brest, had ordered them to the meeting: unusual for receiving orders—and ominous.

"Gentlemen, the commandant will receive you now. If you will, please come this way."

A walnut table ran through the center of the meeting room. At its head sat the commandant and, to his right, his adjutant, looking over several papers and sea charts. The three captains entered and stood by chairs at the far end.

"Sirs, be seated. I realize this is unusual, however, your next assignments require supplemental information." The adjutant then returned to his seat.

Du Guay stood, grunting to clear his throat. "Gentlemen, I'm sure you're aware the British are transporting armies into Holland, and we expect them to march on Bavaria. We've already engaged them over issues in the American colonies and elsewhere, and should not expect a political resolution. This portends a state of war will exist between our two countries in a short time.

"The Admiralty is preparing for the defense of our ports and convoy routes. These will include line-of-battle vessels with fifth-ranked frigates and smaller ships used as patrols, scouts, and dispatches. Frigates will harass enemy shipping, moorages, and warships of equal tonnage. I expect all ships to report any movement, in particular convoys of troops or large fleets." Du Guay paced along the side of the table. "This reconnaissance is crucial and takes priority over engaging the enemy. Every week, dispatch ships will rendezvous at pre-designated locations to inform you of our political standing with the British. Do you have questions?"

The captains glanced at one another; the commandant had answered what they needed to know. "No, Commandant Du Guay, we understand," François spoke for them.

"Fine, the officer outside will assign your orders."

As François left the building, he heard his name. "François!" René approached, waving. "Tell me, are we at war against the British?"

"Not yet, but it's inevitable. Du Guay is anticipating it will happen soon. I hate to see it."

The two brothers had different approaches to life, René favored adventure whereas François favored practicality. They were separated in age by ten years, yet they always enjoyed their time together, sharing their seafaring stories.

As they traded their most recent tales, they relaxed with glasses of wine outside a café near the Penfeld, drinking until dusk. Soon, François noticed a young woman and an older man nearing them. The man he didn't recognize, but the female he did —Yvette.

"Ah, René, let's cross over to that shop window for a moment." François hoped to distract René, but he had acted too late; Yvette's eyes focused on René; a moment later, he caught sight of her, freezing in place. François flinched.

"How pleasant to see you again, Yvette," René said, overcoming his shock.

"Monsieur de Saint-Alouarn." Her greeting was hard as stone, and Anton looked about to burst. "Or I should say Chevalier de Rosmadec since you received a knighthood, I heard."

"Please, Yvette, I prefer René. The knighthood is traditional."

"René, you remember my father?" She gestured to him, bracing for a potential fight.

René bowed to him. "Good evening, sir."

"Hello." Anton spat it with a steady glare. He'd have said more if etiquette had not held his tongue.

"Yvette, you look wonderful," René continued, warming immediately. "You must tell me what's happened to you since we separated. As usual, my life is chaotic—the life of a seaman."

"I've heard unbelievable stories about seamen's lives." She showed no emotion, but time had not eased the pain of his betrayal. Not a month passed in which she did not chastise her foolish, younger whims. But here was a chance to find her error, to avoid it in the future. After hearing his side, she thought, he could go to the devil.

"You mustn't believe everything you hear." René groped for words. "If possible, we should get together to update one another. A seaman's tale should come straight from the seaman and not gossips."

"It's time to go, Yvette!" Anton insisted. "Papa, just one moment," Yvette demanded. "René, we must meet. At our last parting, things needed to be explained. Tomorrow evening at seven I'll be free. If you wish you may call then."

"Of course, tomorrow. My ship doesn't leave for a few days and I have much to tell you." René smiled charmingly.

"Until then, good evening, sirs." Yvette took her father's arm and continued along the street.

Once she was gone, François grabbed René's arm. "This meeting isn't wise. Your relationship ended years ago, and what might a meeting resolve?"

"François, I need to speak to her to settle what was misinterpreted. You remember how I cared for Yvette. Usually, I don't care what women think of me afterward, but she is different and I must impress on her my feelings."

The men walked in tense silence until they reached the river. "The wind is changing northeast," François noted. "If it holds I'll be departing tomorrow. It'll be better where I'm going than where you'll be heading."

René did not miss his quip about the meeting but did not respond to it. "Good voyaging, my brother. Let's both hope the British decide not to fight."

* * *

The next morning the winds came out of the east and *la Naïade* set sail with François aboard, already missing his family.

"Abraham," Yvette said, interrupting his nightly visit around the family fire. "Will we stroll today? Papa, is it all right if I steal him from you?"

"Go. You both have much to discuss." Anton grumbled, disturbed over her plans with René.

The two ambled north from the bay, arm-in-arm, stopping and sitting upon a wooden bench facing a church. The light coming through the clerestory windows on the other side of the church backlit the stained-glass windows into brightly hued but indistinct shapes of the saints.

"Abraham, do you remember the ship's officer I mentioned who courted me?"

"The married one who lied to you?"

"Yes...well, and no. René hadn't married as I learned later. He was betrothed although he barely knew her. The family arranged the marriage."

Abraham put his elbow on the bench rail behind him and leaned his jaw on his hand. "And?" He expected something grave.

"By chance, I met him again while shopping with my father. I asked him to meet with me and he agreed. I pray this will resolve the confusion that has vexed my confidence. When we broke up, he was at sea and we never discussed the reasons. I must end this distrust of myself. We are meeting tonight at seven in my home."

"What's his name?" Abraham tried to block his fears and anger at the interloper.

"René de Saint-Alouarn, a noble family from southern Brittany and a well-recognized name. I'm over any feelings for him, so you needn't worry. My sole emotion is contempt when I'm with him. Feel assured, Abraham—you're the man I love."

"Yvette, I don't understand why you want to meet after so much time. But since you're being honest, there's no reason for me to worry." Abraham was being truthful, yet he couldn't help not worrying. He had shown her his commitment and didn't see her need to analyze a previous romance.

"You're too sweet. I promise after this I shall never talk to or about him again. The visit probably won't last more than a few minutes." Yvette only wanted to hear René's real feelings and determine where the fault had laid—a simple task.

But Abraham was less than reassured, the phrase "a few minutes" ringing a warning. Much can happen in a few minutes. He had no logical defense to prevent her from seeing René or sway her decision. Although it took courage to tell him, he wished she hadn't.

"Dear, I was afraid you'd object, and I hesitated in telling you. Few would accept it as gentlemanly as you did," Yvette said, kissing him gratefully on the cheek.

Abraham forced a smile and abandoned the subject, instead engaging in one he knew Yvette would appreciate. "This church reminds me of Saint-Sulpice in miniature. Saint-Sulpice is large but smaller than Notre-Dame."

"Do you want to come to mass and see my church?" Yvette offered, hoping the exposure might, in time, sway his agnosticism.

Although the music would entertain him, the sermons were boring and useless in facing the real world. Also, the joy of forgiveness that he felt as a child no longer affected him. "One day soon," he replied in the hope of pleasing her.

"If it's alright," he added, "I'll visit you tomorrow night after work."

Yvette put her hand on his neck. "I know you are fearful of René. You shouldn't be. He is just the past...you are my future."

* * *

Yvette wanted to dominate the confrontation with René, dressing in modest, dark colors and a crucifix. She knew better than anyone how charming he could be and sought only one answer: had he stolen her heart and virginity on a whim, or had he ever loved her for who she was?

She waited by the fireplace with her mother, reading. When the church bell rang seven, Louise said, "Yvette, you must be careful tonight. Make wise decisions about what's right for your future. Take everything into consideration, especially your beliefs." Louise joined Anton upstairs and left Yvette to contemplate the advice. Her mother, she knew, preferred René, a Frenchman and Catholic with a noble name.

Yvette recognized René's arrival, an unusual pause between two knocks, and opened the door.

"Hello, Yvette. I've been looking forward to tonight."

"Come in, René. You remembered the way to our house." She regretted his civilian clothing matched the color of hers.

"Please...I'll never forget. You look very nice tonight, Yvette. I'm pleased you're wearing the shawl I gave you."

Startled, Yvette recalled the gift. It undid her attempt to appear impersonal.

"I'm surprised at how much lovelier you are than I remembered. That's not flattery, it is a fact." René had planned his words hours earlier and executed them with impromptu flair, the initial step in his strategy.

"Kind of you to say so, René, though we met to understand what happened and be done with it." Yvette's fingers fidgeted and a persistent twitch started in her eyebrow. The emerging signs of stress betrayed her poise. For the first time, she considered the meeting could be ill-conceived.

"Yvette, you shocked me when you suggested we meet," René said over the orange glow of the fireplace. "After we separated, you cannot know the suffering I went through when you refused to let me visit. I'd have done anything to explain the predicament into which I had gotten myself." René's eyes lowered as though confessing a horrible sin.

Yvette sympathized yet answered in a detached voice. "Well, the opportunity is here now."

"Many times I wrote while at sea describing how I loved you and never found another like you. When the unopened letters came back, I knew someone had informed you of my betrothal. I'd intended to tell you. Yet I feared it might end our relationship, and I guessed right. Your decision to shut me out kept me from explaining why the engagement was a secret."

"When you left for the sea, René, you proposed marriage to me. Within a week I discovered you had a placée in the West Indies. My heart broke. Then before your letters arrived, I learned of another betrothal here in France. It was humiliating. How could you have offered me your hand when two others already had it?"

René furrowed his brow. "I had no placée in the West Indies and don't know how the rumor started. It still vexes me. No one else ever heard that. Although true I was engaged to a noblewoman here when I proposed, I planned to end it after you accepted."

"Ah, so you'd break off the engagement to the other lady after I gave my answer. Mine was an option of sorts."

"Yvette, my family decided long before whom I should marry. Had you agreed to the proposal—yes, I would have nullified the other betrothal. You weren't a choice but the only woman I'd ever wish to marry. If you rejected me, it'd be impossible to replace you, so it didn't matter whom I wed. My one chance at happiness, having you, had passed. I see now how wrong it might seem. In reality, it's a sign of how much esteem and love I held for you. And...I still do." René's eyes were moist and Yvette accepted the honesty in his voice. Something inside her pitied his misguided decisions.

"René, why didn't you marry your betrothed when I left you?"

"Upon returning, I realized marrying anyone other than the one I adored would be a sin. I sent word ending the betrothal and searched in vain for someone like you. When we met yesterday, I prayed for a chance to clear up the misunderstanding. As God is my witness, you were and still are my heart's only love."

"Strange the twists life takes when only one side of the coin is seen," Yvette said, almost to herself. "I'm glad you came by to tell me this. It so confused me when later I heard you had no placée and still didn't marry your fiancée." Her voice had softened and the rock wall around her heart fell, tumbled by his impassioned words. Yvette's eyes, seeing René's handsome chiseled features, awoke long-forgotten feelings. They crept into her mind and swept away the pain of deception and suspicions.

"Yvette, I loved true. What can I do to prove my sincerity? Ask anything." He moved closer and took her hand, looking deep within her. "How can I heal the injury I caused you?" René sensed the changes of her seasons: winter—she was cold; spring —she started to bloom; summer—she grew warmer; and if fall comes—she'll be harvested. Yvette just needed a little more reassurance.

The explanation dizzied Yvette's mind. She wavered on the cusp between the known past with René and an unknown future with Abraham. "Oh, René. If we could jump back to those heavenly moments and correct them before they slipped through time...but too long...too much has passed." Yet her old feelings were nudging away caution.

"Only if the past comes between us. Please, Yvette, remember our love and it will return. All that's needed is to accept this small bit of our history as a humor, a silly detour. We can be in bliss again. Our opportunity is now. We must act upon it. Such will not come again."

René, sitting on the chair's edge, cradled her hands. He leaned forward and kissed her.

"Oh, my," she said with eyelids closed. "René, you mustn't. I've met another man whom I love." The kiss worked magic. Yvette's memories of his tenderness and her caring, not René's words, seduced her.

"I can understand. Yet, his love can't equal the feelings I've held for you after so long a time and believe you still hold for me. My sweet Yvette, don't allow another mistake to keep us apart. We're fated to be united. After all, we're together at this moment on the verge of being happy forever. Let it happen to share our lives as one with God's blessing in a holy reunion." René used sincerity, passion, and moreover, cleverness, by engaging her strong religious convictions.

It had always bothered Yvette that Abraham was a lapsed Anglican, whereas René was French Catholic, a belief nothing would change. She loved both. Yvette chose the past and her religion.

"René." They fell to their knees between the chairs embracing in the soft glow of the embers. Within fifteen minutes, they had turned the meeting into a tryst.

* * *

Abraham's work on the sloop dragged the entire day while thoughts of Yvette and her old beau tormented him. In his distraction, he almost chopped his leg with the adze. After work, he arrived within half the usual time at Yvette's door.

"Hello, Abraham." Louise smiled. "Good evening, Madame Façonneur. Is Yvette at home?"

"No, not at the moment. She left this message for you." Louise held out a folded and sealed paper.

"Oh, do you know when she'll return?"

"The note will explain, I'm sure. Good night." With a wide grin, Louise closed the door.

Abraham stared at the road as he walked up the dark street, unconscious of his surroundings, focused on a growing panic. In minutes, the familiar café stood before him. Drawn to it by happy memories of Yvette, he entered and ordered tea.

Placing the paper on the table, Abraham sipped the hot drink. He broke the seal and unfolded the note, holding it so the nearby lantern cast light on it.

My Dearest Abraham—

I have wrestled with my conscience about how to tell you what my heart is saying without hurting you. That is impossible. I cannot meet with you tonight or ever again because something unforeseen has happened. Believe me, I still love you. You are a wonderful man. I will always consider our impassioned and caring moments together with the kindest of memory. Last night my reunion with René unexpectedly revealed an acute lingering affection for him that had remained hidden within my heart. You have every right, and I can truly understand your emotions, to be upset with me for my incomprehensible actions. Unknowingly, I have fallen in love with two most exceptional men. However, I may only profess love to one.

For this, I am honestly sorry. For having made your attention, love, and time come to naught, I can only pray you will forgive me.

Your loving Yvette

"Naturally, you're forgiven." Abraham put the tea to his lips but lowered it again and left.

The next day, Abraham labored hard in the cool air, focusing on fairing the beam under him. This didn't keep snatches of Yvette from slipping in to strike between the cracks of his crippled reality. He only returned to the shop after most workers had left.

As he put his tools away someone approached.

"Abraham." Anton drew close. "I wanted to talk to you but didn't see you at noon."

"No, I ate alone." His face was dead, a mask carved by deep sorrow.

"Yvette told me of her decision. I can't tell you how unhappy it's made me. That René, he's no more than a scoundrel. What can one do? She's stubborn and sets her mind, even if she's wrong." Anton's ears burned red.

"The woman does have her own mind." Abraham locked his toolbox and walked away.

"This isn't over, Abraham. I'll set things right with her." The impossible promise trailed after him as Anton continued mumbling.

Weeks passed and the warm days of May helped Abraham overcome the longing for Yvette. He avoided Anton as much as possible. This did not escape Anton's notice, who hoped Yvette might guide her affections back to Abraham. But if she thought of Abraham, she kept it to herself, for she never mentioned him.

One day at the shop, as they discussed work and exchanged news, Caffieri said to Anton, "Warship repairs and constructions are going well. We'll be prepared if they fight us."

"And our troops have flooded into the Germanic states." Anton, although accepting Abraham, hated the English. "They say their King George is leading the British army himself. Does he think he's Julius Caesar?"

Not an hour later, bells rang and soldiers posted proclamations. "Well," Caffieri announced, "the waiting is over. Great Britain and France are at war!"

For all, it came as no surprise. Within a week, more damaged warships entered the harbor for repairs, forcing Abraham to work longer hours at a faster pace. Memories of Yvette peppered much of his free time, causing him to spurn all other romantic pursuits in favor of reading science books. The opposite of René's over-indulgences, Abraham avoided women altogether to forget.

At the end of June, more bad news filtered in from the battlefields: the British army and their allies had overpowered the French forces and the Bavarians at a battle in Dittingen. This setback frightened the population. For the rest of the summer, however, both sides withdrew or settled into their gained territories. Still, by the fall of 1743, Britain had seriously hurt France's chances of winning the war. Abraham felt fortunate to still have a position at the yard. No orders had come to dismiss foreigners, likely due to the increased workload and shortage of craftsmen.

On Christmas Eve, Abraham dressed in his best clothing and arrived at the boardinghouse dining room for the feast. Others gathered on either side of the long oak table, arrayed with garlands and candles, talking and laughing, awaiting the first course.

"Ah-ha, Abraham!" Hendrik caught his attention; he was one of the more bibulous tenants who lived on the first floor, and always seemed to have a glass of wine in hand. "So, you've descended from the heights to join us mortals."

"Hendrik, a Happy Christmas to you."

"Same to you."

"How did you do at your meeting at the hospital? Did you get any sales?" asked Abraham.

"Oh, the hospitals haven't enough supplies with the war hampering shipments. Ach! Such a business for those poor suffering patients." Hendrik, from Amsterdam, spoke French with a heavy Dutch accent. "What will happen when I deplete my inventory in the warehouses? I can't bring more into the country. I'll be living on the street. The war is ruining my business and had better end soon."

"In truth, I'm waiting for Minister Maurepas to boot me out, Hendrik. Being English when Britain is at war with France is not a safe position at the shipyard."

The landlady, at the head of the table, rose to give a speech. "Attention, everyone. Let us bow our heads and give a prayer of thanks to our Heavenly Father."

She began the *Pater Noster* and concluded with "Amen." Then she banged on her metal plate with a spoon and a serving girl brought out the first course of the meal.

By the end of the feast, the pure white tablecloth lay disheveled and stained. Goblets, serving ware, crumbs, and bowls filled every space. Hendrik, next to Abraham, pushed himself back from the table, his large stomach extended out in front of him—a bomb ready to burst.

"Hendrik, that must be Madame d'Aché," Abraham said, gesturing to one of the ladies present. Abraham had heard about an aristocrat living at the boardinghouse. This lady was very old and dressed in fashions at least twenty years out-of-date.

"She's from a noble family but hasn't money anymore. Four years ago, she arrived from Paris friendless." Hendrik rubbed his rotund belly in discomfort.

"She looks out of place here."

Abraham moved to the carafe sitting on a serving table and overheard the old lady.

"The customs differ greatly from those in Paris. That extends to the landowners, too. In Brittany, the *haut monde* plays around more than in Paris. My niece had an experience with one of the sort, the Chevalier de Rosmadec—quite a rogue he is."

Abraham's ears pricked at the mention of René. Madame d'Aché's diatribe made Abraham sorry for Yvette both betrothed and taken advantage of by the "rogue."

She added, "He makes promises that will get him into a chamber and flees back out to sea. He's here in Brest often enough I hear, engaged to a common girl of no title. The whole while he flirts with those of wealth and keeps company with others. Such a fine family, too. He's a Saint-Alouarn, you know. He couldn't behave that way in Paris. Nobility has an image to uphold."

There was nothing he could do to help Yvette, but the sadness Abraham felt from Madame d'Aché's words had exposed old wounds.

* * *

René and Yvette had reignited their passionate courtship and planned for their future as man and wife. This, however, was not to last.

By the end of the year, Yvette's romantic bond with René was crushed. She learned of infidelities while he was away. The engagement he proposed a second time was even hollower than the first and left her devastated. For days, she pondered over a suitable reaction to this new humiliating situation. Then he arrived back at Brest.

Yvette suggested celebrating the New Year at the hotel and entered on René's arm, hoping to embarrass him with a loud rebuke of his actions in front of Brest's high society. Every table was taken in the room and they stood waiting for seats by the entrance.

René scanned the lobby and spied an attractive lady at one table, kissing a man. If he could, he'd get her aside to suggest a later rendezvous.

Yvette followed his eyes as he lingered on the young woman—Charlotte. Her mind flooded with anger. In a flash, she pulled René back toward the exit.

"Why leave? Can't we wait in the lobby for seats?"

"No, let's go! It'll take too long. There's a café half a block from here." She rushed him from the hotel on the verge of tears. René, who hadn't noticed, continued recounting his last voyage and professing how much he missed her.

Yvette ignored his fawning chatter. She knew he'd been with Charlotte in Saint-Malo. The lurid report filtered along from noble to servant, from servant to gossip, until reaching her, and his wanton ogling proved it. Although he was a most appealing man, René was, most importantly, untrustworthy.

A block away, she slowed the pace, drained of emotions over days of rage, disappointment, and self-loathing. Revenge, she realized, was sinful; trying to win a philanderer back was foolish, and both took too much effort for what she'd get in return. Yvette simply wanted to be rid of the ogre as fast as possible.

She stopped a half-block away and he turned to face her, wondering. Yvette's profound hatred deflated. She spoke with a forceful, but sad voice. "René, I know you were unfaithful to me with Charlotte and with other women. Twice you've made a fool of me but I cannot forgive you a second time. There is nothing you can say. You are a damned cad and I shall never speak to you again."

René stood mouth agape, stricken by the words. Yvette, anguishing over René's betrayal, her naiveté, and spurning an innocent Abraham, walked home alone, too sorrowful for tears. Again René had fooled her, but, more devastating, her poor choices had destroyed the blossoming love Abraham had pledged to her. She felt it was she who had committed the crime of infidelity to a true lover.

* * *

François arrived at his manor a week after the beginning of the new year. Although the holiday was over, the family enjoyed celebrating both a second New Year's Day and also his recapture of a warship while on patrol. Marie and François relaxed in the salon, exchanging news.

"François, I guess you needn't worry over René and Yvette's betrothal. The engagement ended on New Year's." Marie's face spread in a triumphant grin.

"Yes, I guess that is for the best," François said, smiling. "René told me about it when I got to port. Yvette caught him in an affair with someone and called it off for good. Thank goodness."

"As I said, he may be a fine seaman, but he's a terrible mate." Marie abhorred René's actions and relished a bit in his misery. The broken betrothal was evidence of his knavery.

"He is brokenhearted over it. I told him that her mainsail was set and already on the horizon. I find it an unusual facet in him; he's madly in love with Yvette, yet he risked it all for some uncontrollable whim. And now he regrets it as if his actions are out-of-step with his deepest emotions."

"If he's miserable, then I'm delighted. René deserves to suffer for the pains he inflicts." Marie had no sympathy for insincerity.

"How callous you sound. René alone is not the one to blame. Women throw themselves at him and that can weaken any man's will. Those who tempt him should receive part of the fault."

"No, he decides to bed them. René alone is responsible, no one else." Marie's voice had risen and François was too wise and too aware of the truth she spoke, to argue. "Plus, think what will become of poor Yvette. He's soiled the girl, twice. Now she's a leftover and even worse, a poor leftover."

"Too bad she got involved with my brother; he's limited her prospects for marriage now." François empathized with Yvette. René's irresponsibility reached far beyond those directly involved like ripples spreading on the sea. Today it affected him and Marie, and no doubt, unknown others in the future.

* * *

In early 1744, Abraham began work on a new project, a frigate named *la Renommée*. He walked along the keel and inspected his scarfs in the long backbone of the ship. The cool weather made hewing difficult as he shaped the beams. This warship was different from earlier ones, designed with a lower gun deck and narrow hull.

"I see iron braces in place of wooden knee braces to hold the upper deck," Abraham said to Anton, to whom he had begun speaking again.

"To reduce the weight, no doubt. They'll still provide enough strength to hold the weight of the guns overhead. Also, the gun deck is port-less with just four feet of headroom."

"I noticed that too. Other frigates are built much heavier than *la Renommée*."

Anton nodded his approval. "The ship constructor is breaking from old traditions to get a lighter frigate for more speed, replacing heavy wood with iron wherever he could. She'll have less draft than her sisters."

Abraham frowned, unsure if he approved of changes that challenged the old customs; ships were constructed through trial and error, and it could be dangerous to sail a new design.

Caffieri permanently reassigned Abraham to hull work, fairing timbers, and erecting *la Renommee's* frames. In the workroom one day, he noticed a figurehead not yet finished, bathed in sunlight.

"The sculpture is magnificent, isn't it?" Anton said. "It's the figurehead for *la Renommée*. How is it said in English?"

"It means *fame* or *renown*."

"Ah-ha, *renommée* sounds a bit like *renown*, doesn't it?" Anton answered. "Master Caffieri designed it and is carving it himself. This is one of the best designs he's ever executed. He did the stern and quarter galleries too." Anton pointed to the sections a short distance away.

Abraham inspected the figurehead for faults in craftsmanship. The figure rose above him and its unpainted wood glowed against the darker interior of the shop—*La Renommée* rivaled any masterpiece. A winged female, draped below her waist in loose folds, holding the trumpet of triumph and a royal orb. Her figure floating on clouds in bas-relief repeated on the taffrail panel. Both pieces were magnificent.

"How different from the ships I worked on in Woolwich. Most figureheads were a lion or knight and were amateurish in comparison. Few had the majestic design and artistic sculpting like this one. Abraham reverently glided his fingertips across the smooth wood. "I've never seen another figurehead that embodies the goddess Fame as well as this."

A month later, Abraham and Anton attached the figurehead to the frigate. At last the ship, nearly complete, took on an identity and personality of its own. The figurehead attracted one's gaze. She was now *la Renommée*.

But as they finished the work, Caffieri climbed onto the ship, expression bleak. "Abraham, I'm afraid I have upsetting news. Minister Maurepas just declared no Englishmen can work on French naval vessels. They still fear sabotage and spies because of *le Royal Louis*. You'll have to leave your job. I'm sorry. You can pick up your pay tomorrow."

Abraham was disappointed but not shocked and nodded respectfully to Caffieri, thanking him for allowing him to work at the shipyard. He squeezed the handle of his wooden toolbox in anger, making his fingers hurt as he climbed off the frigate.

Anton stayed silent, knowing what the job meant to him. Nothing could console him. They pushed their tool carts along the dock back to the shop side-by-side.

Abraham, head low and shoulders hanging, laid out his plans to Anton. "I'll leave for England. Maurepas' edict has ruined any chance of finding work in France. Perhaps they've started hiring again at Woolwich." Anton listened and said little.

The next day he collected his pay. Caffieri wished him a heartfelt goodbye. The other carpenters waved but kept working on their tasks; it meant more work for them. Only Anton approached him and expressed his regret.

Anton handed Abraham a pocketknife with a worn golden handle. "Here, take this knife. I was going to give it to André, but I want you to have it. Maybe it'll bring you luck and at least it'll remind you of us here. Before you leave, is there anything you'd want me to tell Yvette?"

Abraham refused with a shake of his head.

Anton did not tell him the engagement had ended. Yvette still cared for Abraham, and Abraham still cared for her, but fate had doomed their relationship.

Saddened, Abraham watched Brest fade away on the sea's horizon a few days later, he mourned. He had lost his love and now his place at the shipyard. There's not much else left to lose, he thought to himself. I'm back where I started before coming to France.

The carriage from *Dover* sped northward, and Abraham arrived in Woolwich with Brest as a far-away memory.

He visited old friends and fellow shipwrights while searching for a job, but found nothing. Abraham decided to spend his last two nights at the Lion's Head Tavern where he had rented once before and then try his luck in Portsmouth. In a rough part of the dock, most landsmen avoided the inn that served rowdy sailors their first shore-leave drink.

At the inn's tavern, two men motioned Abraham to join them after he ate.

"Celebrate with us, mate!" called the heavier of the two. He wore a marine's bright red coat. The other dressed as a seaman in a loose shirt and wide-legged short trousers.

"Thanks, what are you celebrating?" Abraham sat on the bench next to the sailor.

"We're celebrating our taking of a fat French merchant ship off the coast a month ago." The marine grinned, showing several prominent holes of missing teeth. "We'll buy you a pint." He motioned to the tavern keeper to bring another mug.

"That's kind of you." Abraham had drunk one pint already and could hold a few more if they were free. "What cargo did she hold?"

"Oh, tons of rum from the West Indies, along with tobacco, Peruvian wool, and a huge shipment of Jesuit's bark. The capture will make our captain a rich man. We'll be none the worse for it either. My friend here can afford to buy a house with the prize money he's made over the years. You should join the navy."

"No, that's not for me. Although I work onboard ships all the time when they can't sink." The marine blinked slowly and Abraham saw that he couldn't meet the mental challenge—too many ales.

"What do you mean? When can't they sink? There's not a ship afloat we couldn't blast full of holes." It was as though Abraham had insulted his honor. "Not three months ago we took on a French man-of-war, huh?" He looked to his friend for confirmation.

"Aye, and it would have been ours if the wind hadn't changed and pushed her off," said the other. "What ship did you say you sailed?"

"Mate, he said he crewed the ship that can't be sunk. No such a ship." The voice now sounded like mumbling.

"When can a ship not sink?" Abraham continued the game, laughing.

"When it's filled with French nuns." The drunken sailor's eyelids were barely open.

"Let's see..." The bigger one, ignoring his friend, tried hard to concentrate on his tough riddle. "What if it's filled with empty rum barrels? No, that wouldn't work. What if it's stuck on a reef?"

"Hmm, I suppose it shouldn't go down then. Still, that doesn't fit. I said I was on them all the time and they can't sink." Abraham wondered how many tankards they'd had.

"All right, that's true. And we're talking about big warships that sail the seas." The big man's eyes glazed over in deep thought.

"That's right. The ships I'm on are big and sail the seas." Abraham enjoyed the fun. "While I'm onboard they can't sink in storm or battle." Other marines at a distant table listened and laughed at their mates' drunken answers.

"I just can't get this one, matey. You've got me."

"What do most men do at Woolwich? Not the men in the armory."

"Ah, they build ships." The marine still had a problem making the connection.

"And that's done..." Abraham waited for him.

"On the slips—on dry land where the ships can never sink!"

"Good, you got it! I'm a shipwright, although I don't have a job now." He tried hard not to laugh as the tavern keeper smiled and shook his head. Abraham had known him for years and he was honest, as innkeepers go.

The marines across the room had enjoyed it even more since they knew the two drunks. One called to the marine, "Send the carpenter over this way so he can talk to someone sober!"

Abraham got up and joined them. For hours, they told of their travels over the seas and the action they'd seen against the enemies of the crown. They all drank pint after pint and, the last Abraham remembered, they helped him to bed where he promptly fell asleep.

Abraham awoke after fitful dreams of jumbled images and conversations. His body protested the previous evening's abuse, but an odd feeling prodded him awake. His bleary vision in the darkened room showed familiar yet out-of-place objects, and the inn's room had changed. He swayed, or rather the floor on which he lay swayed, in a long roll to one side and then the other. Abraham feared the worst

.

Chapter Three

The Shilling

The *Northumberland* rocked to and fro with the rhythm of the sea as she rested at anchor. The first lieutenant had a scant hour remaining to make certain everything appeared perfect to impress the captain during the inspection, including the crew and stores.

He unlocked and opened the carpenter's storeroom. There sat Abraham on the floor with his back against a tool chest, his hands cushioning his aching, bowed head. "When an officer enters the room—salute!" the lieutenant ordered.

Abraham, bewildered, blinked at the young lieutenant. "I'm not in the navy. I'd never enlist in the navy." But, admittedly, he remembered little after he sat with the three marines.

"Check your pockets. There's a shilling for enlistment as a ship's carpenter. You're aboard the king's ship, *Northumberland*. In less than an hour, the captain will be inspecting, so make yourself presentable on deck or take a flogging."

As the officer left, Abraham shook his head in disgust at what he'd always feared might happen. A Letter of Protection would have shielded him from being pressed. The marines must have heard him say he didn't have a job. He wondered about the payment and reached into his left pocket and pulled out the shilling.

Abraham wondered if a marine had slipped it into his pocket. He'd never enlist in the military whether drunk or sober. Maybe he could make himself presentable and take his case to the captain during the inspection.

Stretching upright on protesting legs, he staggered out of the carpenter's storeroom onto a long darkened deck. No one was present, and he looked around, recognizing the other storerooms and cribs common to a 64-gun ship. A few moments later he saw the lieutenant at the opposite end.

"Make yourself ready and get topside or the marines will come for you." The officer locked the small carpenter's storeroom and left.

"Yes, sir." Abraham made his first salute. He'd play their game until the captain rescinded the fraud.

Abraham found a scuttle barrel of fresh water outside the carpenter's storeroom and washed and arranged himself. Noises at the other end of the empty deck drew his attention. He ventured aft and knocked on a cabin door.

"Aye?"

"Excuse me, might I ask you a few questions?" The door opened and a man wearing civilian clothing appeared.

He stood an average height, balding, and was about thirty-five years old. "Hello, I'm the ship's surgeon, Mister Lake. You're the new ship's carpenter, aren't you?"

"Yes, I'm Abraham, a carpenter. Whether I'm the ship's carpenter is unclear. An officer told me I enlisted last night, although I don't remember it. I hope to talk to the captain or master." His ears and cheeks were still flushed over his predicament, but he controlled his anger.

"Aye, I see. Well, captains and shipmasters punish trouble-makers. I'd have to mend your back after a flogging. You don't recall coming aboard singing with the marines, without protest?"

"Now I remember, although I wasn't sober." Abraham put his hand on his forehead. "The captain will understand. He must!"

"An honorable man is a man of his word, drunk or not. Last night you pledged to serve the king. Accept the fact—you're in the navy." The surgeon shrugged and added, "We lost the carpenter's mate in battle and you're all we have except for the ship's master carpenter and a few carpenter helpers. The marines had a right to take you whether or not you agreed, and a volunteer gets much better treatment than one forced into serving.

"If you impress the captain, he may someday commission you as a ship's master carpenter, a warrant officer. You'd get shore leave, a bonus, and more wages. Anyway, you're in the navy for at least four years, longer if the war continues."

"I wanted shipyard work," Abraham snapped. "I can't believe this is happening!"

"Relax, my friend. There's plenty of time to sort your thoughts. We aren't due to set sail for days." The surgeon led Abraham to the upper gun deck and a midshipman showed him where to stand with the crewmen.

The captain arrived with due ceremony. After the inspection, Abraham and Mister Lake, the surgeon, chatted and he realized he should be thankful to be a ship's carpenter; they could have made him an ordinary seaman. If so, he'd be pulling grueling watch duties. As a carpenter, he'd only have to work day watches. Since the captain declared it a ship's holiday, topmast seamen, masters, and officers got shore leave until nightfall. Abraham had to stay onboard, so he paid sixpence to an honest sailor to fetch his belongings, including his tools, from the Lion's Head.

That night, although exhausted, the day's stress left him uncomfortably awake, swaying in a hammock, rump-to-rump with others belowdecks. Waves of emotions flooded his mind: self-pity forefront, followed by self-disgust.

On his first workday on the *Northumberland,* the ship's purser assigned him a pay number and introduced him to the master carpenter. Abraham protested his forced enlistment to both men, but they just smiled and told him not to waste their time. A backlog of work existed for the ship, and they expected him to get right to it. Abraham had always worked on ships in slips or at anchor and lacked the knowledge for repairing parts in use. As the days passed, the carpenter helpers assigned to his crew showed him the clever tricks he hadn't needed for repairs on shore. He also learned the futility of pleading a case that refuted what a marine officer claimed. As a constant reminder of his foolishness, he put a hole in the enlistment shilling and wore it hanging from a cord around his neck.

A week later, the order came to set sail. He didn't know their destination or when they'd return. How strange, Abraham mused, weeks earlier he'd wanted any carpenter's job and now he couldn't get out of the one he had. In the end, it assured him of years of steady employment; that was the nub of it. Even though it wasn't what he had planned, for now, he'd do his best as a *Northumberland* carpenter's mate.

* * *

During the year since Yvette last saw Abraham, she often looked back with regret for rejecting him. The disappointment over her foolhardiness hadn't subsided, although religious training taught that penance healed the soul. Yvette had a long way to go before forgiving herself for being deceived by René, who'd lied to her, and for hurting blameless Abraham, who'd loved her.

On reflection, it surprised her to find that her deep religious beliefs might have led her to false conclusions. She had chosen René over Abraham because of Abraham's agnosticism and René's Catholicism. Her mistake was in believing words over actions. René professed to be Catholic but behaved like a heathen. Abraham was agnostic but acted saintly. She had measured them on a very inaccurate scale, and the epiphany rocked her to the core. How could she have let her beliefs lead her so astray?

Anton received a letter from Abraham describing his impressment into the navy and the day it arrived, he took a walk with Yvette.

"Yvette, I must ask you this question and please answer it as truthfully as you can." He realized his news would cut her deeply. "I've received word from Abraham. Now that René is no longer engaged to you and back at sea, do you still hold any interest in Abraham? That is to say, when you ceased the courtship with him, was it conclusive?"

The boldness of her father's inquiry awakened the contrast between Abraham and René. He did not know, but all her aspirations since New Year's Day had centered on the only other man she had ever loved. Anton had stirred buried feelings nothing could restrain.

A choking sob came from her throat. More followed until her eyes were pools of tears and her lips trembled with the sorrow of past delusions. Her head bowed as she sobbed in loud convulsions, startling her father.

"My dear, I didn't understand! I'm sorry." He saw the display was truth enough of an answer. A sadness grew in Anton, who knew there was little he could do to ease her pain. "Come, come, now. Let's see how we can correct things."

"He...," she muttered, "he..."

"All right, all right." Anton sympathized with a gentle touch on her bent head. "Don't speak until you're better."

After a few minutes, her breathing returned to normal, soft sighs replacing the gasps. She pulled a handkerchief from her pocket and wiped her nose.

"I'm sorry for that spectacle." She dabbed her wet eyelashes.

"That's all right, my dear. I might have reacted likewise in your situation. Let me inform you, however, things are complicated now. You should understand Abraham has taken a new course. And I mean that literally."

"What's become of him?"

"I guess I should start from the beginning...." He told her of Abraham returning to Woolwich and getting pressed into the navy. "Right now I have no idea where he is. Abraham could be thirty miles from here outside the bays or three thousand miles across the ocean."

She didn't speak, tears still rimming her eyelids. At last, regaining her composure, she asked her father the one burning question to which he hadn't yet provided the all-important answer.

"Father," she said, her head down with eyes shut, "do you think he'd take me back?"

Anton foresaw she might ask and realized she knew the answer as well. He sighed, his voice full of compassion. "I have no idea. That is something you have to ask him yourself."

* * *

By April, the large 64-gun ship had seen no action, although its accompanying frigates had made a few captures away from the squadron. The seas swelled heavier that month and Abraham spent many hours ill from the roll. Others had tricks to help them overcome their seasickness; he tried them as soon as he learned of a new one, but nothing eased the recurring ailment. Often he had to report to the officers and commander, discussing the condition of the ship. He had abandoned his false impressment claim and instead counted the days to when his forced indenture would end. In the meantime, his captain, Thomas Watson, was an amiable and capable officer in his mid-thirties and portly. Many onboard claimed his pleasant disposition emanated from the bottle.

On the seaboard of France, they always kept ten miles from the coast. The land appeared as just a tan or green haze on the horizon. So close to Brest, its nearness and memories of Yvette pestered him. Still, he was kept busy as the ship's master carpenter had taken ill soon after departing Woolwich; the bulk of the work fell upon Abraham.

One day, the captain called him to his cabin for what Abraham thought to be a discussion on a repair. "Robinson, come and sit."

He grabbed a chair from the table and turned it toward the captain's desk.

"Mister Robinson, everyone agrees you're more than a capable carpenter's mate. Truth be told, you're the best carpenter

I've ever had onboard a ship, and I've had many a good one. Today I'm sending a request to consider you for a promotion to master carpenter, a warrant officer." As the captain spoke, Abraham detected a slight garble to his speech, reminding him of the rumors.

"Thank you very much, sir." Abraham was pleasantly shocked. "I do my best." Leaving with the captain's permission, he fantasized over the prospects of master carpenter's pay.

The *Northumberland* was an old ship that demanded many repairs, for which Abraham was now responsible. Aside from expected damages, the sea presented a variety of new problems, most of which Abraham had never had to deal with in the harbor. Sailors claimed a seaman on fair seas can never become an able-bodied seaman; the same applied to good shipwrights—tribulations teach the best lessons.

After the ship escorted a convoy to Lisbon, the master carpenter, his illness worsening, disembarked to a hospital ashore. Abraham was, in every practical sense, the new master carpenter. The *Northumberland* and the flotilla sailed north.

On May 8th, in early dawn off the coast of Ushant, Captain Watson was ordered to intercept a nearby ship to discover its nationality. Topmen hung more canvas to catch the slow breeze. Before noon, the wind strengthened and the warship gained speed. The convoy was left far behind them.

"Captain," said the first lieutenant, "the Admiral is signaling us to cease the pursuit and return to the fleet."

"Really? You can make out his flags? Lieutenant, I prefer not to see them through the haze." The captain smirked. "Continue the chase."

"Sails starboard!" they heard a few hours later.

"What have we got here?" Captain Watson asked as they neared the unknown ships.

"Two two-deckers and a smaller one, a frigate, corvette, or perhaps a merchantman, sir."

The shipmaster, overhearing the comment, added his concern. "They're French by the looks of them. Two are likely third-rate, our size, and the other has a deck of guns. We're out-gunned and should abandon the chase and return to the fleet as I see it, Captain."

"French?" The captain slurred his words, betraying too much wine. He watched the distant warships in a trance, almost smiling.

"Sir, they look to be heading straight to engage us. Shall we return to the fleet?" said the first lieutenant.

"I've never run from the French! Keep a steady course. We have good wind and we'll be on top of them in no time."

"Should we beat to quarters, sir? We're closing on them fast," the first lieutenant said nervously.

"Of course. To quarters, take in topgallants and stunsails! Clear decks, and stow hammocks! Let's discover what stuff these Frenchmen are made of. Make for that one!" He pointed to the more distant of the two closest ships. The smaller ship had veered off.

It alarmed the shipmaster, who commanded sailing when not in battle, that Captain Watson had not chosen the closer ship to attack. Attacking the farthest, gave the closer warship time to turn and attack their stern.

But as the drums called the men to their stations, those topside had too little time for everything that needed to be done. The command had come late and they were rushed.

"We'll take them one by one." The captain saw the second warship approaching head-on. She was a 62-gun maneuvering to give him a broadside in passing abeam. The blast of her cannons echoed loud in the ears of the crewmen on both ships.

Abraham manned his station below to check for hull damages on the orlop deck and in the hold. He overheard the battle above and, for the first time, experienced what sailors felt in terrifying engagements at sea: fear. The quaking of the ship was tremendous as the *Northumberland* replied with her guns and Abraham grabbed a plank to steady himself.

"Head for the 64-gun!" Captain Watson tore for the French warship. As he made for her, the first ship turned about in the English ship's wake. "This will be a day they'll remember, Lieutenant," he said as they prepared to strike again. "Keep an eye out for the 62-gun astern."

"That's the *Mars* ahead, Captain. I've seen her before."

Within a minute, *le Mars* was passing and firing its port-side guns. Likewise, Watson's ship returned the fire with greater accuracy, shredding sails and raking the decks. The *Northumberland* turned for another run as the first French ship caught it halfway and blasted away the foresail of the *Northumberland*. Her huge foresail yard, falling and lying across the deck with a limp web of lines, made it difficult to man the fore-guns.

The first ship, *le Content,* navigated away from the *Northumberland* to wait for *le Mars*. Then, together, the enemy warships attacked the *Northumberland* from both sides in a continual shower of cannonball and musket fire. The carnage was everywhere; nevertheless, the firing continued with exchange after exchange—very ship showing more damage with every volley.

THE SHIP'S CARPENTER

Belowdecks on the *Northumberland,* the roars deafened the gun crews, who depended on hand signals from their officers, and the thick smoke of the cannons often blinded them, making aiming difficult. Men carried the injured below for the surgeon and his aides to attend. A few powder monkeys, boys as young as ten, were wounded in the firestorm while running powder canisters up from the magazine storeroom. Deep in her belly, the carpenters ran and crawled on the decks and in the hold inspecting the hull. Removed from the mayhem above, they checked hits below the waterline for leaks or other structural damage.

The power of the heavy iron thrown through the planked sides was devastating. Nothing had prepared Abraham for the continual pounding of doom upon the great wooden shell. His blood burned with excited, terrified energy. He hurried from side to side, fore to aft in search of damages. All the while, over him, cannon exchanges covered the decks with wood splinters, fallen lines, and wounded men.

The horror ground on for over three hours as the ships locked together in a contest of dominance and death. In the late afternoon, *le Mars*—crippled—withdrew from the action. Even so, *le Content* continued the barrage as injury to the ships and men mounted still higher. Captain Watson eventually staggered and fell upon the poop deck. Crewmen carried him below to the quarterdeck where he leaned against the mizzenmast, alive, though gravely wounded by a musket ball.

"Cease firing, we have struck!" A shout came from the poop deck above him.

Angered, Captain Watson turned to his first lieutenant, who was just as puzzled by the command. "Who called the strike, Lieutenant?"

As the first lieutenant climbed the stairs to figure it out, a blast from *le Content* shattered the helm. It instantly killed both helmsmen and took away the wheel in splinters. The ship lurched as the wind spilled from the sails, freeing the ship of any control.

"Damn the rascals. Leave firing and house your guns, we've struck!" The curse bellowed from the poop deck. It was the shipmaster trying to surrender. He and the gun master came running down the stairs followed by the first lieutenant.

The three hurried to the ashen captain, the shipmaster was shaking with fear. "We will all be killed! They are going to rake us fore and aft, Captain. Strike and let us cut away the masts, we'll be retaken tomorrow. The ship is without a helm and can't continue."

French cannons continued firing through the dense powder smoke, unaware the *Northumberland's* shipmaster had struck its colors. The officers carried the pallid captain below to the purser's cabin for the surgeon to tend. In a faint breath, Captain Watson gave a weak order. "Put her before the wind and continue the fight."

Unsure whether the existing damage put their warship in any danger of sinking, the first lieutenant sent for the master carpenter. Within a minute, Abraham arrived in the purser's cabin. "There's not an inch of water leaking in, sir. She's in fine shape below."

The shipmaster and the first lieutenant returned to the poop deck to consider Captain Watson's order, but the firing subsided just as the captain fainted dead away.

Abraham started back for the orlop deck when the ship bumped something. Shouts of "Cease your fire!" came from the upper deck, then the tromping of feet from French marines. The shipmaster had struck the colors, and the French had boarded.

"My God, we didn't strike, did we?" Captain Watson asked as a French lieutenant came to accept his surrender. Mister Lake, working on his wound, ignored the French soldiers, too busy to care.

"*Oui,* sir. Your ship is surrendered," said the French officer in English.

"The fool." Captain Watson, with little strength left, motioned to the doctor to hand him his sword; while still in the surgeon's hand, the captain pushed it toward the Frenchman. "Here, I won't need it any longer."

"He's finished," said the lieutenant to two marine guards as he took the sword. "Get the English officers on the upper gun deck so I can instruct them. Unarm the crew and take them to the gun deck. Careful, many will want to continue fighting!"

Abraham, understanding the exchange, was aghast: his ship had surrendered, his captain was seriously wounded, and worse —he was a prisoner of war!

The enemy ships tied up alongside and transferred the crew onto the *Northumberland* to sail her to France. Meanwhile, French marines forced the English crew to the gun deck bow with Abraham joining the throng of captives.

The battle-weary sailors on the prison deck stretched out for the night wherever they could find room. An ominous silence blanketed the cramped deck as the crewmen, exhausted, contemplated their grim futures. Fresh guards at the first light of dawn replaced the old ones, and prisoners awakened after frightful dreams of the battle.

Abraham and the others were forbidden to stand unless accompanied to go to the head. Besides the closed gun ports and cramped deck, the heat of five hundred men became unbearable, many of them moaning with wounds. The only relief came in the afternoon when marines brought kettles filled with beans and mounds of hardtack for the famished crew.

The same procedure repeated every day as the three ships headed east to the nearest port to claim their English prize. On the fifth night, the ships halted as anchors dropped into the sea.

The next day, Abraham peeked out of a splintered shot hole. He could make out just sea and sky with no sign of land but rumor had spread that they were near the coast of France. The ship might be sitting in the harbor of La Rochelle, Lorient, or any of a dozen smaller port towns along the coast.

By the seventh day, the temperature was sweltering, and French guards began to fear revolt. Prisoners were allowed in groups of twenty-five to the upper gun deck. The first group reported the *Northumberland* lay amidst French warships in a bay. Abraham was in one of the last groups and didn't get above until evening.

When he climbed into the breeze on the upper gun deck, he couldn't help but survey the ship's condition; it had suffered much damage and needed months of repair. Abraham gazed starboard toward the shoreline and saw many two- and three-masted topsail ships floating in the bay. Further to the east, he spotted a river leading inland and atop the hill surrounding the shore appeared to be a castle.

It was the château at Brest. He recognized its familiar features. The *Northumberland* was in the Road of Brest. They'd likely be sailing up the Penfeld River itself for repairs.

Abraham's head hung and he avoided the scene, remembering his life there, and wondered whether any of the carpenters he used to work with might be assigned to repair her. They'd be coming aboard soon after anchoring to assess the damages and take tallies of cargo. A parade of workers would be coming and going for days; then the idea occurred to him— escape!

Instead of sitting out the war on a prison hulk or in a disease-infested prison, he'd disappear into the milieu of Brest. He spoke the language and was familiar with the dockworkers, even many of the guards. All he had to do was avoid those who were aware he left France or was on the *Northumberland*. Just Yvette and her family knew, if Anton had told them, and perhaps a few at work or at the boardinghouse. The suddenly hopeful thoughts tumbled through his mind and tore back his sullen mental shrouds.

First, Abraham had to find a hiding place; the French wouldn't search for him if they didn't know he existed onboard. Since leaving port, Abraham had scrutinized every small nook and locker, every cabin and crawl space throughout the vessel in search of leaks and repairs. The French guards had yet to tally the prisoners or estimate a death count so, if hidden before the count, they couldn't miss him slipping away. Carefully reviewing what he knew about the ship's layout and the guards' stations, he devised a plan.

When it was Abraham's turn again to go above deck, he took the enlistment shilling from around his neck and palmed it in his right hand. Lingering, he went up last in the group and stopped on the third step, bending as though to put on his shoes. As expected, the rear guard nudged him with his musket; Abraham feigned falling forward and slid the coin behind a stair baluster, then continued to the upper deck.

He knew his entire plan depended on timing and stealth, so he was too anxious to enjoy his time in the fresh air. When the marines called the prisoners to go below, he took off his shoes.

As the men descended, he positioned himself as the fourth in line. The front guard was facing forward so the only guard watching the men was the staircase guard.

As Abraham reached the step with the coin, he slowed and kicked it toward the staircase guard. The coin landed with a ring. The guard turned right, seeing the coin, and reached for it. At that instant, Abraham lay on the railing on the other side of the staircase and rolled over it onto the deck. He was hidden from the guard's view and slipped under the staircase, crouching. Four of the men behind him saw his exit, but they said nothing and smiled. Picking up the coin, the guard returned to take his station watching the men. Abraham hid until they had all descended. The staircase guard turned forward, and Abraham slipped back behind the mainmast, perfectly still. Overall, he had been as quiet in his bare feet as a cat stalking a mouse; his plan had worked without flaw.

Once he heard the changing of the guard, he pried up the oakum sealing a deck patch of an old common pump hole with Anton's pocketknife, and climbed into it, pulling the patch back over him. As he stood on the orlop deck, laughter erupted from above: the crew knew he'd escaped. The French were befuddled but, as nothing was amiss, everything returned to normal.

The orlop deck was dark. To stay safe, Abraham had to get to the powder magazine one more level below. He crept to the bow until he found the magazine hatch. The grating was still unlocked. He lifted it and stepped onto barrels filled with gunpowder, slipping under the decking where he couldn't be seen by the fire watches that occurred three times a night.

During the second day in his hideout, Abraham felt the jar of a ship coming alongside. It was a prisoner transport. Hundreds of men shuffled above and Abraham anticipated that the *Northumberland* should weigh anchor to enter Brest. Not having eaten in two days, Abraham hurried in the darkness to the lockers that held the food stores. He fumbled his way to a hardtack barrel, soaked some biscuits in water, and filled his stomach, weevils and all.

The next day, French sailors descended to the hawser locker, adjacent to the powder magazine. First came the sound of a turning windlass with deep shuddering groans. Then the hawser pounded, heavy with seawater, striking against the side of the locker as they hauled the anchor upward from the rocky bay bottom. Once docked, the carpenters would come onboard to assess the damage and costs for repair; he'd walk off at day's end as any other carpenter.

When they anchored at the dock, they searched again for leaks, took a tally of the hold contents, and checked the lockers. No one sought an escaped stowaway hidden within a powder keg den.

Early the next day he sneaked up to the prisoners' gun deck to find out where they anchored. The bright morning light of May blinded him as he peeked out of a hatch. The ship was moored dock-side with a long gangplank. One guard stood with his back to the ship. Beyond that was a route to freedom.

However, in the full light, Abraham realized for the first time how dirty his clothing was. If he attempted to leave the ship dressed in such filth, no one would believe he was a carpenter. Abraham needed to get to his leather bag and belongings in the carpenter's storage room.

At the sound of footsteps, Abraham scrambled for the nearest safe spot, stepping outside onto the head gratings at the bow. Only the guard by the gangplank stood duty, so he stepped to the riverside. Now he had to wait before going back inside to retrieve his leather bag, clothes, a book, and money. He'd have to leave his precious tools.

A clattering caught his attention. The inventory takers had gone below to the orlop deck. Abraham left the head and climbed down the stairs to eavesdrop. The men were near the carpenter's toolroom and carried a large clanking ring of keys, swearing as they tried to unlock the door. In frustration, they pried it off with a cannon worm and began to list the tools. Eventually, the men left to check other storerooms and Abraham tiptoed down the staircase. They'd make counts in the aft lockers for some time, so he slipped into the open storeroom and changed.

He shaved off seven days of beard, straightened up his appearance, and got ready for the final step of his plan. Abraham now had a game of hide-and-seek to play with the inventory takers and fire watches.

The deck being silent, Abraham went to forage in the captain's pantry for decent food. Halfway along the deck a voice bellowed. "Halt! What are you doing here?" A fire watch approached with his pistol half drawn out from his belt.

"Oh, you startled me." Abraham feigned surprise and hurried for an excuse. "I'm taking the repair survey with two other carpenters. They're to meet me. I guess they haven't arrived yet."

"Other carpenters, huh? What's your boss's name?"

He replied with the most influential name he could think of: "Master Sculptor Caffieri. We have to make an evaluation of the ship and assess its damage."

"Caffieri, huh? What do you have in that bag?" He pointed to the leather bag.

"Just technical things I'll need; papers with charts and an instrument to measure the lay of the ship." He'd lied himself into a corner: how could he explain a compass, English books, and papers?

"Show me." The guard withdrew the pistol from his belt, cocking the hammer.

"Of course, sir." Abraham pulled out the compass and spun his cock-and-bull story. "I take this into the hold. First, I lay it on the keelson and take a direct coordinate reading of the lay of the keel juxtaposed to the north magnetic pole. Then I calculate using geometric formulas in my books if it's affixed true and straight in dimension all up and down the timber. It's rather technical, but I can show you if you don't mind the climb all the way to the ship's bottom. Come, see how I do it. Just don't step in the bilge water."

"Oh, no bother, I get what you mean. I think I've heard of it—the keelson and the pole formulas. That's right. All right, go to your business then. Sorry to have frightened you. If any other guards stop you, say Eduard checked you to do your work." He tucked his pistol back in his belt and walked away to search the rest of the ship. Abraham sent up a silent prayer to his agnostic god and a mute thanks to the ignorant guard.

With Eduard's approval, he could now wander the ship under the guise of an inspector himself: this was better than his original plan. Ecstatic, he headed to the forecastle and discussed with an inventory taker the damages to the spars and freeboard, pretending to take notes on the back of letters.

After fifteen minutes, Eduard returned. "Have the others come onboard to help you yet?"

"No, they'll arrive later in the afternoon to do their assessment. I've finished my share."

Eduard smiled and Abraham bade him goodbye, walking down the gangplank and off the *Northumberland* for the last time.

At first afraid, Abraham discovered his near invisibility, laughing while ambling out of the shipyard. In Brest, he didn't exist as an English prisoner, a carpenter, or a lover. No one was looking for or expecting him to be there.

The inn where he'd stayed when he'd first arrived in Brest was a safe place to hide, located far from the dock, friends, and coworkers. After paying for a room and a bath, he chose a cafe a few doors down and ate a large meal—his first in over a week—while he organized his plans. Afterward, he relaxed outside, enjoying the sounds and traffic. Abraham wanted to return to England, not just to avoid being a deserter but also to continue as a ship's carpenter. Before being pressed, he never thought a shipwright needed to work at sea. His sailing experiences, however, completed a circle of skills that would make him a better shipwright.

When Abraham got up to start back for the inn, he saw a large woman exit a shop across from him. She glanced at him, then walked away. At first, he didn't recognize her, but then realized it was Gaëlle, André's wife. He hoped she hadn't recognized him, and with the distance, it seemed unlikely. But anyone noticing him in Brest might have serious consequences, and he would have to be more careful.

Now, though, he'd have to concentrate on more important issues, like getting back to England.

CHAPTER FOUR

The Passports

Gaëlle sat with a smug smile and a raised eyebrow as she leaned over her emptied dinner plate toward André.

"Yvette told me her old beau got pressed into the English navy."

"Yes, my father said so. Abraham sent him a letter," André replied as he finished his meal.

"Well, however she learned it, can you guess who was eating today at a café?"

"Hmm, I'd say Yvette, but that wouldn't be a surprise. Who?"

"Abraham." She sat back, satisfied with her claim.

"No, that's not possible." André shook his head. "You made a mistake."

"It was him, I'm sure of it!"

"Well maybe, but don't tell Yvette. She's still sensitive over Abraham. And if he's smart, Abraham won't have anything to do with Yvette again regardless of her change of heart." He loved his sister, but the demands she placed on beaus drove him mad.

"It's not for you to say, though, dear," said Gaëlle. "They may amend things. Who knows what might happen?"

"I do. Yvette's bad luck for a man and has broken off every chance of marriage she's ever had. I pity the man who marries my sister because there's no long-lasting commitment in her. There's always a flaw somewhere. She'd find fault in Saint Francis." André crossed himself mockingly with a frown.

"Well, Yvette should discover if Abraham lied to her."

"I'm telling you—don't do it, Gaëlle—don't get involved!"

"You deal with Yvette your way and I'll do it my way. Tomorrow I have to visit your mother and I plan on telling Yvette. She has every right to the truth."

The next day, Gaëlle dropped by her mother-in-law's to leave some children's clothes for Louise to mend and took Yvette aside.

"I happened to notice someone yesterday and I thought I should mention it. André doesn't agree, and although we shouldn't dwell on old hurts, wouldn't you want to know if someone told you a lie?"

"Gaëlle, what is it?" Yvette laughed.

"Abraham wrote he sailed away with the English navy. It's not true! Yesterday I caught sight of him at the café by Moineau's shop. It was him—I'm sure of it. So, if he said he was in the navy, he lied."

"No. I wish it might be true, but no. He's a sincere person and I believe him. Abraham's in the navy and you must have seen someone who looks like him, that's all." But Yvette dearly wished Gaëlle was right.

"Yvette, I guessed you'd say that. I recognized him, and he recognized me, too, and hurried away." Gaëlle's fingers made a walking motion as she spoke.

Yvette, confused, assessed her claim. Gaëlle's eyesight was excellent, especially at a distance. But why should Abraham lie to her father and to what end, she wondered? Unless Abraham had heard her engagement had ended and lied because he didn't want to be involved with her again. Her face fell.

"I see what you're thinking, Yvette. Don't go assuming the worst. There could be a logical explanation to the whole affair."

"You're right. There are three possibilities: you're mistaken; Abraham lied; or, and the one I'll pray for, something else happened and he's back in Brest."

"I'm not mistaken, Yvette. I saw Abraham."

"If so, he may return. What time was Abraham at the café?"

"Around nine o'clock in the morning."

"Then tomorrow at nine I'll visit the café and decide for myself! Thank you for telling me, you acted as a genuine friend." Yvette couldn't eat the next morning so headed out early to the café. It was empty other than a woman drinking coffee, so she circled the adjoining blocks four times over the next hour, searching. When she couldn't find him, she remembered his first lodging in Brest and headed there.

"Excuse me, is there a Monsieur Robinson staying at the inn?"

"Monsieur rented room three, madam. Shall I tell him you're here?"

"Monsieur Robinson is here now?" A tightness formed in her chest.

"Yes, his key isn't in the room box." The housekeeper pointed to the empty cubbyhole. "He's probably still sleeping. Shall I knock him awake?"

"Well...no, I don't want to disturb him." Her heart pounded in her ears, excited and afraid. He still might have lied to avoid seeing her, but there was a chance for a third explanation. "May I leave Monsieur Robinson a message? Is there a quill and paper I may use?"

The housekeeper motioned to the little escritoire in the foyer. Yvette sat at the desk and wrote:

Abraham—My sister-in-law, Gaëlle, by chance spotted you in the café yesterday and told me of your return to Brest. I pray you will be kind enough to forgive my previous transgressions. I entreat you to meet with me for a conversation. Please yield to my request tonight at six at the old café. If however, you do not come, I will understand and respect your desire to stay detached from me.

In kindest loving esteem, I remain, your Yvette

Then she handed the note to the housekeeper who placed it in the key box, and Yvette walked homeward, anxious but overjoyed.

* * *

As Yvette finished her message, Abraham awoke after almost ten hours, his mind still groggy. The extra sleep had been needed. Afraid of seeing someone again who might recognize him, he decided to eat at a different café. So he hiked further toward the edge of town for breakfast and, in half an hour, found a small café.

"Good day, Abraham." Just as he finished eating, Hendrik glided to his table.

"Hendrik, how are you? It's been months!" Abraham marveled at running into another acquaintance.

"So, you're back in Brest. I heard you sailed for England."

"That's a long tale. It's enough to say I'm here for a few days and I'll be leaving again for London soon."

"Too bad. The boardinghouse misses you. There hasn't been a good card game since you left."

"Sit for a while so we can talk, Hendrik. I'm wondering what the best routes to England are with the war on in full. You traveled the Channel. Do the Calais passenger boats still sail to *Dover*? Or did they stop?"

"Not long after the war started, they discontinued them. Though experienced men still can get to where they need to go." He placed his finger aside his nose in a knowing way.

"Well, that's helpful news. How?"

"There are two ways. One is with a smuggler, but that's dangerous during the spring and summer with such good visibility. The second is a neutral merchant ship. It's legal and safe. If I had my choice, I'd go with a neutral ship. Yet, there's a problem."

"And what's that problem, my friend?"

"Too few neutrals come into Brest. The English patrols stop most of them and send them back, whereas in Le Havre there might be more neutrals and smugglers. And if you're going to Britain you'll need a passport." Hendrik shrugged and then added, "You can't travel these days unless for a good reason."

They continued discussing the war until noon and then parted ways. Abraham wanted to tell the navy about Captain Watson's fate, so he took a ferry to the arsenal's hospital across the river.

Captain Watson, he learned, had died from his wounds three days before. Even if his drinking had caused poor decisions that led to the capture of the *Northumberland,* Abraham still pitied the captain.

Back at the inn, the housekeeper gave him Yvette's note. As soon as he recognized her handwriting, a dilemma arose. If he communicated in any way with Yvette, she could be unknowingly abetting an escaped prisoner of war. If he didn't, she'd assume he didn't wish to see her again. Prudence told him not to meet with her; however, his longing overpowered caution. He decided he would depart by coach for Le Havre at once after meeting with her, regardless of the outcome. Abraham picked up his leather bag from the hotel and rushed to the station to buy a fare for that night.

* * *

Louise Façonneur didn't like the implications of that English heretic returning to Brest. Gaëlle had mentioned it, and she worried for her daughter. Yvette always allowed men to manipulate her, she felt, and this Anglican was the worst of the lot.

She even suspected that, if he hadn't lied about the British navy, he had been a spy the entire time, setting fire to *le Royal Louis*. To apprise the police of this possibility would be the patriotic and right thing to do with Catholic France at war with Anglican England.

That evening, both Louise and Yvette lied to one another about their destinations: Yvette claimed she was taking a walk, and Louise said she was visiting a friend when she actually headed to the police station.

Yvette, fretful over what her future might hold, ordered tea at the café and wondered if Abraham might not show. Then, by the doorway, she recognized the outline of a man carrying a leather bag. Her heart leaped.

"Hello, Yvette."

"Abraham." She stoked her courage, although sick in the stomach with foreboding. "Gaëlle was right, you're in Brest. I'm happy you came."

"It's something best not explained here." Abraham glanced around the café and offered his hand to walk outside.

While passing shop windows, Yvette asked, "Abraham, the letter said the navy impressed you in Woolwich, then Gaëlle said you were in Brest. So why are you here?"

"Yvette," he sighed, and slowed the pace, "both are correct. After I sailed to England, the navy pressed me into service. Over a week ago, the French captured the *Northumberland,* my ship, and I escaped. The French navy doesn't know it yet. I hope."

"Oh, my dear Abraham. I have so many questions and things to tell you." Yvette began her confession, relieved he hadn't lied. "I'm sure you think I'm an idiot for going back with René. He appeared sincere, and we were once so in love. In our meeting that night, he reminded me of things that I held close. Not just feelings for him, but my religion. Believing in his false sincerity, I refused to see his infidelities and real nature."

"When we last spoke, you said you loved me and not René," Abraham said. "Then in the letter, you confessed to love us both yet chose René. Today in your note, you wrote of affection for me and no longer for René. Not a night passed I didn't want to be holding you, but..."

Yvette interrupted, "'But why should I trust you?' you were going to say. Because my emotions did not stand still after we were last together. Now I realize my love for René was based solely on the fact that René was a strong Catholic. It had bothered me you weren't. You can't understand how deeply I hold my beliefs." She struggled for words. "My family has always been rooted in our faith," Yvette pressed a hand to her heart, "and I still am. I rejected you but I was wrong. My convictions are mine alone, and if I can be so mistaken in this, then it is not my place to judge you. It's not an error I'll make again."

"I see." Abraham paused, considering what Yvette said. It sounded sincere. Although it wasn't proof of her convictions for him or a guarantee it might not happen again for another deep-seated belief.

"I'm torn, Yvette, and still care for you. Yet, I'm aware of the futility of planning a future together regardless of our feelings." He clenched his jaw. "I've committed myself to serve in the navy —an enemy navy. Even if they discharged me next month, we couldn't be together until the war ended. Could our affections last that long?"

"They'd last that long on my part, Abraham. There's no doubt in my mind and heart that I love only you."

"So much has happened to us these past months. And the war will postpone our plans for years." His face dropped.

"Not if I were to go with you!" Yvette startled herself but she meant the words.

"What? How and where would you live and work? You don't speak English. Besides, I'll be leaving tonight for Le Havre." He shook his head, refusing to dwell on such madness.

"Learning English and finding employment will come. I want to be with you even if you're only home on leave."

"Yvette, that's unreasonable! You've never lived in a foreign country, let alone one at war with your native land. And there are other problems." He held up his hand and counted off his fingers, frowning. "I'm in the navy; you want to sail with an escaped prisoner to England; we aren't married; and you're French. I'd say things are against us."

"They appear on the surface as such, but compared to our chances of being together in January, they're an improvement. I'll make whatever sacrifices are needed." She grabbed his shoulders and gave him a gentle shake. "I want you more than before, do you understand?"

Abraham wasn't as sure of it as she, and he could not bring himself to allow the vision of being together to put her in danger. Abraham answered her longing gaze with a heavy heart.

"Going with me, I'm afraid, is impossible. No."

* * *

As Louise spoke, the long-nosed police officer listened and nodded. Inspector LaBrouche was polite and thanked her for the information, promising he'd investigate.

Louise felt she had done not just her family good, but had also helped the national cause. Even if he hadn't been a saboteur, one less Anglican on French soil, the better, she told herself.

When she got home, Anton was filling his meerschaum pipe. "Good evening, dear," he said.

"Hello, I was over at a friend's house."

She fiddled with the pewter utensils, raising Anton's suspicions. Her words, he thought, sounded wrong and hesitant. Anton could read her body language and tone of voice easily after decades of marriage. Something wasn't right, and she was hiding it.

"Did everything go well today, dear?" he goaded.

"Oh, just fine."

"Nothing new to tell me?"

Louise paused; she knew he had caught her fib. "Oh, no, nothing new."

"Are you sure?"

"Quite sure." She never could lie to him.

"Well, if there was something to tell you, you can be sure that I would. I've always trusted your opinion."

She broke. "Gaëlle did tell me your carpenter friend, Abraham, was back in town. Imagine, first the scoundrel wrote he was in the navy and now he shows up here in Brest! What rascals those English are. Nothing—only lies!"

The news bothered him. Anton trusted Abraham well enough to not suspect him of lying. Maybe his mangled hand had gotten him out of the navy. Anton decided to ask Yvette.

"Where's Yvette?"

"Oh, she was going for a walk. I suppose she's disturbed over what Gaëlle said. I hope she doesn't do anything rash. It won't do good to rekindle that relationship. The poor dear is still brokenhearted over René's engagement ending. And now this."

Anton hadn't heard her ranting about Abraham for months, and the issue irritated him. "Well, let it be. Yvette will handle it. She's a grown woman now." He took his seat by the fireplace and lit his pipe, satisfied the subject was closed.

* * *

"We can't let your parents find out I'm in Brest or escaped. It places them in jeopardy. The military or police won't care if they're aware of my escape or not. If they're helping me, that's enough to put them in jail. Did you mention I returned?"

"No, and I hope Gaëlle didn't either."

Abraham put his arm around her shoulders as they stood looking over the Penfeld. Both were happy for the moment, even if anxieties clouded their hopes. Yvette turned his head toward hers and, pulling his hat off of his head, kissed him for the first time in over a year.

After they embraced on the overlook, they walked back toward the coach station.

"I have only a little more money left to get back. Crossing the Channel may be a problem if I can't find a passage out of Le Havre. Perhaps I can bribe a captain to let me hide until we leave port."

"Must you go? Stay here and find a job until the war ends."

"That's desertion. I want to finish my naval service now. It's benefiting my career in ways I never expected, and will benefit me later. I must go back." It was the frustrating reality of his future.

"Then you must take me!"

"If we got caught in Brest, they'd put me back with the other war prisoners. If you got caught helping an escaped prisoner, they'd toss you into a dungeon for life, or worse! No, you can't come. It'd be too dangerous." Though they were true, Abraham regretted every word.

"I won't make the mistake of letting you leave me again. If you must return to the navy, it's just for a few years. Afterward, we'll start our own family." Yvette could not see a life without him now. She had rediscovered happiness, and it centered on being with him.

"After marrying, I assume. That will be in England or France? You see, we're restricted on how we can proceed."

"A wedding can wait. Here we are, Abraham, arguing over marriage and you're an escaped prisoner of war in an enemy country. Let's plant the seeds before reaping the harvest. First, you need to get out of France. Second, we'll figure out how to be together." Perhaps, she thought, both could be accomplished at the same time.

"I must leave tonight. I can't be in Brest for long without more people recognizing me." He rubbed his forehead.

"If you need a neutral ship, my brother could help. André knows every ship in the harbor." He might even know one that could stow away two people, she mused.

"No. We can't get him into trouble. I'll find a ship in Le Havre." Her family didn't need to jeopardize themselves for him.

"André knows you're here. Gaëlle has told him, I'm sure. He'd be happy to help us to leave. We'll have a better chance with his help."

"We? Getting me out is the priority. I haven't accepted the notion of you going along. No, it's too dangerous for you, and him."

"Abraham, it's not as if André never commits crimes. How does his family afford luxuries? The pay isn't that good. Smuggling is a big business in Brest. Merchants and captains pay pilots and customs inspectors bribes to ignore what's seen. André's never said, yet that's how things get done in Brest, and every port in France and England, too, no doubt."

Yvette was right of course, Abraham thought. Bribery was so rampant even police committed the crime. Still, he didn't want André involved.

When they turned the corner near his inn, Abraham suddenly jerked Yvette back from the street into a shadow. Standing by a storefront across from the inn were the same two police inspectors who had nabbed him that dreadful morning outside his boardinghouse.

"The police! Now there's no way to leave. They will check the coach station." His eyes darted around for others.

"Come home with me. We'll find a place to hide you," Yvette offered.

"The police know of our relationship and might be watching your house. No, I'll go to the docks or maybe the sellers' stalls and ask if any neutral ships are in port."

"Do you think the police won't be watching the docks?"

"That's a chance I'll have to take. I have no alternatives."

"There is one other, I can inquire," Yvette said. "They aren't looking for me. You stay hidden until I get the information and afterward, you can go to the ship when it's dark. You're familiar with the back alleys."

"That's placing you in a terrible position."

"You must agree I'm right, Abraham. There's no other way." Both saw the truth in it.

"How did they figure out I escaped? I don't get it. Gaëlle didn't tell them, did she?"

"No, not Gaëlle. I can't imagine how they found out, either." The only logical conclusion sprang to mind. "Oh, no," she said, her face drained. "She wouldn't."

He sighed. "Your mother."

"Gaëlle may have told her. She had no idea how Mama felt about you, damn!"

The curse word surprised Abraham, showing how her faith was changing. "My, Yvette, you're different since I last saw you. Well, if they found out from your mother I'm back in Brest and that I'm in the British navy, then..."

"The police presume you're either off of the *Northumberland* or here to burn another ship!" Yvette finished.

"This is not good. Being an escaped prisoner is one thing. If they speculate again I burned *le Royal Louis,* that's a whole different affair. I must leave Brest. I'm going to the stalls now."

"No! Asking at the dock will ensure police catch you. Go hide yourself, and I'll come get you when everything is safe. Don't worry, I'll watch out for those two."

Abraham thought for a moment. "We'll meet near the church that looks like Saint-Sulpice. Don't come until it's dark, say around ten or eleven. And for heaven's sake, be careful, Yvette!"

"If I can't get the name of a ship, I'll find a place to hide you overnight without implicating anyone. Don't worry, I'll find a way for it to work, Abraham."

Yvette kissed his cheek and sped off. When she got home, she set out dishes for dinner and sat to eat, not saying a word to her mother.

"How was your walk, Yvette?" Anton sat, wondering about what Louise had said.

"Fine, Father, I ran into an old friend today." She said tersely, still upset with her mother.

"Really, who was it?"

"Mother, can you guess?"

"Why, how should I know?" Louise answered flustered.

"Oh, I believe you do."

Anton detected a pending explosion and interjected, "Yvette, tell me. It was Abraham, wasn't it?"

"Yes, Father, it was. He's been in terrible predicaments since leaving Brest." Yvette glared at her mother.

Louise shook her head, grabbing her fork tightly. "Don't get involved with him, Yvette. Abraham is a lawbreaker. You must stay away from the Englishman."

"Lawbreaker? Why think that? Did you talk to someone about him, Mother?"

"Abraham is the enemy! If you help him they'll come after you." Her hands were on her cheeks, fearing the worst for her daughter.

"They? My God. What did you do?" Anton hissed.

"Mother found out Abraham was in Brest. She's told the police he's in the British navy." Yvette, with a frown, pointed a finger accusingly at her mother.

Louise crossed her arms. "Yes, I did. The inspector thinks he might be an English saboteur and came back to cause more trouble."

"Mother, you're not familiar with the matter and your suspicions are wrong. How could you not trust or ask me?" Red in the face, Yvette stood from the table.

"Yvette, sit and tell me what's happening," Anton pleaded.

"I can't, Father. I must go help Abraham." Yvette hurried to the door with her cloak in hand and tears in her eyes.

"Wait, I'll go, too. It's getting darker and you shouldn't be out alone so late." Anton grabbed his hat off of the hall peg, shaking his fist at Louise.

As they both hurried out of the house and down the street, Anton convinced Yvette to disclose the entire story. When she ended, he knew what to do.

"The stalls are a terrible idea. Most likely they will help for a bribe and then take another from the police to inform on Abraham. We have only one choice—André."

Yvette agreed, and they ran toward the docks to catch a ferry across the Penfeld. Soon they were knocking at André's door. Gaëlle answered.

"We have to talk to André right away," Anton puffed.

André, hearing his father, rushed to the door. "What's wrong?"

"Tell us what neutral ships are at harbor and sailing for England. We need to send somebody on one."

"Does this concern Abraham?" André asked.

"He's in Brest and needs to leave as soon as possible," Yvette confirmed.

André put a finger to his jaw. "A couple of neutrals are in port, but they're not sailing to England. There's one departing for Scotland though."

"Close enough. How can we get Abraham on it?"

"Oh, that's not a problem. The captain will be happy, or at least obliged, to take him for me. He'll get a forged passport for Abraham, too. Every time he comes into port I do him favors." André winked.

"How much will it cost?" Anton asked.

"Not much, maybe six livres. I probably can get it for less, say four or five. The captain owes me lots of favors."

"And for two?" Yvette asked.

Yvette's family turned to her, astonished, knowing what was in her mind. "I'm going with him. It's what I should have done when he left Brest the first time. I love him. Don't try to talk me out of it."

"Well." Anton had a lump in his throat. "I guess we had better hurry then."

André, excited by all the drama, quickly instructed Yvette. "I'll go to the ship to make the arrangements. You and Abraham come to the dock by the horse fountain at midnight on the stroke. The ship is in the Road of Brest so we'll sail out to it. Take whatever you can carry onboard."

"I'll go tell him."

"I guess I'll go home and pack your things," Anton said. "By God, Louise will help me, too!"

The sky had darkened to night when they got closer to the house, and Yvette parted from her father. The church was four or five blocks ahead and she became cautious of what was around her. Suspicious of everyone, she eyed people in the street and balconies and even faces in windows.

Finally, she came to the little park near the church. Yvette looked in the shadows but couldn't find Abraham or anyone else. Then, peering inside the church, through the disciples in the stained glass windows, she spotted the outline of a man. Distorted and lit by the glowing votive candles, he looked like one of the saints portrayed in the windows.

Abraham stood with his back to the altar in the central nave aisle, facing her when she entered.

"You're back so soon. Don't tell me you have the information already." Pleased by her fast return, he started for her.

"Better—the ship arrangements are being made as we speak. Let's sit here." She pointed to a pew and knelt, crossed herself, and Abraham sat down beside her.

"There's time. We'll meet my brother at midnight by the dock and he'll take us out to the ship. Don't worry, André isn't aware of why you're in Brest, just that you have to leave. Papa said it'd be best he didn't find out."

"Yvette, you told your father?" Abraham said, disappointed. "My father was bound to learn it when I left with you."

Abraham startled. "Oh, no. I never agreed to that!" He drew back. "What will you do in England when I'm on a voyage?"

"I can find work doing something. Like it or not, I'm shipping with you, sailor." She laughed and poked him in the stomach.

Abraham weighed the benefits. Despite the danger to Yvette, traveling with her might throw off any looking for a lone fugitive. What would his future hold being married to such a determined young woman? It brought a smile to his face.

They arrived at the dock just before twelve o'clock. Both stood in the blackness hidden by a looming stone buttress facing the river. Out of the dark, they picked out the shape and lantern light of a small pilot's sailboat approaching and made out André's shape at the bow. From further away, Anton shuffled along the dock with cases under each arm. Everyone climbed onto the boat.

The night breeze blew strong enough to push the sailboat down the Penfeld and out into the Road of Brest. As the lights of the merchant ship's lanterns grew closer, Yvette turned and wondered for a second if she'd ever lay eyes on her family or Brest again.

They climbed up the ladder onto the deck, and the captain greeted them with smiles and a Portuguese accent. Their compartment was not in a hidden hold locker, which both expected, but next to the captain's own. He had no fear of the customs officials and, like André, said most of the officials owed him a few favors; they'd overlook the two "Scottish" passengers and leave them alone.

Yvette bade goodbye to her brother and father as tears streamed down her cheeks. "Tell Mother I understand what she did. Tell her I love her and always will."

"Abraham and my dear, Yvette, this has all come about so suddenly. For the sake of expediency, a hand-fasting, the old custom, must do until you return to France for your wedding." Anton pronounced with tears. The brief ceremony was witnessed by her father and brother, and the captain. Abraham gave her his mother's locket as the token of his vow to wed.

With that done, she took Abraham's hand and waved as her family sailed back on the pilot's boat.

They made love that night in their cramped berth. To add more proof to her discovery of freedom, Yvette felt not a scintilla of guilt over it, a carnal sin or not in the eyes of the Church.

For Abraham, Yvette was worth all the torments of his escape. The binds of family, navy, religion, and propriety were severed. They'd do what they wanted to do, at least for the next few days. And they did—often.

Since they planned to go to London, the captain dropped them off at *Dover*. Abraham and Yvette went ashore and rode in a coach heading toward the great city.

Yvette, having never been more than thirty miles from Brest, was overwhelmed by London, her first big city. Buildings and streets flowed in every direction like wheel spokes. That night, they stayed at an inn not far from the coach station.

The next day, Abraham hurried to the Admiralty buildings near Westminster. After explaining the happenings aboard the *Northumberland,* Abraham was sent to the Admiral of the Blue Fleet's office. A very pleasant lieutenant discussed the battle with the *Mars* and *Content* and took him to a clerk who transcribed his account. Word had reached the Admiralty of the capture of the *Northumberland;* however, no one had learned of Captain Watson's death, and this news caused a stir among those listening.

The officers who heard his tale congratulated Abraham on fleeing his captors. Abraham mentioned that Captain Watson had recommended him for a warrant officer commission before his death. An officer found the request and sent him to

Shipwright Hall for the required master carpenter examination. Hours later, another officer told him to check back at the office for the results and his new assignment.

The next day, he showed Yvette around London and they looked for a place to live. As they inquired about flats on the east side, they met an attractive French woman who overheard Yvette's Breton accent. She lived nearby, but in a wealthier neighborhood, and they talked for almost an hour about people back in Brittany. Afterward, she asked Yvette to call on her to keep up her Breton language skills, offering in exchange to help Yvette learn English.

Yvette's livelihood was their major concern. Although well-educated for a female, she had no contacts to find a job even as a servant or maid. Anton had given her enough money to last a few months, but finding a job would be difficult for one who spoke no English. Pay for Abraham's voyages might be months or even years apart. And more unsettling, the navy seldom paid on time.

Abraham visited the Admiralty daily, anxious over his commission and next assignment. With every passing minute, he came closer to leaving Yvette and felt guiltier and guiltier about it. She was willing to wait for his visits after his long patrols, work in a foreign country, and even put off marriage, all to prove to him her devotion. But these sacrifices were also atonement for her guilt over jilting him.

One day while Abraham visited the Admiralty, Yvette made good on her promise and called on her new friend in London.

Madame Goubert, not quite five years older than Yvette and unmarried, resembled her so much they could pass for sisters. Her uncle had been a clockmaker in France who moved to

London many decades earlier. She had inherited his estate and moved to London permanently from Quimper, south of Brest.

At the end of the week, Yvette received a note from her friend telling her of a bookshop on Birchin Lane near Cornhill whose proprietor needed a French-speaking clerk. Yvette rushed to the shop on the east side of London with Abraham as her interpreter.

"Good day. We're here to see Mr. Willocks." Abraham smiled politely.

"That's me, what can I do for you, sir?" He was an older, spectacled man, whose too-small wig barely covered a balding head.

"A friend informed my wife of your open position. Are you still looking for a clerk?" asked Abraham.

"No, no. I'm seeking an assistant for buying. An educated man who speaks and reads French fluently."

"Well, my fiancée speaks and reads French and just arrived in London. However, she speaks little English," Abraham admitted.

"Hmm, I'm looking for a man." Mr. Willocks' examined Yvette; it was her smile that did the trick.

"Can she read well?" He handed her a book in French on science. Yvette flipped it open randomly and read a passage on the chemical properties of zinc until the owner motioned to stop. Then he turned to her and spoke in perfect French. "Good, you can read, and your numbers? Is your math good as well?"

"Yes, sir. And I learn faster than most."

"Do you tire of walking? How are your legs?" He pointed at her skirt.

She pulled it up, showing him her muscular calves. "I have strong legs. I love strolling."

Somewhat taken aback by the immodesty, he laughed, shook his head, and continued. "I didn't need to see them." Her

99

openness tickled him. "What I need is someone to visit other booksellers, negotiate a good price, and buy French books. I don't have time for it or the strength anymore. It doesn't pay much, but the work isn't very demanding."

"Will I shop the whole time?"

"Only as long as the sellers are open. When you return, you will help me close up my shop. Climbing up the ladders is getting harder with my weak back. If you are interested, you can start tomorrow. I'll pay you eighteen pence a day."

"That's low. A common laborer makes twenty pence a day," Abraham said, frowning. "And they can't read their own name. Yvette is educated and smart."

"She's a woman."

"But also attractive, that alone will reduce your costs when she haggles."

"Agreed, twenty pence a day. That's if she can learn to speak enough English within the month." Mr. Willocks would have paid more for such a pretty assistant, but he was a businessman after all.

"Fine, I'll learn English well."

Having her first real job thrilled Yvette. As they left the shop, she tried to allay any worries Abraham might have. "I'll be fine not knowing English for a while. Other French speakers are around. Many Protestant Huguenots live in the Spitalfields near here. Madame Goubert told me they own the silk weavers' shops and lots of others."

"Although she's right, from now on we should speak in English. It'll force you to learn it faster."

Yvette's first workday began with Mr. Willocks telling her what French books to buy and how to get them for a good price.

His was one of many foreign bookshops in that section of the city. The Cornhill area held a diversity of nationalities and was a poorer, somewhat crime-ridden part of London. The Royal Exchange, however, was close to the shop and the well-heeled frequented the popular coffeehouses and tea rooms in the area.

That afternoon Mr. Willocks sent her for biography books. After expecting Yvette to return with four or five books for the money he gave her, she returned with seven.

"Well, you *are* a good haggler. And these are nice books." He looked over her purchases, smiling.

"One thing I do well is bargain. The Royal Exchange's tower makes a great landmark, too, so I don't get lost."

Daily, her skills improved and by week's end, she was familiar enough with the streets to hurry back to help in the shop. Yvette's enthusiasm and sprightliness, not to mention her dickering talents, impressed Mr. Willocks more and more.

After scouring the area near the shop, Abraham found a small flat they could afford on Castle Court Street, only four blocks from the bookstore. It came with a stove, an old table, and two rickety chairs.

The next morning, Abraham visited the Admiralty to ask if his new assignment or commission arrived.

"Your orders have come and you're to proceed to the naval docks at Plymouth and board the *Lark,* a 44-gun. She's new out of Liverpool and will be fitted out in Portsmouth for duty in the Blue Fleet. Report no later than five days from today. It will take four to get there."

"Aye, sir. Oh, did they say if my certificate for commission as a master carpenter came?"

"You need your Master Carpenter Certificate to show to the purser when you board," the officer answered and motioned for Abraham to sit again as he walked out of the office.

After fifteen minutes, he returned with a folded document and handed it to Abraham. "Here's the commission. The navy is overlooking the rule for a full six months' duty due to your experience at Woolwich and your temporary master carpenter duties on the *Northumberland.*"

"Aye, sir." Abraham saluted and left. The warrant officer's pay would afford to make Yvette comfortable. However, this good news came with regret; Abraham would be returning to sea.

When Yvette got back from her work, she broke down hearing they had just precious hours together.

"Abraham, I know this last year and a half has been hard for you, but I'm here now no matter what." Yvette reached her arm around him, kissing his neck. "Remember, I will always love you and be here to care for you. Maybe knowing this will help you during some dreadful time."

Her impassioned words comforted him, driving away many of the apprehensions he had carried about returning to sea and leaving her alone. The next day, their final embrace lasted long. Abraham gave her money and took the four-day coach to Plymouth.

The *Lark* was a large new vessel with two decks of guns. The painted bulwarks and gunports were still bright, and the rigging was fresh. Routine tasks would have to be performed each day, but until the sea wore away at her there would be little for him to repair.

Abraham found the officer on duty, Lieutenant Burston. He requested the carpenter's storeroom be opened for his inspection, so Lieutenant Burston walked with him below to unlock it. Even as a warrant officer, the master carpenter couldn't use the key until a higher-ranked officer inspected the locker.

"Sir, have you sailed with this captain before?" Abraham asked.

The lieutenant replied smiling, "It's my first voyage with Captain Wickham."

"I was on the *Northumberland,*" Abraham explained. "The French captured her a month ago, sir."

"Yes, I heard of that. She was a rebuilt ship, I believe."

Abraham poked his head in the tool locker and inspected everything. "Aye, sir, and now she's a newer rebuilt French ship, although in terrible shape the last I saw of her."

"They exchanged you quickly enough," Lieutenant Burston said, surprised.

"I escaped in Brest. The crew is still in France."

Lieutenant Burston's eyes widened. "Quite brave. I'm impressed."

"Thank you, sir." Abraham put away some of his things. "Do you have an idea where we are headed on this voyage, sir...the French coast, the Mediterranean, or the Channel?"

"No, I'm not sure where until the captain opens the orders."

Abraham completed his inspection. "Everything in here looks in good shape, sir. Thank you for the information." Abraham gave the key back to the lieutenant, hoping Captain Wickham's orders would be for a short patrol.

* * *

Shortages of commanders forced the French to promote more, including René, to the rank of *ensigne de vaisseau.* Earlier in the summer of 1744, the navy ordered René's ship, *la Fine,* to accompany François's *l'Emeraude* on missions. When they returned to port, he and François met at a favorite tavern to discuss their joint patrol.

"As I recall, *la Fine* keels somewhat," François noted, seeing her in convoy.

"She's not the easiest to handle, but decent. Truth be told, I'd prefer a larger and faster ship."

"They're building a frigate now called *la Renommée* that's supposed to be fast, and another similar one in Québec, *le Castor*. She's made of Canadian wood, though, and won't compare to a vessel built here. Polish and Russian masts are best; I wouldn't spit for Canadian lumber."

"Good masts may be hard to get in the future from the foreign timber merchants," François sighed. "The English pay in gold and we offer promises and paper."

"I've always liked your new ship, *l'Emeraude,*" René said.

"For a 24-gun frigate, she's smart enough. Our next mission will be a test for both of us." Without regret, François had accepted the transfer off the cramped *la Naïade* onto the larger vessel. The more guns one carried, the better the chances of survival.

The fraternal bond between François and René gave them an advantage in sailing patrol together. In the first few weeks alone, they encountered four unescorted merchant ships and captured them with little difficulty. The brothers rose in regard among Brest naval officers, receiving commendations for their bravery in battles; it was not the norm for the French to embrace such an aggressive policy on the seas.

In January of 1745, François spotted the foggy ghost of a ship in his spyglass. A lookout called her out and the sailors leaned port side to catch sight of the vessel. Through the haze, it was impossible to distinguish her colors. *L'Emeraude* had separated from *la Fine* during a squall the night before and this vessel might have been his brother's; François gave an order to follow, hoping the winds might change.

Soon, the distant flag revealed itself to be distinguishably darker than the all-white French flag. As soon as his warship gained on the other, the red field of the flag stood out, most likely, a merchantman. François ordered the crew to quarters. Still an hour away from engaging, the ship appeared to be heading in the direction of Plymouth.

"It'll be an easy catch. She's an old ship and crank with uneven ballast. Lieutenant, keep a glass on the horizon for the enemy or *la Fine.*"

As they gained on the ship, François weighed all the different factors: the currents, roll, and wind direction, before deciding to take the English ship on her leeward side. This would allow his gunners to aim at her masts if she ran. A chase gun fired a warning shot but the merchantman did not surrender. *L'Emeraude* closed in on her.

Within musket range, a port side cannon on the forecastle put a lucky shot through the merchantman's main topsail spar, and it crashed upon the deck with a thunder. The merchantman, out-gunned and out-maneuvered, stood defenseless against the superior warship. It fired a few disorganized volleys at *l'Emeraude,* missing her. Then the English ship wisely struck her colors.

"Not bad. A few days into the new year and we caught one," François boasted to his lieutenant. He sent a boarding party to take over the ship, and word came back that she carried dried cod and rum in her hold. "They were probably sold to the English captain by the French in Louisbourg in Cape Breton, and now are French again," he joked.

The joking did not last long. The lookout shouted, sighting two more sails westward on the horizon.

"They're merchants. British!"

"Place this merchantman between us and the oncoming two ships, lieutenant, and hoist the English flag. Get everyone off of our decks." François planned to lure in the two distant merchant ships under the guise of being a British warship.

When the two merchantmen advanced within gun range, François sailed out from behind the merchantman, hoisted his French flag, and headed straight for the two unsuspecting small vessels. The captains had approached together, a serious blunder, as even together they stood no chance against the warship. If one had gone ahead to investigate, the other might have fled. But both within range of the warship left neither an escape.

The closer of the two opened fire with a small gun, and the shots missed. François wore to expose his starboard side guns and returned fire at both vessels. On the farther vessel, one shot took away the jib, and François circled for another run at the merchant ships now turning to flee with the wind. The slow merchantmen lumbered compared to *l'Emeraude,* and she caught up to them before they had completed the turn.

"Fire as you bear!" He shouted to the gun crews. The cannons thundered as the damage mounted on the two British ships.

"Come about her stern on a broad reach." His ship cut across the stern of the closest merchantman, cannons joining in a devastating fire at the stern of the ship. Although a hundred yards away, *l'Emeraude* loosened the merchant ship's rudder from its pinions and it hung in the sea, dangling from preventer chains. The merchant captain couldn't steer, reduced his sails, and took down his flag in surrender.

François headed for the last fleeing quarry. Half a mile ahead of *l'Emeraude,* the remaining merchant ship's speed couldn't match the deft French warship. In less than ten minutes, François's ship overtook her and blasted away at her port quarter and quarterdeck. His chain shot destroyed her mizzen shrouds, and his marines with musket fire drove much of the crew below deck. After another twenty minutes of continual fire, the final merchantman likewise struck its colors.

"That's incredible—three in one day!" François realized the absurd luck that afforded him such success and without any deaths of his crew. Two and a half months earlier, when he'd captured a corsair called *Godolphin,* it had cost him seven men. Illness rested in God's domain, but battle was strictly man's realm. As captain, his decisions sent men to their graves. Crew deaths always bothered him.

Not long after the victory, *la Fine* appeared to the south and joined them. René had picked up on the sounds of the guns and feared a clash. They soon discovered that all three captured merchant ships contained full holds and, at a celebrating Brest, François received congratulations.

That night, François met Marie in Brest with the news of his accomplishment. She, as usual, focused on her relief that he'd returned unharmed. His praise of René as a commander brought a weak smile.

"Mama," said Louis on François' last day of shore leave, "I'll be a captain, too. Won't I?"

"Oh, most certainly you will." She would have to pray harder, she thought, to change his dream. She didn't mind Louis in the navy, but she didn't want him at sea.

"Do you have to go so soon, Papa?" Louis pleaded. Marie Charlotte shook her head, her eyes widened hopefully. "I'm afraid I do. Perhaps I'll be back within a month, though it might be longer." François regretted his answer.

Under low gray winter clouds, François returned to his ship, rechecking his charts and lists. The *la Fine* had sailed alone southward earlier on patrol. François, now used to his brother's company, wished that René could have continued sailing with him.

L'Emeraude sailed the next day to patrol south of the Irish coast to harass the shipping routes. Then later he'd join up with two other frigates in the Channel near Le Havre.

On the 19th of January, François outran a pursuing enemy frigate and a sloop coming from the east. Enemy warships now filled the seas as the war dragged on. They'd have alerted other ships that *l'Emeraude* prowled nearby, so he increased the lookouts.

The next morning, just after sunrise, his men spotted a merchant. The vessel, 120 tons and not a match for his frigate, sped toward the west coast of England. Within three hours he had caught up to it.

"Lieutenant, fire one to let her know we've got her." François watched the imminent catch through his spyglass.

As the cannon roared its threat, he saw the captain of the merchantman on the quarterdeck turn to the noise and raise his fist in defiance. The *Marborough's* captain prepared his ship to put up a vain fight. When *l'Emeraude* swept astern windward of the merchant's port quarterdeck, it stole from the merchantman's sails, slowing her, and François ordered the ship to surrender. Nevertheless, even out-gunned, the captain of the vessel remained defiant, promising a blood bath for his crew.

François noted the crew manning their few guns and lining up along the midships with muskets. He ordered marines to fire a round at the quarterdeck. The loud volley sent splinters raining upon the foes. Their captain, grasping his chest, staggered to the rail and fell hard, blood spilling along the deck planks.

A young officer, seeing the captain had died, informed the shipmaster and they struck their flag. It turned out later the captain owned both the ship from Bristol and its cargo. He didn't intend to give it up and face ruin, a futile gamble with the lives of his crew.

François took over the vessel and sent it to Brest. When night fell, he set a course westward under an English ensign toward the Irish coast.

As they turned south, a lookout called from above of a topsail ship, and François sailed in an intersecting direction until he could determine her size and purpose.

She turned out to be a merchant ship of 140 tons, larger than the last. François lowered the English flag and hoisted the French one. At once the merchantman attempted to flee northward. The chase began. The two ships ran course changes that did little except allow the more maneuverable *l'Emeraude* to get closer.

François closed windward and told the gunners to aim high with bar shot on weather rolls.

When they were less than a mile away, François fired a warning volley that ricocheted off the deck and splashed on the starboard beam. After firing one defensive shot for honor, the merchantman accepted the unavoidable reality and surrendered.

The *Swallow,* out of Cork, carried a consignment of cotton from the American colonies to Plymouth. The captain knew French well enough to ask his crew to be released on the many fishing vessels dotting the waves. François obliged since captured men might cause trouble if an English warship tried to retake her.

The week of patrolling along the Irish coast had been profitable with two captures. By the end of January, he had seized six merchantmen and returned to Brest to renewed praise.

The navy ordered René on *la Fine* to go with François once again on patrol at the start of February. In addition to the previous month's glorious achievements, the next one hundred and fourteen days held even more success for the brothers. On May 30th, *l'Emeraude* and *la Fine* returned from their cruise guarding their convoy. They took fourteen prizes of which ten arrived as captures and four others considered recaptures. Of the ten enemy vessels, four were well-armed with one being another corsair, the *Prince of Wales* of 10 guns. François's larger ship, *l'Emeraude*, captured most of the ships with René assisting.

François and René were the toast of Brest. The navy held a ball in their honor which every naval officer of high rank attended.

"You're quite the upcoming commander, Monsieur de Saint-Alouarn," Marie whispered into his ear as she observed the frequent glances of officers and ladies.

"Glory is fleeting," he quoted as yet another officer introduced himself. As the local hero, François, for the first time

in his life, garnered more attention than his younger brother. It flattered him, though it made him uncomfortable.

Even Captain Guy de Kersaint, the most prominent Brest naval officer, congratulated François on his triumphs and indicated he may receive a knighthood in the *Ordre de Saint Louis* for his bravery over the last six months. François had been hoping for the news; without such an award, a naval career was commonplace. With it, one could be an admiral in time.

When he told Marie, she smiled and said he deserved it for everything he'd sacrificed over the years. She, of course, would rise to a new social level, too.

A month later, François received confirmation the Admiralty had listed him as a nominee of the *Ordre de Saint Louis*. Not long afterwards a letter from Versailles came which read in part:

...the good conduct of this officer, his vigilance in taking advantage of all opportunities, took to sea without remaining in safe bays, and his conviction, pleasing His Majesty, is deserving of praise as he is an inspiration for other officers.

Beyond the sudden attention, naval law also entitled François to one-tenth of the value of the ships captured. This enriched him by four thousand livres, a huge amount he gave to Marie to handle. To François, money had always been irrelevant because it was available to him since birth; Marie, however, held money as a precious commodity, a tool. Regardless of how much one accumulated, it had to be spent with prudence.

* * *

For six months, the *Lark*'s tours provided no time to visit Yvette. With winter's seas rough, damage to the hull and masts became frequent.

Off duty, Abraham made small wooden accessories for the London flat. Cabinetry, which had never interested him before, now turned into a pleasant pastime. After being forced into doing both structural and decorative work onboard the ship, he had become adept at fancy swirls and carving in the round. He wondered if he might someday be good enough to sculpt a figurehead like *la Renommée*'s—true mastery of the craft.

Newspapers followed a naval court-martial concerning the loss of the *Northumberland*. In January, the British made a prisoner exchange with the French after only six months for the crew. The Admiralty scheduled the proceedings to take place on the *Lennox* to determine if the crew, officers, and, in particular, the shipmaster should be held at fault for the surrender. Abraham received a summons to attend and Captain Wickham relieved him of duty when they returned after a Channel patrol. Ample time permitted him to get to Portsmouth, the *Lennox,* and a visit to Yvette.

In January of 1745, he boarded the ship in Portsmouth harbor along with the men and officers of the *Northumberland*, though no one could rationally claim that crewmen following orders were to blame. If they had continued fighting when the shipmaster struck, they'd be guilty of disobeying; now it appeared the Admiralty suspected them of obeying orders.

Over the next few days, Abraham attended a preliminary hearing and testified about his actions.

"When the shipmaster sent for you, tell us what you reported in the presence of the officers and the mortally wounded Captain Watson," the prosecuting officer said.

"Sir, I told him the ship's hull was intact. I also said no water had leaked in from the few hits below the waterline. Those just loosened the oakum with minor seeping."

"There existed no danger of the ship sinking, in your opinion as the master carpenter *pro tempore?*"

"No, sir. Sinking seemed the least risk she faced at the time. Her wheel being shot away..."

"That's all we need to know concerning the leakages, Mister Robinson," the prosecutor interrupted. "How long have you been a ship's carpenter?"

"The *Northumberland* was my first warship, sir. I was on her for a few months. I've only now received my Master Carpenter Certificate." Abraham was unworried, having answered the same questions many times before at the Admiralty.

"Now relate your experience in ship repair before that."

"I had just under ten years of service at the English and French royal navy ports as a shipwright, sir."

His answer caused a commotion among the high-ranking officers. One officer asked, "Mister Robinson, you served building warships for the enemy, the French?"

"Aye, sir. Due to an injury, I lost my position at Woolwich, and after it healed there was no work. A job opened in Brest before the war. So, I took it and when the war broke out, they let me go. Then I returned to England, sir."

"Oh, you left France when the war started. That's all we need from you, Mister Robinson."

Abraham returned to the gun deck, where other members of the crew waited to testify. The crew had listened closely when he told his tale of escape. Most just shook their heads, amazed.

By the close of the day, the admirals determined they should commend the crew for their brave actions along with the officers who followed orders. They honorably acquitted the first lieutenant from any wrongdoing yet accused the shipmaster of striking the colors when the fight should have continued. They sentenced the poor man to spend the rest of his life in Marshalsea Prison, a reprieve from the firing squad.

After the verdict, Abraham hurried to London and Yvette to enjoy what little time he had for leave. When he returned to the *Lark,* they shipped out the next day. Although the crew dreamt of taking prizes, to date, the *Lark* had seen little action. Abraham, unlike most of the crew, was content with this; he wanted to see his service through in peace and return to a life ashore. To him, the choice between safety and prizes was heavily weighted in favor of the former.

CHAPTER FIVE

The Citadel

Captain Wickham admired his work, and Abraham liked him and the two lieutenants onboard, Burston and Lovelace. One April day, as Abraham repaired a split deck plank astern, Burston let him in on the current rumors.

"They've been saying a squadron will sail to blockade Louisbourg on Cape Breton. Now that's a fray I'd love to join. Imagine capturing the largest French fortress in the Americas. The Citadel of Louisbourg is so well-armed, that it might take years before they'll surrender. I can't imagine the army taking the citadel by force. We'll have to starve them out."

While the lieutenant fantasized about glory in battle, Abraham's thoughts were on Yvette. "True, Louisbourg is France's door to Canada, but the *Lark* blockading for years would be horrible."

"Ships do get relieved though," Burston assured him, "for maintenance, new assignments, or crew exchanges on long blockades."

In early May, the *Lark* put into port for refitting, allowing

Abraham to be with Yvette. In the back of his mind though, he suspected it was for the blockade and dreaded telling her. When he arrived at their little flat, he tried to enjoy what might be the last time he'd see her for a year or more. As his leave wore on, Abraham confided about the possibility of the long tour.

"Yvette, you know we've been lucky my patrols have been short and I've come home often."

"We have been!" she agreed. "In Brest, my friends had husbands who left for months and even years. I guess your ship is just for patrols."

"So far, but they might send us on a longer voyage this time. I hate to think of not seeing you for many months." It made him sick.

Yvette didn't share his gloom. "Of course, I'll miss you, too, but it's what you must do. No matter how long you're at sea, I'll be here waiting. And you mustn't worry over me, dear. I have a good job and my English is improving. The war isn't in England, and no one would ever attack London. Our concerns must be over your safety, not mine. Do you expect danger?" She knitted her brow.

"Nothing too perilous, I'm glad to say. We might sail to the Americas or the Orient. I won't find out until we're at sea."

"Well, don't worry over things until they happen. Let's just enjoy the next few days together." Her buoyancy deflated his fears.

"You have a wonderful way of chasing my worries away." Abraham grabbed her and pulled her to him.

When his ship weighed anchor, he unhappily learned they were joining a fleet as a stores ship to blockade Louisbourg in the chilly waters off Cape Breton. Weeks later, Abraham stood on the deck and watched the coastline grow closer. With only the sounds of lapping water, chattering men, and creaking wood, he remembered how a few years earlier the thought of traveling to the colonies frightened him, just as he feared working on ships at sea. Abraham chuckled at how interesting his life had become as a seaman.

The fleet arrived in June off Cape Breton with the ships forming an impressive blockade. It was the largest squadron of warships in American waters in over thirty years, comprising eleven ships of the line plus a host of transports, snows, and sloops from the colonies. The ships anchored three miles from Louisbourg, which appeared as a foreboding clutch of tan dots on the distant shore with a small lighthouse across the bay on low rocky hills. It was an unfriendly place for an Englishman. Crewmen talked of the hostile Mi'kmaqs' savagery and the Acadian loyalty to the French.

The next afternoon, orders came to assemble the majority of the fleet in nearby Gabarus Bay to prepare for an all-out attack. Such a formidable fleet, even with all its cannon, could not assault the fortress without massive losses. The colonials had been laying siege to the fortress since the start of May; most were militia and civilians from various New England colonies—an army composed of shopkeepers, farmers, fishermen, frontiersmen, and few qualified officers. These untrained, inexperienced colonial soldiers were supposed to conquer Louisbourg, now defended by well-trained French infantry. Scaling the citadel walls was sure to be a massacre.

After the crew cleared and barricaded the *Lark,* removing everything unneeded from the decks, Commodore Warren gave a speech to encourage the colonial troops and, upon returning to his flagship, confirmed everything was in readiness.

"Seems as though, sir, the plan to starve them was a short-lived strategy." Abraham stood near Lieutenant Burston watching the bombardment the next morning.

"We have to begin an assault immediately. Canadians attacked Annapolis Royal on the northern coast of Nova Scotia, but our troops rebuffed them. So instead, they are marching to reinforce Louisbourg. The commodore plans to end the siege before they arrive. And we've silenced most of the batteries and redoubts. With luck, we can take the citadel." Lieutenant Burston stood with his fists on his hips. "For now, we'll stay out of range of their cannons until Commodore Warren signals. Then we'll pay for every inch with lives. At least the colonials and fleet have broken them down with our bombardments."

"Aye, sir. The red-hot shot put a good deal of the town to ruin as well. And the colonial infantry has kept them from repairing the walls and manning their cannons." Abraham watched the flame and smoke belch from the guns on the ships of the line. The *Lark,* filled with troops and landing rafts, wasn't taking part in the barrage, but they had an excellent view of the battle.

"Surely by now the French have little powder and shot left. When we captured the *Vigilant* in May, she was filled with powder for the fort's guns. Powder our colonials desperately needed as much as the French," Burston said. "The morale inside the walls must be by the board, too. The only thing left of the great Gibraltar of the North is their flag upon the staff and pride as Frenchmen."

Just before the attack was to commence in full, a solemn group of five French officers marched out from the fortress to the beat of drums under a flag of truce.

General Pepperell, in charge of the colonial troops, negotiated with the French delegates on terms of surrender. With absolute annihilation on the horizon, the French Governor Du Chambon asked for an honorable surrender. This permitted the officers and citizens to keep possession of their personal property in their homes until they sent it to France. They also requested the surrender be an Honors of War before boarding transport ships for France; this allowed the garrison to march out with their flag unfurled, carrying their weapons and beating drums. The British accepted the terms, allowing the French their dignity versus the loss of more colonial men in an attack.

All morning long, the blockading ships navigated into the harbor beside the fortifications. The *Lark* put in near the ships of the line along the docks while frigates and smaller ships bobbed in the middle of the harbor. When they finished dropping anchor, a calamitous din of roaring cannons celebrated the victory. Commodore Warren, having accepted the golden keys to the city from the French governor, then opened the south gate. Officers in spotless bright uniforms and colonial soldiers clothed in rags marched into Louisbourg.

When Abraham stepped ashore and entered the surrendered bastion, he was horrified. Dead-eyed civilians staggered among blackened beams where buildings once stood. During the siege, they'd pulled down many of the damaged homes to provide fuel for heat, and the entire town was in shambles. He assumed it'd take years to rebuild. Over nine thousand cannonballs had fallen on the hundred acres of the town and four thousand inhabitants.

The surrender agreement prohibited colonial soldiers, who had visions of pillaging the great fortress, from doing so. Now they guarded the homes they had planned to loot and so, no real gain came with the victory for any of the citizens, soldiers, or sailors—whether French, colonial, or English—except praise for the victorious officers. Five hundred soldiers and civilians died during the forty-six days of the siege and the final assault, yet not a man on the *Lark* suffered. The years-long blockade and sea battle Abraham imagined never happened. The greatest calamity was his seasickness on the crossing, arriving just five days before the invincible citadel surrendered.

"Lieutenant Burston, look! They're replacing our flags with French ones." Abraham watched in confusion as the all-white Bourbon flags again flew on the staffs a few days later.

Burston grinned, nodding his head. "It's a ploy by Commodore Warren to attract French merchantmen into the harbor. He'd make great profits in prize money if he lured French captains into port for a bloodless capture. No one asea has learned yet of our taking Louisbourg."

"That's clever," said Abraham. "I wondered why the commodore sailed from the West Indies to join such a siege. The poorly trained men should have stood no chance in capturing the fortress even with so powerful a blockade. I guess he gambled that if they succeeded, he'd set up this spiderweb for prize ships."

"It was a small gamble that went his way," said Burston. "Louisbourg had a dry and warm spring, which was unusual and allowed healthier camps. Ice blocked the harbor so French relief ships couldn't get in before the blockade. Then we captured that warship carrying the cargo of gunpowder. Their troops were near mutinous, and the governor was an old fool. We caught them unprepared. Warren had everything to win and little to lose."

"Sir, I suppose many French ships will come to Louisbourg before they learn of its fall," Abraham remarked.

"Of course, and who can say how many? The French ships coming from India or the Orient may not hear of it for months. Imagine what they might carry in their holds. Seeing the French flags flying, they'll sail right toward the harbor, unsuspicious. Instead of a French man-of-war welcoming them to port, it'll be one of ours capturing them."

"I've never put too much faith in getting rich at sea. Not that I'd refuse to take prize money, but I doubt as a master carpenter I could get rich from the shares in only four years. I'll pin my fortune on my trade after I get out of the navy."

In the cloudy, cool morning hours one July day, Abraham noticed two warships raise anchor. They sailed out and soon returned with the *Charmante,* a French East India Company ship that had taken Warren's bait. Within a few days, the word spread that the huge five hundred-ton vessel had in her holds over one hundred thousand pieces of eight.

This incredible catch added to the bursting coffers of Warren and richly rewarded the two ships' crews. But Abraham heard the grumbles from colonial militiamen dockside. They felt it unfair to sacrifice so much to capture a fort they were forbidden to plunder. While the English sailors got prize shares using Louisbourg as bait, they received nothing.

It seemed unjust to Abraham as well. It encouraged taking ships for profit rather than for strategy or duty. It caused dissension between officers and crew, and complaints from ships with little chance of taking a prize. Eager to return to England, Abraham was glad when the *Lark* raised anchor and left Louisbourg. Once at sea though, the ship headed west, not east.

They sailed for New England, passing by the rocky shores of Nova Scotia. Four days later, as they approached the coast, Abraham made out the green of the trees in the distance and buildings along the shore. America, as he'd seen so far, was an unrefined and wretched place with primitive towns devoid of elegance. Louisbourg, the jewel of Acadia, had been bare of any adornments or culture even before the siege's destruction. Abraham wished some American city offered more than a gathering of log cabins or stone huts.

"We're going to Boston," Burston informed him. "We'll drop anchor later today."

"I'll look forward to it," Abraham replied, though expecting little.

By evening, they were turning into a bay leading to a huge harbor. As they sailed toward the Charles River, Abraham's hopes rose when he realized how wrong he had been. Boston's expansive layout and its large brick buildings thrilled him. Abraham counted over a dozen tall church steeples. Ships filled the harbor and trade crowded the wharves along the shoreline. Boston could easily have been a major port along a European coast.

They moored near Town Dock and Abraham rushed ashore to buy fresh bread, fiddleheads, and berries, the first fresh food he'd eaten in over a month. Boston's residents, unlike those in the ports in France and Britain, lived in peace, seemingly unafraid of the faraway war. His previous fears of being attacked in the colonies by enemy soldiers, pirates, or natives now seemed absurd.

"Mister Robinson," Burston said, interrupting Abraham in his carpenter's crib the next morning, "did you enjoy Boston? This is your first trip to Massachusetts, isn't it?"

"Aye, sir. And it's nothing as I expected. It's far more cultured than Louisbourg."

"We were seeing Louisbourg at its worst, even if it was never as nice as here. Boston is one of my favorite towns in the colonies."

"Do you think we'll return to Plymouth soon?" Abraham asked, hoping for good news.

"No, I'm afraid not. Although it's not official, we're to lay up at the Newfoundland station of St. John's next." Indifferent to the assignment, Burston merely shrugged.

"Do you have any idea how long we'll stay there, sir?"

"Since parts of the Gulf of St. Laurence freeze and the snows begin at St. John's in October, we must leave by then I should think. I doubt they'd have us there the entire winter."

"That's still a couple more months away." Abraham puffed out his cheeks. Visions of returning soon to Yvette vanished.

* * *

It was early November of 1745, and François and René were back in Brest for new missions. When René reported to Du Guay's office for his orders, he joined two other captains.

Du Guay stood tall at the conference table, imposing in his commandant's uniform of deep blue with bright red lapels trimmed in gold. The red sash of *Commandeur de l'Ordre Militaire de Saint-Louis* draped conspicuously under his coat across his chest; he was one of just twenty-eight of that rank.

"Due to the complexity and importance of this mission, I will outline your next assignments," began Du Guay, peering at each in turn. "We have a great opportunity to end the war and your participation is to be kept in absolute secrecy. Prince Charles needs reinforcements before he pushes on to London. His Scottish troops have met with remarkable success and a victory looks to be in the making. His close alliance with France will have a profound effect on future British and French political and economic affairs if he reinstates the Stuarts as legitimate heirs to the crown. Your mission will be to blockade the port of Montrose in Scotland and assist in the debarkation of *Royal Écossois* troops onto shore there, and at Stonehaven and Peterhead as well."

The commandant described the movements and which troops they'd designated for each ship. *La Fine* had the honor of transporting Lord John Drummond, the leader of the expedition.

Later in the evening René and François met up at their usual tavern.

"Scotland, you said?" whispered François.

"To Montrose in convoy and blockade duty." René twisted his mouth, unhappy with his assignment.

"You might have received worse," François taunted. "You'll see a little action regardless, although not much chance of getting a prize. I'll be off on patrol duty taking the prizes and having the thrills while you sit in the harbor watching soldiers march around on shore. I do sympathize with you." He cackled.

"You pig," jibed René. "When we're old and full of arthritis, we'll see who came away with more prizes and medals."

"If we include women as prizes, then you won years ago, dear brother," François laughed.

"If children and family are prizes, then you have." René smiled. Though René had a restless soul, he admired his brother's maturity and found, more and more, that maybe he too desired a wife and a family. If only his psyche did not revel in such a carefree approach to life.

As he approached his ship, René saw hundreds of *Royal Écossois* troops boarding her. While the officers were French, glistening pointy spontoons resting upon their shoulders, most of the troops were Irish and Scottish, choosing to return for their cause as part of a French battalion. René's orders were to sail as soon as the winds were right, which came in late November. After several false starts, the three frigates guarding the convoy, departed for Scotland, slipping past British warships in a night fog.

Five days later, while passing *Dover* in rough seas, a small British squadron chased and set upon them. The two fleets closed, with the enemy warships outnumbering and out-gunning them. *La Fine* and the other frigates separated and shielded the transports from the oncoming enemy. Sailing close to his foes, René did his best to draw the enemy away from the transports, engaging the British sloop *Chance* and two frigates. He disabled the frigates and fought broadside to broadside against the sloop.

During the fight, he boarded and took the *Chance* and used her to assist in protecting the convoy. The British, however, captured two of the transports armed with fewer guns than normal, *en flute*, including *l'Esperance*. Her cargo, Irish and Scottish troops, would never get the chance to fight for their homelands. That night, the remnants of the French fleet regrouped and continued onward to Scotland through a misty rain that concealed them.

For days, British warships followed René's *la Fine*. René used every tactic to keep the warships from the transports until a foul gale separated the ships and hid them from the enemy. At last on the seventh of December, the first of the ships arrived to unload their human cargoes along the River Esk outlet near Montrose. The privateer frigate beached, unloaded cannons and men, and later captured a British sloop-of-war, the *Hazard,* in the Montrose harbor.

La Fine arrived the next day with the remainder of the ships.

"Lord Drummond, you may debark your men," René said with satisfaction.

By late morning, the troops assembled on the beach and marched inland to aid the Jacobite army of the Stuart Pretender, Bonny Prince Charles.

In turns, the convoy anchored along a dock on the Esk's riverbank to unload. *La Fine* unladen after the rest of the ships left for the harbor. The last of the baggage, supplies, and arms made it ashore by evening when lookouts warned of a British warship approaching less than four miles off, hugging the shoreline. The French rushed to set topsails to flee.

"She's a 44-gun!" the lieutenant lowered his spyglass and called up to René on the forecastle. "Twice our size."

"We've no leeway and must go upriver before she gets into it. Make headway for the deeper middle. Easy as she goes, though, we've no idea its depth." The enemy ship, still in the harbor, had spotted them and headed for the Esk's outlet.

La Fine cast off, and the topsails caught a good, stiff breeze to pull her from the shore. All eyes kept looking back to see if the British would venture into the shallower waters.

"Sir, they're still coming and almost at the mouth of the river," the lieutenant warned.

René at the bow, searched for submerged dangers in the water before them and shook his head with a grimace. "His draft is at least two or three feet deeper than ours. He'll stop soon or ground himself. The best we can hope is that we can get far enough where his guns can't reach us when he does break off the chase."

Minutes later, *la Fine* reached the stronger current in the river's center and made slow headway from contrary winds. Less than half a mile behind them, the 44-gun drew nearer the river.

In the fading light, René spied a mudflat dead ahead, just inches above the water. "To port, to port," he cried back to the helmsman.

His vessel turned toward land, but as it did, the stronger current flowing around the bar forced their direction too shoreward.

In a panic, René shouted, "Starboard, now! Hard to starboard!" No amount of rudder or sail changes could stop *la Fine's* momentum from continuing straight for the muddy shoreline. The bow rose two feet in the air as a loud cracking shuddered along her length when she hit moments later.

"Damn! Carpenters below!" He peered seaward in haste, fearing the foe's imminent bombardment.

"Captain, we're stuck and they're within range, sir!" The lieutenant looked at the menacing ship of the line, his mouth open.

"Lieutenant, I'm aware. We have no time. Lower boats and get the crew to shore. I'm afraid we may have to set *la Fine* afire if they try to board and capture her." René had performed well under duress after years at sea, but here, the odds were against him. "Shit!" he cursed to himself.

The British *Milford's* captain observed *la Fine* drive into the riverbank to set up an easy victory and continue onward toward their prey. It would take only minutes before he could open fire upon the helpless French frigate.

As René watched the two-decker draw closer, his eyes sprang wide when he realized the ship of the line had stopped dead at the mouth of the river. She had been stranded as well on an ebbing tide. Although in cannon range, with the bow facing *la Fine,* she'd be no threat at all. Then he heard the British officers shouting orders at their crew; they faced the same misfortune of running aground.

The enemy captain directed gun crews to shoot alternating broadsides to rock the ship out of the mud. After ten unsuccessful minutes, they lowered a boat and let out a cable.

The longboat's crew rowed to a pinnacle protruding from the deeper water behind the grounded ship and fixed the cable around the stone. Then the British hauled in the cable on their capstan and pulled the warship backward and off the bottom into deeper water.

The *Milford's* captain, fearing another grounding, left *la Fine* and sailed off in search of the ships that had fled to sea.

Hoping for a miracle, René surveyed the damaged hull and found her filling with dirty water and beyond repair. In addition, deep mud held her fast. With no cranes or winces to extract her, *la Fine* was doomed. He chose the only action he could, empty the hold and torch her. Just before midnight from land, he glumly watched his frigate burn to the waterline. The brown muddy Esk defeated him where no British warship had.

Later that evening, the French frigates returned looking for *la Fine.* The other captains, commiserating with his loss, came up with the best solution for the shipless René. The British sloop they had captured earlier in Montrose Bay, the *Hazard,* they had renamed the *Prince-Charles.* Rene, with his crew, took command of the sloop and the fleet now departed for France, their mission at an end.

But the journey back to their home port was even more challenging. The British ports, now all alerted to the presence of the French squadron, sent their ships to destroy them. Rene's fleet fought through enemy patrols every day returning to France.

After they finally berthed in Brest, the story of their campaign brought praise for the captains' unflinching determination in confronting overwhelming adversities. During his adventurous assignment, René had survived a collision, fought ten battles, took twenty-seven prizes including five corsairs, and still completed the mission.

Such outstanding heroism, the same as his brother's, deserved a reward. Before the month was out, Brest welcomed René as a hero. Versailles recognized his skills, too, and awarded him a knighthood in the Military Order of Saint-Louis presented by King Louis XV. At the many balls after his return, the medal on Rene's uniform drew great admiration from the ladies. Although suffering the shame of losing his *la Fine,* Rene had learned valuable lessons on the mission to Scotland, none the least of which was that defeat in one area often came hand-in-hand with victory in another.

* * *

When the joyous news came, blazing bonfires, pealing bells, and booming cannons in the Tower of London celebrated the great victory at Louisbourg. Yvette, being French, didn't rejoice as the others. She enjoyed watching the festivities but hoped, most of all, that her love was safe from danger.

One night, a knock beckoned her to the door.

"Hello, Yvette," said her neighbor, an old lady. "Since you were at work, I wondered if you heard the news of Parliament today?"

"News? No, what's happened?" she gasped.

"Oh, my, you'll not like this." The lady placed a finger to her downy chin. "The Parliament is enforcing the old penal laws and Catholics have to leave London within three days."

"What? Why?"

"Because of the Jacobites. The government is afraid the Catholics will help the Scottish rebel armies."

"I'm not Scottish, I'm French! Why should I care what the Scot rebels do?" Yvette replied. "What do they think I'll do— shoot someone?"

"Prince Charles took Edinburgh and they think he will soon attack England." The woman put her hand to her mouth, afraid. "With our troops fighting on the continent, who's here to protect London? If you're Catholic, you must go. Not too far; they said ten miles outside the city."

"Where can I live outside London? I have to go to work! My employer needs me, and I need money to live." Her face reddened.

"Yvette, you must go or they'll put you in Newgate. I'm sorry."

"Oh, thank you. I'll talk to a friend who may know what to do."

The next day Yvette asked Madame Goubert for advice.

"So I've heard, Yvette." Madame Goubert did not seem bothered by the ordinance. "If you seek help from important people or adapt your beliefs, you can avoid such nuisances."

"I don't know any important people," Yvette answered, pouting.

"Well, the Countess Huntingdon might help. Selina is a member of the Methodists and they accept Catholics into their church. If you are, should I say, a temporary visitor, then they do not consider you a Catholic any longer." Madame Goubert winked.

"Oh, I see. So you trick the constables into believing you are a different sort of Protestant and not Catholic." Yvette held back her surprise at her friend's open confession of renunciating her beliefs.

"That's right. After this messy business ends, we can be Catholics again."

"Aren't you being unfaithful to the Church, professing to be a Methodist?"

"I don't swear an oath or even pray with them. If one attends a few of their meetings, they assume you're a convert. So, if anyone were to ask, I could say in honesty I attend the Methodist church. That doesn't mean I'm a Methodist in my beliefs, though."

"Well, I doubt I could do it that way. I'd feel as though I was cheating the Church or an apostasy. I can't even bring myself to marry in an Anglican church."

"Yvette, we have to decide what is best for us. Right now we're in twice the jeopardy—we're French *and* Catholic. No doubt you've read of the beatings and looting in the Catholic shops. Well, it may get much worse if the Scottish Pretender attacks London. Being a Frenchwoman, you'd stand out like a poppy among periwinkles."

Madame Goubert added, "We're not allowed to practice our religion here, although I have a few friends who do it in secret. It's dangerous. I believe hiding my faith for a while is justified and an obligation so I can survive to worship again later. There's nothing wrong with hiding from those who wish to do you harm. Why don't you come to a meeting with me? There's one in two days on Fetter Lane. Lady Huntingdon will be there herself.

Consider it exploring another's beliefs. One doesn't have to join them," she said convincingly.

"Perhaps if I look at it as expanding my knowledge I'll be all right with going to another church, not to pray or worship though," she decided.

"Good," said Madame Goubert. "Come and we'll take my coach. It's not far, just west of Saint Paul's."

As a matter of perspective, Yvette thought, legal advocates often manipulate the law by word definitions. So too could the belief in her faith be untouched by attending a meeting as an intellectual foray, not a spiritual compromise. It wasn't as if she were going to an Anglican church.

Yvette accompanied Madame Goubert to the gathering and sat listening to the blasphemy. Between 200 and 250 people attended, sitting in pews in the chapel. When they finished, Madame Goubert led Yvette to a smaller room where followers continued their spiritual discussions.

"Oh, there's Selina," she said to Yvette. "Come and meet her; she's a wonderful speaker herself. She's become so well-known." Madame Goubert grabbed Yvette's hand and led her toward the tall slender woman. Lady Huntingdon looked to be in her late thirties and dressed in a modest gown despite being a countess. Her face was plain with a serene countenance, and her dominant forehead gave a serious and intelligent accent to her appearance.

"Selina, that was a marvelous presentation today. Allow me to introduce you to a new member, Yvette Façonneur, who arrived from France not long ago."

"Lady Huntingdon, I am pleased to meet you," Yvette said, curtseying. However, Madame Goubert's introduction of her as a "new member" offended her somewhat.

"Welcome, Yvette. Please, call me Selina. In the house of God, we are equals. How did you enjoy our sermon today? This is your first meeting with Methodists, I presume."

"My first. Well, it's different from what I'm used to hearing at church—no Latin," she laughed.

"Well, I'm sure you could detect many other differences even in one sermon. Don't let the words put you off. Look into the meaning and let your heart decide what you consider is truly right for you. Sincere followers do not aim to convert others by force but through example and love. If you are used to Latin services, you are a Catholic and not a Huguenot?"

"Indeed, I'm Catholic. I'm curious about others' religions and found the speakers interesting. What they said reflected many of my feelings. The roads to our faith may be different but the persecution of Catholics and Methodists by Anglicans is something we share in common."

"Things will change. It takes time for one religious faction to accept another. And we must make efforts to curb discrimination. Just last month I wrote to Lord Carteret, who is the secretary of state, to intercede in the abuse of Methodists. Lord Carteret said he'd send my grievance to the king. Pray King George sees it as his Christian duty to ban the practices injurious to any religion. Yvette, have they persecuted you for your beliefs since you arrived in London?" Lady Huntingdon reached over and touched Yvette's arm.

"No. Other than a few mean comments from people upset over the war, I've had no trouble. Although I received word a few days ago that I must leave and live ten miles from the city."

"Then you are one of the fortunate ones. There are even deaths for many who are not Anglican. I pray not just for the victims' souls, but more keenly for the perpetrators. They are the ones who need salvation."

Lady Huntingdon seemed so sincere and compassionate, and Yvette wondered how a woman, born into title and wealth, could turn to an unorthodox religion with such conviction.

"Please, Yvette, you must visit us again. Contemplate what you heard today. Be sure to sign the visitors' book upon leaving," Lady Huntingdon added, and left to mingle.

"Lady Huntingdon's pleasant," Yvette said to Madame Goubert. "Someone mentioned she has children."

"They're an exemplary family. The earl is devoted to Selina, and she has four children yet living. Two sons died over the last few years. It affected her greatly. Although she remains charitable. She's giving to the poor and even prays with them. The needy call her 'Lady Bountiful'."

"These English are so strange. In France, the king would have stripped her husband of his earldom for allowing her to behave so. She also said she wrote to the secretary of state? Such conduct is baffling!" And yet Yvette found herself impressed.

"It's the Protestant upbringing promoting such rebellious behavior, I believe. As you've noticed, she's a zestful woman," said Madame Goubert. "People respect her strong passion and honest beliefs. If anyone can get something done, it's Selina."

What Yvette found most interesting was the crowd she attracted: all social classes mingled together as equals. This was more eye-opening than their beliefs.

As Yvette and Madame Goubert waited outside by the carriage step for their coach, Lady Huntingdon found them once more. "Yvette, if you find you have trouble leaving London, please consider that I can help. Just drop me a note and I'll see what I can do." Lady Huntingdon smiled again, stepped up into her coach, and left before Yvette could reply with more than a nod.

"Goodness," Yvette said, "she seems concerned for everyone!"

"Not seems, Yvette," Madame Goubert corrected, "Selina is concerned."

After the coach dropped off Yvette at her door, she met her neighbor on the stairs.

"Yvette," she whispered, "Deputies came from the King's Messenger's office looking for you, and want to know when you will leave London."

"They'll just have to wait until I decide what to do," she said, frustrated. "I should have it figured out by tomorrow night. But thank you for telling me."

Declaring herself a Methodist was tempting, but Yvette was still certain it was wrong. Those at the chapel, she realized, were too radical in their approach to Christianity. Perhaps Madame Goubert's important friend, Lady Huntingdon, might know a way to get around the penal law edict, she thought. She drafted a note describing her problem and, in the morning, dropped it off at Lady Huntingdon's London residence.

She received a reply from Lady Huntingdon by messenger. The note invited her to stay at the countess's home in Leicestershire, Donnington Hall. Lady Huntingdon was leaving for it the next day, and while Yvette had little time to prepare for a long trip, she gladly took up Lady Huntingdon's kind offer. The only worry remaining was her job.

"Mr. Willocks," she said, "I'm afraid I must leave for a little while because of the penal laws forbidding Catholics to stay in London."

"Damn!" he cursed.

"Oh, sir, I'm so sorry..." Yvette's heart raced.

"No, no! It's the fools in Parliament I'm upset with, not you, my dear. Their stupid mandates come crushing down on everyone and protect no one. They tax us for armies and navies and then leave the back door open so the Scots can walk in and steal the crown. But where will you be going?"

"My friend will give me a place to stay in the Midlands until I can return to London. This will leave you without an assistant, however."

Mr. Willocks smiled. "I won't need an assistant until you return. The wealthy are fleeing London in fear of the Jacobites. And they are my buyers. So, you see, I must wait until everyone returns. Your position will be waiting for when you come back, Yvette."

At noon, two constable deputies came to the shop in search of her.

"Yvette Façonneur? By statute, I'm informing you that you are violating the Catholic expulsion laws and must leave London at once."

"Sir, as you can see, I'm not carrying any weapons or gunpowder." Yvette smiled, hoping the constables might find it humorous.

He didn't appreciate her jest. "Since you haven't attempted to leave, you must come with us."

"I have attempted! This afternoon, I'm leaving with the Countess Huntingdon. The countess and I are going to Leicestershire."

"Well then," the sour deputy grumbled, "be gone by day's end."

"By the end of tomorrow, I'll be fifty miles away. I promise.

Without another word, the deputies left to track down other delinquent Catholics.

After lunch, Yvette hurried to Madame Goubert's home, a big stone house on a pleasant street lined with tall trees. They were to meet Lady Huntingdon, and Yvette carried a large bag with enough clothing for at least two weeks.

When Lady Huntingdon arrived, Yvette thanked her for her assistance. "I don't know what I would have done without you," she admitted. "The constables came to the shop where I work to arrest me!"

"Oh, it's little effort for me," she answered. "Let's visit Madame Goubert a while. There's good news for us."

Madame Goubert had tea and cakes served as they sat and discussed Lady Huntingdon's news.

"This morning, I received a message from the secretary of state. I'm so thrilled to tell you King George has guaranteed me he will put a stop to the harassment and persecution of non-Anglicans at once. Now our work can go on unimpeded. The moment I heard the news I prayed thanks."

"Do I still have to leave London?" inquired Yvette.

"Yes, I'm afraid that matter is out of his hands since it was a law passed by Parliament. The king will, however, order sheriffs to arrest those breaking up a religious meeting or doing damage to the property of others because of their religion. This is the first sign of tolerance for religious beliefs in many years and perhaps sets a precedent we can build upon.

"This means much to preachers dedicated to spreading the gospel. They have a hard time when the law officers disrupt our meetings or look away when mobs attack. Now intimidation will end."

"Because of you, Selina," fawned Madame Goubert. "Your influence with those in power will be the foundation for a new road of religious freedom."

"No, no. My hand merely wrote the letter; it was God's hand that delivered the message to the king's heart."

Yvette didn't understand why the British king paid any attention to Lady Huntingdon unless she had real political power behind her. She wondered whether that power was her husband or the influence the countess had over the people. If the poor called her Lady Bountiful, she must have some control. Or was it the large Methodist population she influenced?

Yvette spent two weeks with Lady Huntingdon at Donnington Hall, envying the luxury the countess lived in. Yvette's only worry was for Abraham, wondering if he'd returned to their flat to find her gone. But soon enough, word came that the Scottish rebel army had withdrawn northward to protect their homeland; this meant Catholics could return to London!

Eager to be home for the Christmas holiday, Yvette and Lady Huntingdon rode back to the city. They returned on a cool, wet afternoon in mid-December. Disappointed, Yvette saw that Abraham hadn't yet returned from his tour, but a letter was waiting for her.

My Darling Yvette—My voyage first found me on the distant shores of America in a blockade of the French fortress of Louisbourg where we witnessed their surrender. I was in no danger of any harm and in September I was stationed in St. John's, Newfoundland. We patrol the coasts and my greatest complaint is my seasickness and the lack of novelties. Reports of three

French ships of the line in the vicinity caused much excitement, although our ship never met up with them.

A few weeks ago, three men who had the great fortune to escape from the French ship, le St. Michel, arrived in St. John's. One evening, at the sole inn in town I met one of them named McMallin, also a ship's carpenter. There we exchanged the tales of our escapes from the French, to the delight of the other patrons.

The weather here is the worst I have ever encountered. The warm waters of the Gulf Stream meet with those of the polar north to create horrible conditions. The fog, or sea smoke as the crew calls it, is so dense it makes walking the street treacherous and sailing hazardous. Collisions are a constant threat throughout the spring, summer, and early fall. Now that winter is upon us, freezing rain, sleet, or deep snows with high winds and rough seas make our cruises along the coasts and our anchorages in St. John's miserable.

I had hoped to leave Newfoundland soon; unfortunately, we are to remain the entire winter. This sentence of drudgery will give me time, however, to afford the luxury of a new pursuit. I am determined to learn the art of furniture making with wood I have purchased in town. When I complete these useful objets d'art, I will ship them to London after I find a low freight fee.

I am again disheartened for us to be apart for the holiday celebrations, yet I am anticipating our reunion when this tour ends. Your loving and humble fiancé, Abraham.

The letter carried a date a month earlier, in November.

* * *

The *Lark* had weathered the worst of winter at St. John's; Abraham still hadn't found out when he'd be returning to England. In February, the *Lark* left for Boston once again. As he walked the narrow streets of Boston and listened to the daily chatter of the citizens, he sensed a fear that wasn't present on his first visit: a French attack on the well-established village of Saratoga in the New York colony had created a near-panic. Now the people in Boston were afraid that a similar French attack might occur there, and handbills were crying out for revenge by invading Canada.

A few days later, they again set out for Plymouth. Many of the crew were getting sick with chills, rashes, and fever, and a few even died from the illness. The surgeon diagnosed typhus as the cause. Then Captain Wickham became sick himself, and the crew seldom saw him on deck.

By mid-April, traversing the icy North Atlantic, they sailed by Ireland on to England. Captain Wickham was still sick when they reached Plymouth and he, along with many crewmen, sought aid in the hospital, leaving Burston in command. Abraham, still healthy, was allowed shore leave and set off for four days in London.

Yvette, was at work when he returned with the handcrafted furniture he'd made while away. To surprise her, he arranged the two maple chairs and a large chest of drawers in the flat. When evening came, Yvette's steps tapped on the stairs and Abraham hid.

Yvette entered and walked past the new chest of drawers, her mind set on the kitchen and making dinner. When she saw the two chairs, she exclaimed, "Oh!" and spun around to find him leaning against the wall. "Abraham!" She rushed to him and they embraced.

"Does my absence make you long more for me?" he whispered in French.

"I was on the edge of madness without you," she assured him. "Now tell me when you have to leave."

"In four days." Despite the short stay, he was happy to be home.

"I've missed you greatly. So much has happened, I can't tell you it all in a week let alone four days. When did you get the chairs? They're wonderful."

"I brought them back with me from St. John's. These are the ones I made during the winter. Do you like them?" He ushered her to the bedroom, pulling her hand. "Let me show you something else."

"Oh, my! This is exquisite!" His abilities surprised her as she glided her hand across the top of the chest of drawers.

"Well, it took a bit of doing, most of the winter," he chuckled, then pulled open a drawer to show off his perfect dovetail joints.

"You have talent, my love. Why do you want to build ships? You should make these. This is beautiful."

"It still needs a nice mirror to go with it. We'll have to wait until we can afford one, I'm afraid." But he was still quite proud of his efforts.

The next day, Abraham slept late and met her at work for lunch. He accompanied her to the various shops in search of books. Yvette told him she was looking for English books now that her vocabulary was improving. Her prowess in bartering surpassed even Mr. Willocks', and he was handing over more tasks to her, not just buying, but selling. When he had other places to go, he had her running the shop on her own. The old man even taught her how to enter items into the ledgers and allowed her to handle the money. Like Abraham, she felt pride in her own acquired skills.

When they returned to the bookstore after her last purchase, Mr. Willocks was sitting at his counter entering numbers with his quill. "Abraham, so you're back from the sea again. Good seeing you in such fine health. I have something for you." He rushed smiling to the storeroom and returned with a book.

"Yvette says you read scientific books. Here is a copy of Voltaire's *Lettres Philosophiques* where he describes Newton's theories on gravity. It's over ten years old now. This copy is beaten up, but it'll fill in the boredom of a long voyage."

"Thank you, sir! I'm sure it will." Abraham, surprised at the generosity, took and tucked the book under his arm. He and Yvette helped the old man close up the shop.

Days later, when Abraham returned to Plymouth and the *Lark,* they informed him that Wickham was still ill and onshore for an indefinite period to recover. Captain Cheap, previously on the *Wager,* where he'd survived a shipwreck and mutiny, became their commander.

Sadly, Abraham soon learned, that Captain Cheap was not a tolerant man nor deserving of admiration. Stern and abrasive, he lacked cordiality with even fellow officers. This put him in contempt of the crew. As the complete tale of his shipwreck and the mutiny spread among the crew, each telling made the captain's reprehensible actions even more nefarious. Confused over the many versions of the story, Abraham approached Burston for a more truthful account.

"An officer attending the court martial told me," started Burston with a casual tempo. "Off the coast of Chile, their ship ran aground just a musket shot from an island. After a few days of attempting to raise her off the reef, they abandoned the ship and swam ashore—marooned. Part of the crew became mutinous because they wouldn't receive navy pay after the day they abandoned the ship. Rebellious, the crew and marines fought over the salvaged supplies, and each hoarded his share. The officers had lost control. Captain Cheap, to quell the mutiny, shot and killed a belligerent midshipman. Soon the food ran out, and they began starving. This split the men into two groups. Twenty crewmen sailed with the captain up the coast in a long boat while eighty crewmen lengthened a long boat to sail for Brazil. Of the twenty men with the captain, just four survived. Of the eighty men who had sailed for Brazil, twelve survived. Most drowned or starved, or savages killed them."

"So, Captain Cheap survived with only three of his men? Those twelve that sailed for Brazil got convicted of mutiny, I suspect," said Abraham.

"No. The Admiralty absolved them due to the conditions and exonerated Captain Cheap of any command errors."

"Well, I hope we aren't sailing for Brazil or Chile soon." He was joking, but the full tale had bothered him.

"We'll be patrolling along the coast of France and Spain looking for a French squadron that's forming. The Admiralty fears an attack somewhere. Reports said they might even attack the New England colonies."

Abraham returned to sea with little enthusiasm. Captain Cheap was a cold-spirited man whose only virtue was his meticulous sense of duty. Abraham seldom spoke to him and preferred it that way.

Along the coast of Portugal, the *Lark* sailed in company with the new *Gloucester,* a 50-gun ship. The seas were mild and

Abraham enjoyed a seasick-free voyage as the two ships continued their southward patrol for the French squadron. He made the most of his free time by reading and learning the sea lore from his fellow crewmen. Lookouts saw few square-riggers, and the voyage was a peaceful one.

The day after Christmas, heading west, the *Gloucester* signaled the approach of two ships. Hands rushed to their assigned tasks to prepare for a possible fight. Abraham stood on the forecastle near the sail master, peering out to see if he could discern the flag the ships flew. He had gathered tools and posted his carpenters belowdecks. They still had a few minutes before the caulkers and carpenters would hurry along the hull with hammers, canvas, plugs, oakum, and planks in hand to repair leaking hits. The air was cool and clear that afternoon, and the sun was high and brilliant, giving everyone a good view of the distant vessels.

The ships were Spanish. Abraham, somewhat disappointed that he'd have to go below, watched as the enemy ships began a maneuver to avoid the approaching cruisers. But the wind favored the British, from the north.

The Spanish ships, a small frigate-sized vessel of 32 guns, and another larger one of 40 guns, came within cannon range. They changed directions to catch a better wind but were out-sailed by the two larger British ships. Abraham went below with his carpenters at the first roar of cannons from the *Lark*.

The smaller cannons of the foe were still out of range when the iron shot exploded from the *Lark*. The roars of the cannon were accompanied by cheers of the gun crew. Then, as the frequency of the cannon discharges increased, the first hit of an enemy ball pounded into the side of the *Lark*. It caused no damage but the loud thud drew the carpenters into a higher state of alarm.

Abraham and two carpenter's helpers rushed along his section of the ship, inspecting the hull near the sound of the increasing hits. They listened for the rumbling sound of seeping water behind the planks but every hit was different. Some penetrated the hull through feet of planking, blasting fragments of wood inside; others simply bounced off the side of the ship. The holes from the cannon balls might produce clean holes all the way through or be filled with splinters, closing up after swelling with seawater, sealing themselves. One hit at the stern produced a leak, and they plugged it with oakum and a shim. Another fair-sized hole was impossible to fix from inside the ship, so Abraham ordered two men to lower a rice bag on a line into the sea from the deck to the hole location. Pressure from the sea flowing in sucked the bag into the hole and the gushing water slowed to a trickle. It would do until repaired later. By far, most only loosened the oakum, made of tar and old frayed rope, from between the hull planks to produce small leaks that were easy and fast to fix.

The two warships had engaged the Spanish ships' weather side, so the Spanish maneuvered to cross their sterns. The sharp sailing of the captains prevented the smaller ships from doing so by slowing. Both enemy vessels found themselves between the two British warships, battered from both sides.

After forty-five minutes, they destroyed the foresail of one foe, and the mainsail yard of the other swung loose over the midships. The useless sail dragged its canvas on the deck, blocking movement. Though the battle favored the British, the Spaniards continued to fight. The larger of the enemy ships lost three cannons unseated by volleys and hove to, parallel with the *Lark*.

When her crew attempted to board, the *Lark's* marines fired lethal musket volleys upon them, forcing the invaders to seek cover behind the bulwarks.

Abraham heard a loud thump on the port side. He expected *Lark's* crew to be preparing to board one of the Spanish ships, and there was thunder as the cannons above blasted into the sides of one another, muzzle to muzzle. Then everything grew silent—the stillness of surrender.

Abraham checked the hull one last time and reported to the captain the condition below. He tallied the damages to the ship for repairs as he rushed toward the stern, relieved there were so few. Captain Cheap was on the main deck, inspecting damages himself and giving orders to the boatswain. The captain had stationed marines on his captured Spanish ship, and the *Gloucester,* a few hundred yards off beside her captured ship, did the same. Although the harm to their warship was minor by comparison, the *Lark* had taken the brunt of the fighting and had fought closer to the enemy than the *Gloucester.* Abraham reported the major damages, which were few and set off to supervise the patching of leaks. He assigned men to every damaged part of the ship and was going aft when he encountered Burston near the stairs.

"Glad to see you didn't get injured, sir. That was a fast capture."

"It was! I was a gun captain; we gave them a good thrashing today!"

"We didn't take in many hits, either!"

"I have to tell you, and you're one of the first to know," whispered Burston, "our Spaniard is a treasure ship! She sailed last from Havana and chests of gold and silver, plus a cargo of cochineal, snuff, sugar, and indigo fill the hold to its top!" He smiled from ear to ear, expecting Abraham to react.

He was less enthused. "That's fine news, sir. I wondered if we might catch a worthwhile prize. Maybe the crew will stop complaining about the captain."

"The cargo is worth hundreds of thousands of pounds!"

"Well, sir," Abraham said hesitantly, "it could be in prize court for years. We might not receive a penny."

Burston's face fell. "Abraham, don't crush the dreams of the crew. Spoils are why many seamen crew warships."

Abraham let out a sheepish, "Aye, aye, sir."

The *Lark*'s captured Spanish ship of six hundred fifty tons, named *le Fort de Nantz,* carried two hundred men, but her small escort, the *Havana,* had taken far more damage than any of the other ships. Throughout the mess, the triumphant crewmen guessed the worth of the treasure and calculated their possible shares. The average sailor made less than a shilling a day, but the slim chance of prize shares kept the navy minimally manned without widespread impressments.

The four ships headed northward, sailing to Plymouth to claim their prizes. They would arrive in mid-January but Abraham found the holidays he had once missed were of no consequence now, as they were for lubbers to enjoy.

CHAPTER SIX

The Moonlight

Washington Shirley, at moorage in Plymouth, stood near the helm on his *Fox*, a 24-gun frigate launched earlier that year in 1746, and fretted over the crew shortage. Although promised more men, the captain was soon to depart with no replacements, an all-too-frequent problem.

Washington was heading below to beat the rain when there was a loud thud at the waist. The frigate had suddenly listed in the quickening wind of the coming squall and, at the mainmast, there lay the carpenter upon the deck, having fallen from the lurch while inspecting the masts.

Washington rushed to him, but the fall had broken his neck. The purser, following routine, ordered the body ashore. He held a deadman's auction for the crew, who bought the carpenter's pants and shirts at inflated prices as charity for the carpenter's family. Washington even purchased a few pieces, sorry for the fellow's passing.

By age twenty-four, Washington had been at sea for eight years and made post captain early, partly due to his grandfather's legacy as the first Earl Ferrers. Laurence, his older brother, had become the current Earl Ferrers after their uncle died, but Washington himself had never desired a title. He was a seaman through and through. Although the Shirleys were old nobility in Britain, he had received the promotions on his own merits.

Like most captains, however, he was short-handed. Washington entered the naval office and handed the lieutenant a second request for more men. "We'll do what we can," the clerk frowned.

"How long shall I be in port before sailing?" He needed a full crew before shipping out.

"Perhaps a week, Captain Shirley."

Washington sighed and departed, guiding his horse along the cobbled road to East Stonehouse, a village near Plymouth, to visit his lady friend. Anne Elliott was an infatuating miss whom he had met a year earlier. Although endeared to her, his resolve to stay single and career-driven was a point of conflict for both. Anne was the daughter of a wealthy landowner and though she had an uncommon Scottish fire in her, she had the common desire to marry. She believed it was just a matter of time before Washington would change his mind.

"Washington!" she greeted when he arrived. "You make a lonely maiden jubilant." Anne dragged him to the parlor. "Fill me in on your adventures."

"Oh, there was nothing exceptional this trip, although I lost my carpenter from a fall after we docked. When I returned home, a shocking letter was waiting for me from my brother. Laurence wrote he might get married soon." Washington cringed at his slip-up. As much as possible he avoided the topic of marriage with her.

Although Laurence kept a mistress, to wed a commoner was unthinkable. At least Anne, from titled lineage, was quite acceptable for Washington to marry.

"And did the Earl Ferrers say to whom he is betrothed?" Anne hoped Laurence's change of heart might influence Washington, but she also hoped Washington hadn't picked up any of his brother's traits. Given every opportunity to become a gentleman, Laurence left Oxford College to spend years in Paris drinking, womanizing, and gambling. Washington had told her his brother had fathered two daughters by his mistress.

"No, I don't think he has anyone in mind, just contemplating his future. Strange, he vowed he'd never take a wife."

"Well, I hope the bride is a fit for his choleric temperament," Anne huffed.

"Dare I say there will be a match for him. Many an uncouth woman would endure hell for wealth and title."

As he rode home later, worry and guilt infected Washington over how long he could keep Anne interested in him without the prospect of marriage. Although he had often struggled with the idea of wedlock, by the time he reached home, he again put career before all.

* * *

The *Lark* and *Gloucester* entered Plymouth harbor escorting their prizes. Now that the prize ships were safe, the two victorious warships were to return to sea.

"Lieutenant Burston," said Abraham after they left port. "We'll be going to the French coast again, I imagine." He hoped so, as a journey to America or Africa would take much longer.

"The *Gloucester* is to sail in convoy. Our *Lark* will patrol with the frigate *Fox*. She'll meet up with us due south of our current position in a day or two. She's been at sea for a week now and is a smart little ship, just launched this year."

"And her captain, sir?" Comforted with the news of another short tour, he was curious.

"I know little of him. His name is Shirley and our age. I met him ashore when he was a lieutenant. He made post captain fast enough, probably because the Shirleys have tonnage in the Admiralty."

"The victuals taken onboard should last us for weeks."

"A month, the captain told us when we weighed. I suppose Yvette will be more appreciative when you return." He winked.

"Hah, if she remembers who I am." Abraham sighed. "My visits are becoming shorter and further apart. I'll be lucky if she doesn't forget me altogether."

"What about your marriage? Didn't you say you wanted a ceremony soon?"

"We've decided to go back to France after the war to have the wedding so her family can attend, sir."

"Peace could be a long wait. We have to beware of losing our hold in India, and our Italian campaigns are faring poorly too."

"It's never-ending, sir. First, the Jenkins' Ear War with Spain. Then this war lasted years with countries popping in and out, debating war or peace. There is little reason in it." Abraham saw no profit in war except for the wealthy. The inability to influence the larger aspects of life frustrated him.

Burston embraced only his duty; the rest was beyond control and not his business. "None that I can see either. But we're not here to understand the complexities of politics. We carry out our duty to survive another day."

In the distance, they soon spotted the *Fox* and Captain Cheap sailed for her. Signals indicated she was in distress from a dismasting. When the *Fox* reached the *Lark,* her captain, Washington Shirley, came in his gig to talk to Captain Cheap. Half an hour later, Burston summoned Abraham to take two carpenter's helpers and assist with repairs on the *Fox.*

"Mister Burston," Captain Cheap called to the lieutenant a few days later, "is Robinson finished with his mast inspections?"

"Aye, he's below in the bow, sir."

"Robinson," he called down the hatchway, "how goes the repair?"

"Very good, sir! A starboard side beam split, sir. Thompson's been helping me with the repair. We've made it fast; he's on his way out now, sir." The smiling face of Zechariah Thompson appeared in the hatchway.

"We've got it sealed up tight now, Captain," said Zechariah. His thin body popped out through the opening and he saluted.

"Was it serious?"

"Aye, sir, it leaked plentiful. I thought it might be too wide a split to fix at sea. But Mister Robinson caulked it and used the spanner to pull the beam together, sir. It'll hold till doomsday comes." In a moment, Abraham's head emerged from the hatch and he clambered to the deck.

"Robinson, I had expected you back from the *Fox* two days ago. What delayed you?" Captain Cheap snapped.

"Sir, the damages to the spars were much worse than we supposed. The main lower mast had cracked. No one found it until I finished the other work. We bent a fish to her and she'll hold. Plus, the foremast had loosened which required tightening the stays," explained Abraham.

"Just the same, Robinson, when I send you to another ship for a few days I don't expect your absence for five. You jeopardize this ship by delaying your return. It mustn't happen again."

"Aye, aye, sir. It will not." Abraham flushed in embarrassment, even though the *Fox* had warranted far more repairs than the *Lark* needed.

Captain Cheap, his eyebrows furrowed, left Abraham and Zechariah standing by the hawser locker. Zechariah turned to Abraham and shrugged in disbelief, just as Captain Cheap glanced back.

"Thompson, something you want to say?" Captain Cheap bellowed.

"Sir? Ah—no sir," Zechariah answered.

"Perhaps you feel I'm not handling my crew properly. Should a carpenter's helper judge a captain's actions? Do you know how to run this ship better than I do?" His voice rose in tandem with his temper.

"No, sir. Sorry, sir," Zechariah blurted.

"Showing contempt for my orders is punishable, Thompson. It causes disruption and undermines the authority of superiors. I will not tolerate such behavior aboard my ship. See yourself to the captain of the marines and have yourself placed in irons, Thompson!" He turned with a red face and stomped away.

The two carpenters stood in shock. Neither could have predicted the sudden outburst over a simple shrug. Zechariah glanced wide-eyed at Abraham and shook his head, walking away to carry out the captain's order.

Unmerited verbal thrashes and physical lashings were common aboard most of the navy ships. Men were expendable, and whether on land or at sea, those empowered misused their authority with impunity, but Captain Cheap was an entirely new level of cruelty.

The next day, the boatswain tied Zechariah to a grating, and, before the assembled crew, gave him ten lashes with a cat-o'-nine-tails. The surgeon took Zechariah below and rubbed salt into the wounds to avoid infection, and Abraham found that Captain Cheap was the first captain he ever loathed. He understood, deeply, why the *Wager's* crew had mutinied years earlier.

The warships patrolled the French coast for the rest of the month and by the middle of February, they made port. Washington complained the lack of carpenters endangered the *Fox* after the dismasting and, while it wasn't quite true, it got him the crew he needed.

"You're scheduled to embark in two days after taking on supplies, but the *Lark* will be docked longer. I suppose we could transfer a couple of her carpenters, but losing crewmen could upset Captain Cheap and he may not agree to it," the officer said.

Washington supposed the captain, being a disagreeable sort, would object to the plan. "Might you make the request? His men did a fine job when they aided us at sea."

Much to everyone's surprise, Captain Cheap gave up Abraham and the young Zechariah Thompson, and both accepted the new post without a second thought. Although he'd take any other ship over the *Lark,* Abraham rued losing contact with Burston, who'd become his friend. And he told the lieutenant so.

The *Fox,* now on the blue deep sea, sailed calm waters. Washington, having taken his supper alone in his cabin, lit another lantern hanging from a beam when the marine guard rapped on his door and announced Abraham.

"Come."

"You requested me, Captain," Abraham greeted.

"Mister Robinson, be seated," said Washington as he poured himself a glass of wine. "I like to acquaint myself with my warrant officers. The fine repairs you made prompted me to learn of your experiences before joining the navy. You served as a carpenter ashore, I was told."

"Aye, sir, at the naval shipyards." Abraham recapped his background for the captain.

"It sounds as if you've had plenty of experience with damage. Have you seen anything pressing that needs taking care of on the *Fox?*"

"They're minor, sir, but I noticed the parrals on the mizzen." This captain seemed much more congenial than his last one, and this relieved Abraham. "A few of them appear worn, although I haven't inspected them yet or told the sail master. That is the highest priority and I'll get to that tomorrow. Second, I do want to inspect a hull patch they made on the starboard midships below the waterline, that is, if we can afford the opportunity to keel leeward for me to go over the side to check it."

"Good, good. I haven't noticed the parrals causing drag, although a few might need to be replaced. Ask the officer on deck tomorrow to help you look at them." Washington found he quite liked this carpenter. He admired his drive, though he couldn't afford to lose him overboard. "I'll let you know when we will heel so you can send a carpenter's mate over the side to check the repair to the hull. You needn't endanger yourself. You are the master carpenter, after all. Anything else, Mister Robinson?"

"No, those were the biggest issues I had, sir. There are plenty of smaller repairs that we're catching up on."

"Fine. I want you to train more carpenter's helpers. Take younger men, two or three—ask the boatswain who'd be best— and start showing them. We don't have enough crewmen to handle the damage if we get into a scrap. Not to say you haven't seen your share, but it's a struggle to keep from being taken. *C'est la guerre.*"

"*Absolument!*" Abraham answered in French, to let Washington know he was fluent. "I'll begin right away with the boatswain's and purser's approval, sir."

"That should remedy our shortage of carpentry help. Tell me, Mister Robinson, you present yourself in an enlightened manner. Did you get much schooling? You replied *en Français.* Did you learn the langue in Brest?" French-speaking crewmen onboard were unusual, other than a few officers.

He told Washington a bit of his family history, then added, "I was fond of the sciences, and I still am, astronomy in particular. Much of my time is spent reading about the heavens. One of my greatest hopes is to observe Jupiter and Saturn through a big telescope."

"I, too, enjoy stargazing, Mister Robinson." Washington beamed, learning a fellow crew-member enjoyed science. "A few years ago, I had the opportunity to view planets through a large telescope, Saturn and Mars. Both were remarkable. It's good you had an encompassing education."

"As a youth, I dreamed of working in the sciences, sir," Abraham continued. "I took up carpentry before my father's death, although he wanted me to go into the mercantile trades.

Now my heart is in my craft. I can't imagine another path for me. Shaping wood is my life."

"Do you have a wife and children back home?" Washington hoped he didn't; his last carpenter had, and commanding warships that made widows bothered him.

"No, sir, but I'm betrothed to a woman in London. All of my family are gone now." It had been almost ten years since his parents had died, and now the thought seldom saddened him.

After a few more questions, Washington dismissed Abraham to go below; both of them parted feeling as though they'd found a friend. Over the following weeks, they discussed in passing politics and philosophy, natural science and technical architecture. Though they were of unequal rank, they formed an unconventional bond.

When the two-week cruise concluded, the *Fox* returned to Plymouth, and Washington requested they careen, repair, and refit her. While waiting for a careening berth to open, the navy assigned Washington to a new ship, the *Dover*, a 44-gun two-decker, that he was to command in two weeks.

The navy also informed Abraham the captured Spanish galleon qualified as a prize. Although he'd be entitled to a share of its worth, there was a claim against it by an insurance company in Spain. They didn't announce the value of the prize, but the *Lark's* crew hoped for a sizable reward. For the first time since entering the navy, the thought of a prize share excited him. Before, he'd considered it a delusion the common sailors indulged in; now its possibility might relieve part of his financial fears.

While awaiting the *Dover* refit, Abraham had two weeks to spend with Yvette. So much had changed—his ships, his commanders, his potential financial future—but his love for her had not. He still found himself beyond joy when he met her at their flat.

When she heard of the possible prize money and asked how much it might be, to no reply, she laughed. "Well, then don't tell me. When the money is in your hand, then we can celebrate and I can spend it! Otherwise, it's a statue in a cloud, good only for dreaming." Yvette, too practical and skeptical of the navy, couldn't let herself get too carried away.

"So you were with Madame Goubert earlier? That's nice." He was glad she'd found friends to keep her company while he was away.

"Our Methodist friends come to her house to play whist. It's so much fun!"

"Have you attended many of the Methodist meetings?"

"Perhaps once every month, mostly to socialize. I enjoy talking to Selina; she's so special. I don't pray with them or worship. But I have other news to tell you," she said, lowering her voice to a whisper. "I've been to mass." She raised her eyebrows.

"What? Where? It's illegal; they could fine you." Her fool-hardiness surprised him.

"Don't worry. Sometimes there's room in embassy chapels. I took mass at the Portuguese and Bavarian embassies." It was a legal detour around the restrictive laws, and she smiled broadly.

"You haven't attended masses in homes, have you?" he asked.

"No, I don't plan to go to those. It's too risky. Although, last month I heard a man accused a priest of giving communion. The constable asked if he was sure the priest was conducting a Catholic ceremony or was just talking in Latin." She giggled. "I don't think the laws are enforced as severely now."

"Maybe not, yet it's dangerous." He wagged his finger. "Religious intolerance flows in and out like the tides."

They spent their time together enjoying the amusement pavilions at Vauxhall Gardens. Among the nightlife, they fantasized about what they could buy with Abraham's possible ship prize.

"Abraham, we have our entire futures to live together," Yvette finally said. "Someday we may be able to afford luxuries, either way, memories and dreams will always suffice."

Days later, with regret, he once again left his lover for Plymouth. Abraham boarded the *Dover* with Captain Shirley and, by the end of February, they set off to escort a small fleet for Gibraltar and Louisbourg. A trip that would take months.

* * *

La Renommée, for her brief three years of service, had seen her share of action, much more than other frigates. Three times she had sailed to Acadia on unsuccessful but action-filled missions under Captain Guy de Kersaint. Although her battle scars were many, she kept her full sailing ability and well-known speed. Now her new commander, François de Saint-Alouarn, had grown used to her quirky handling and looked forward to testing her abilities in combat.

Marie, fearful for her husband, hoped *la Renommée* would be part of a convoy or large fleet on her next undertaking.

"Dear," Marie said in the salon. "Your ship is the fastest one they have. They'll always send her on the most dangerous missions. How long must you be on her?"

"As I've mentioned, I prefer being on a fast, smaller ship." Though never as much as Marie, he was concerned as well. "Besides, the navy is sending out fewer convoys. They are losing confidence in our abilities, or more correctly, they fear Britain's increasing capabilities."

"*La Renommée* has an unlucky history. I'm afraid they'll continue sending you on risky cruises." Marie had learned of de Kersaint's harsh experiences; although *la Renommée's* attributes had saved the crew on numerous occasions, the frigate's assignments were always dangerous.

"Let them send her into dreadful missions, but with me in command, my dear, you have nothing to fear," he chuckled.

"Yes, I have confidence in you, the navy, no." Too often she read of Versailles' incompetence and inept admirals. Louis walked into the room.

"Father, Pierre de la Roche has left for Brest to be in the *Garde de la Marine*. When can I go?"

The question thunderstruck both Marie and François. "Louis, you're too young, only nine years old, and Pierre must be at least thirteen or fourteen. Isn't he?" Marie couldn't believe what Louis was asking. He was her child, still learning his numbers and vocabulary, not a warrior the enemy might slaughter at sea.

"I don't know. His brother said he was leaving to go to sea. I want to become a captain. The same as you, Father." The boy, like most, wanted to emulate his heroes.

"Louis, you'll sail to sea but not just yet. To be a captain, you must have an education to properly command and navigate. Then when you finish school, you can go into the *Garde de la Marine* to learn how to be a good officer. You needn't worry, the Saint-Alouarn men go to sea. Each has become a great captain," François explained, not wishing to discourage his son. He, too, regretted Louis' premature request.

The reality that her little boy had to leave for the navy someday weighed on Marie. François was right, in a few short years, he'd follow in the footsteps of family tradition. Her son's future faced braving storms and battles. The longer she dwelt on the thought, the worse she felt but she smiled at Louis and walked to the window, pretending to adjust the tasseled curtains. There was no avoiding the inevitable unless Louis changed his mind.

"You know," François said, "as a child, I wanted to study history and travel to see the great pyramids of Egypt and unlock the ancient mysteries. My father guided me into the navy, however. I accepted the role laid out for me. I won't do that to Louis. He'll pick his career to follow."

Marie was grateful for that, although she knew François had glorified the navy all Louis' life. It had done its work in the boy's mind and the sea was his destiny.

As the wind blew west across the Road of Brest, it carried with it François's frigate, and this time, there was a special passenger on board: the Marquis de Conflans, the new governor of Saint-Domingue. The promotion to governor capped the achievements of his long military career.

"Have you been to the Caribbean often, sir?" asked François while they paced the deck on the third day at sea.

"In 1712, I was an ensign there, and we chased the pirates. Now mostly smugglers are in the islands," de Conflans replied.

"Things are much better now in Saint-Domingue. I doubt we'll be seeing any pirates or smugglers on the way. We'll have to keep a good lookout for other dangers."

"We have the advantage aboard *la Renommée*, sir, if it should come to that."

"So I've heard. That's why I'm on her, Captain de Saint-Alouarn." De Conflans leaned on the starboard railing, gazing at the blue sea.

"The wind is changing and coming strong from the south. We can put in at Belle Isle if we don't make better headway," François said, fearing slow progress in waters so near the coast.

"Very prudent," de Conflans replied. "Let's wait and it might change for us."

They sailed onward.

Within a few hours, the wind did shift, pushing *la Renommée* northwest parallel to Brest. By midday, they were nearly a hundred and fifty miles southwest of Ushant when they spotted a topsail ship.

"It's British," said François. "Lieutenant, prepare!"

By the time the crew spread the sand, filled the water buckets, and set them in place, a lookout recognized the ship as *la Panthére*. She was a 26-gun frigate the British had captured from them two years earlier and renamed the *Amazon*.

"It's the *Amazon* for sure. We'll have more to throw at her than she can hurl back. She carries 6-pounders against our 8-pounders." De Conflans was as familiar with British ships as François.

"Sir, it'd be best if you went below during the engagement. I'd hate to have you injured," suggested François.

"Of course," de Conflans agreed, turning to his cabin. "This fight is yours, Captain."

"Helmsman set a course south-by-southwest and see if we can outrun her. Lieutenant, set tops and mains to run." With the prestigious governor on board, François had no wish to engage in a conflict. In addition, a nearby enemy warship might hear the battle and join the action. The frigate's sails ballooned with a good wind pushing her.

La Renommée sped across the waves and outdistanced her opponent. François watched the masts, which strained in the gusting wind. The *Amazon* was now two leagues aft.

"Reef the fore topgallant and the jib, Lieutenant, or we'll lose our topmasts." The slight reduction of sails had little effect on their speed. It was late in the afternoon and he hoped to evade the stalker for good during the night.

But soon, a stiffer wind blew and there was a low crack from the tops. The fore-topmast slanted forward.

"Shorten mainsails! Let topsails fly—mind the stays!" François barked as sailors scurried to assess the damage. To the ship's carpenter, he cried, "To the ratlines and brace it!" His commands desperate, he looked back toward the *Amazon*. Only one thought came to him—damn cheap spars!

"The topmast gave at a knot two-thirds the way up, Captain," shouted the carpenter from the crosstree. "It's split in half and we must replace it. No fish will hold."

Given the damage, François expected they'd have to defend themselves. He was familiar with the chasing vessel. The *Amazon* had lines similar to *la Renommée* but was smaller with an eighteen inches shallower draft. Although a worse sailor in rough seas, she'd be upon them before they could make fast a new mast. He'd have to furl the topsails to reduce the stress on the masts and use just his mains for sailing, not a good choice during battle. As he ordered the commands, de Conflans returned to the quarterdeck.

"Topmast split, huh? I heard it." He eyed the *Amazon*. "Not good, but you can still maneuver. Should I stay above to help?" His years of experience would be helpful so de Conflans stood near the helmsman and directed the heading as François commanded the ship's battle preparations. He decided to stay to the windward side of the oncoming warship; if the *Amazon* came onto his windward quarter, she'd rob him of the little wind he had. This forced the enemy to try the same, and both ships hauled more eastward. Around the time the English warship reached gun range, the carpenter lowered the broken topmast.

The first shot from the *Amazon* hit the mizzenmast, showering the quarterdeck with splinters. The enemy had the wind advantage and the French frigate waited until she was abreast to try disabling her. As the *Amazon* came within pistol range, they both maneuvered to get broadsides off and fired as their guns exchanged roars in a measured pattern. Despite the closeness, there was little damage.

A second blast from the ships was more potent. Three crewmen fell on *la Renommée* from canister shot and musketry. Aboard the *Amazon,* the French shots carried away the top mizzenmast along with many lines that put the foresail flapping.

After hours of firing and posturing, it became clear the French marksmanship was devastating the British crew. Fortunately for the British, a quickening breeze at sunset forced the ships apart.

La Renommée had suffered from the scrap as well, and François withdrew southward before his ship received more serious harm. The enemy warship, which he'd expected to follow, stayed behind. He scanned her decks for the reason and saw a telltale column of smoke. She was afire. François sailed southeast to escape, leaving her a white speck on the distant waves.

After a half hour of commanding makeshift repairs and listening to the wounded groaning, two new larger ships appeared three leagues downwind. They were signaling, and *la Renommée* was the topic. Without proper repairs, his ship was too slow. The chasing warships had set full sails.

François set out southwest before the wind to put the enemy behind him. Just as these ships disappeared, two more appeared up-wind. One was the *Amazon,* who recovered from the fire and back to claim her opponent. She brought another warship with her, a 60-gun ship of the line.

The *Amazon* closed behind *la Renommée* and crossed her stern, firing in passing. François cut his ship hard to the port to run parallel and fired his guns. One shot hit François's mainmast eight feet above the deck and split it from top to bottom with a ringing thud. Passing from *la Renommée's* port, the *Amazon* came about along the starboard aft.

The other warship was gaining. It attacked straight toward the frigate's port side, intending to wear away for a broadside. As she began her turn, *la Renommée* sent her broadside first. Two hits to the British ship's mainmast brought down her main topmast and removed her fore topsail. The big warship, dismasted, retired from the skirmish. The *Amazon* fell back as well.

La Renommée pulled away and the first lieutenant took the quarterdeck as François climbed below to check on the injured. Some had lost limbs, which would end their careers, and others were simply in tremendous pain despite sedatives. Although five had died, François postponed his grief as he returned to his post.

All night they sailed to the northeast, hoping to lose any pursuers. But when daylight broke, the sight of a sail upwind demoralized the crew. One warship had followed *la Renommée* all night in the light of a rising moon. To provide the frigate the canvas she'd need to outrun the enemy, the carpenter attached a studding-sail to a jib boom, fixing it atop the foremast.

The larger warship's threat sailed on toward *la Renommée*.

Around mid-September, Washington Shirley said goodbye to his lover and set off on another patrol along the French coast. His new command, the *Dover,* had proved to be a good ship so far, and he was eager to put her in action. The French, however, remained, for the most part, in their ports, offering no way for Washington to achieve the victories he'd need to rise in rank. To relieve his boredom, he spent much of his free time discussing fields such as mechanics, ship design, and history with Abraham; however, Abraham was far less ambitious than he, content to be a carpenter, and did not understand Washington's urge for action and opportunities to showcase the virtue of uncommon valor.

The *Dover* accompanied four other warships off the French coast near Ushant. It was their fourth day at sea when the sound of cannon fire carried across the waves from the west, where one of their squadrons had engaged the foe. Hurrying westward, the *Dover* reached the fight at its conclusion, as the enemy frigate sailed away.

Another ship arrived to aid the burning frigate, so Washington sped after the French warship. Near dusk, he lost sight of it in the dimming light but, when the moon rose, spotted one fleck of sail-reflected light along the horizon.

"There's the devil—hull down," said Washington. "Follow that little glimmer, Lieutenant, and by dawn, we may be upon her." He ordered more sail and went below, with orders to wake him if they were closing.

Just before sunrise, the lieutenant woke the captain with good news.

"Sir, we're two-and-a-half leagues from the French frigate." Washington, on the quarterdeck, held his spyglass to his eye.

"She's making good speed, and she's spotted us, heading east-south-east toward their coast. Beat to quarters, Lieutenant."

The rattle of the drum sent the men into a rush to prepare for combat. Abraham checked the pump once more and walked amidships to view the enemy. In the mist of the morning fog, he barely made out its shape, but as the sun's edge glided above the horizon, he spotted the illuminated sails and prow. Instantly, he recognized the sleek hull lines and the forward-placed foremast, the characteristic taffrail, and most convincingly, the figurehead. It was *la Renommée*. He turned toward the purser, Collins, who stood next to him.

"I'm familiar with that ship! It's *la Renommée*. She's the fastest ship in the French fleet but rides low in the water, hard to haul."

"How do you know so much about her?" Collins asked, eyes narrowing.

"I helped build most of her."

Overhearing, the lieutenant took Abraham to the captain. "Sir, Mister Robinson says he's acquainted with that ship and helped build her."

"Is that so, Robinson?" Washington asked in surprise.

Abraham smiled. "Aye, sir, at Brest in '44. I built her at the start of the war. I know every plank, beam, and treenail."

"By Jove, tell me more! She looks to have aft chase guns."

"No, sir. The chase gunports on her stern are false. Her lower-deck has no guns."

"How many guns does she carry? What's her tonnage?" This information could be invaluable during a fight.

"She has twenty-six 8-pounders in main-deck gun ports and four 6-pounders on the quarterdeck." Abraham used his fingers to show the configuration. "She's almost six hundred and seventy tons."

"What's different about her?"

"Well, sir. If we had built her in England, she'd have heavier scantling and the masts would be a larger diameter. The designer planned to lighten the ship as much as possible to make her fast and used iron braces for the deck bridges instead of wood knees. After I escaped from the *Northumberland,* I talked to a French pilot and he told me she was the fastest ship afloat. She'll do 15 knots after breaming. But he said she's a wet sailor and bad in heavy seas."

"You understand this ship well. Thank you, Mister Robinson. If there's something else, let me know!" Washington turned back to view the ship through his spyglass, before adding, "What's her name?"

"*La Renommée,* sir."

"Oh, the *Renommée,* huh? So, we've caught the French racehorse. I'd love to make her the fastest British frigate," he said to the lieutenant. "The *Amazon* damaged her badly; she has a studdingsail bent for a topsail."

The *Dover,* however, was only keeping pace with the French ship. He wondered if the frigate's noted speed would save her. But when the studding sail ripped away, his prey slowed. The damages were terrible, so he gave orders to fire two shots to see if she'd lower her flag.

The rumble of the cannons filled the air. She did not strike.

When the distance reduced to a quarter of a league, the *Dover* presented a broadside. *La Renommée* countered with a larboard tack showing her broadside and commenced shooting. The two ships closed and exchanged musket and cannon fire, each ship vying to get a weather advantage or expose the other's stern.

The *Dover* neared to board the French frigate. François quickly saw his intent and put his ship to flight. He realized, as did de Conflans, the perilous situation they faced. His crippled frigate's singular boon, her remarkable swiftness, was compromised. In all his years of sailing, this dilemma was the worst, not only for the jeopardy his crew faced but also for the governor's sake and what it might do to his career.

Though she tried to outrun the *Dover, la Renommée's* damage was too great. Within the hour, she'd slowed and Washington's hopes rose. The French frigate had been the talk of British captains for years; to capture such a prize would be a remarkable feat, one sure to be noticed.

La Renommée sailed to port, slow and lumbering, to protect her stern from an attack. She fired on the British two-decker, keeping her from crossing aft as the ships both closed within pistol range. Cannon blasts landed iron on both opponents and scuppers drained red off the decks.

Abraham, below on the gun deck, scurried searching for leaks, grateful not to be on the upper deck. Not that the deadly balls didn't kill men on the lower decks, but seeing the cannons' flash was seconds of horrid anticipation. Below and oblivious, he had grown used to the anxious tingling in his body before battle, the rush of energy and alertness as he moved around the decks.

As he listened for water seeping, his ear next to the hull, a cannonball smashed through the side of the *Dover*, not five feet from him. Wood chunks and slivers flew from the hole and ricocheted off the gun carriages in all directions. The blast threw Abraham to the deck, covered in bits of wood but unhurt. Shaken, he rose, deafened by the blast, shook his ringing head, and staggered away to continue his search for damage while three of the nearby guncrew were taken to the surgeon.

On deck, Washington, remembering what Abraham said about the frigate's frame thickness, ordered his gun captain to fire low. Dark holes appeared at the water line as shots pierced the hull. Good hits, he thought to himself. A few more and the racehorse would be his.

Aboard *la Renommée,* François and de Conflans both screamed commands, trying everything they could to save their ship from capture. A carpenter's helper announced water rising in the hold. As de Conflans left to check on the leaks, he toppled to the deck with a shout; a musket-shot wound in the thigh soaked his breeches and stocking in crimson. He had received many injuries in battles during his long naval service and was accustomed to the blow's numbness, but each tarnished his bravery with a fear of bleeding to death or dying of infection. It angered him that this time would be no different.

De Conflans hobbled below in pain, aided by two crewmen. There, carpenter's mates and helpers pounded plugs and canvas into holes to staunch the flow of water into the hold; it was already three feet high. De Conflans sent a crewman to inform François that water soaked a third of the gunpowder and that the water was rising faster than they could pump.

François scanned the decks before him when he got the horrible news. *La Renommée* had lost most of her masts, sails, and rigging. They'd lost seventeen men with thirty-three wounded, most of them gunnery mates. To fight on was entirely useless. The stark picture of defeat forced him to whisper, "Why do the Fates move against me?"

As the ship listed to starboard, dead in the water, François ordered the colors struck. At once, with the lowering of the French flag, the fighting ceased. The *Dover* moved up to the side of *la Renommée* and the British captain called out to him.

"Have you struck, sir?"

"Oui—la frégate est le vôtre." François clenched his teeth after admitting a captain's ultimate humiliation.

Washington then lay aboard the ship and directed men to throw grappling hooks to secure her. English marines climbed onto the French deck and the decimated frigate crew, without weapons, moved to the bow under guard. The French ship listed badly so Washington rebalanced cannons and lashed the frigate to the side of the *Dover* to keep her from capsizing.

Abraham and his helpers assisted those on *la Renommée*. He directed the men in both French and English, and they soon stopped the leaks. By late afternoon, the pump was discharging more seawater than what leaked in.

Dover's marines brought the defeated François and de Conflans aboard to Washington's cabin. The two sullen Frenchmen sat facing a captor who felt no mercy, for they were military men bound to the life of martial skills just as he. It might just as easily, under different circumstances, have been Washington sitting before them, but he questioned their identity, home port, and mission, then sent them below to an officer's compartment under guard.

Large holes peppered both sides of *la Renommée's* hull. The mast damages were beyond what Abraham had ever before repaired. It was a testament to the crew and the ship, so torn up, that it had outrun the *Dover* as long as it had.

Once the water dropped in the hold, the ship floated even. This allowed the *Dover* crew to unlash the frigate from its side and attach tow cables to her foremast. With *la Renommée* now in tow, the *Dover* set off for Ireland. The ship, a capture target of many British captains, might fetch a decent price in auction or if the navy purchased her. Washington knew either would delight the crew although he hoped for the latter. He'd love having *la Renommée* under his command.

The main topmast and topgallant yardarm suddenly gave way and came crashing upon the captive deck with thunder.

Washington, hearing the noise, came to the quarterdeck and saw the pile of splintered spars. They could not be repaired; he ordered the split masts cut down and thrown overboard with the spars.

Abraham reported the repair progress. The last serious leakage from high waves splashing through the shot holes was minimal and soon to be fixed, and they had already finished plugging the worse damage below the waterline.

"Mister Robinson, I'm indebted to you," said the captain. "Your knowledge played an important part in our victory today; the information on the light frames influenced where I directed my fire."

The captain patted Abraham's shoulder. "Although we lost three men, it might have been worse if the fighting continued. The breaches in their hull forced them to surrender. In one of my chests, I have a book by Edmond Halley that I'm sure you'd find interesting. Please stop by this evening after dinner and I'll lend it to you."

"Thank you, sir. Halley's work in astronomy and the other sciences fascinates me." Abraham's face flushed at the thought of being invited to the captain's cabin, an honor few received.

"Good, you'll enjoy it then. Once, I met him at a naval dinner. Halley was a Royal Navy captain on half pay, were you aware of that?"

"No, sir." He was amazed Washington had actually spoken to the illustrious scientist. "How did you find him?"

"When you come, I'll tell you more. The two French commanders will be there; you can brush up on your French while we talk. It'll give us something other than the war to talk about. Maybe we'll find out more about their mission, so pay close attention to what they say."

When Abraham arrived, the captain was behind his desk, which sat straddling a starboard cannon's train tackle two feet from its truck. The French captain and governor, and the *Dover's* marine lieutenant, rested across from him in chairs. Two lanterns illuminated the interior and out the gallery windows, the stars dipped and rose with the ship's rocking. The four had dined together, a common courtesy to enemy officers.

"Mister Robinson, join us," said Washington in French. "Let me introduce you to Captain François de Saint-Alouarn and Governor Le Chevalier de Conflans." The captain motioned for him to sit.

"Good evening. I'm happy to make your acquaintances, gentlemen," responded Abraham in French. He bowed before sitting.

"Ah, you speak French as well as a native. You've lived in France?" François asked. He appreciated Washington's hospitality but still mourned his advancement possibilities now that he'd lost his ship and failed the governor.

"Yes, in Brest when I worked at the shipyard." Abraham knew the Saint-Alouarn name and wanted to shout about how René had treated Yvette, but he remained polite.

"Aha, I thought I detected a Breton accent," said François.

"I picked it up from the other shipwrights. As a matter of fact, I helped build *la Renommée*." Abraham pressed the issue. "Excuse me, sir, Captain Shirley introduced you as Captain de Saint-Alouarn. You are related to Monsieur René de Saint-Alouarn, Chevalier de Rosmadec?"

"Why yes. You're acquainted with my brother?"

"In a way. I'm betrothed to Yvette Façonneur, whom I believe your brother courted." Now René would hear of it, he gloated.

Stunned by Yvette's name under such distant circumstances, François blurted, "My God! Yvette? How is she?"

"Yvette's well and living in London. After the war, we'll be returning to Brest to be wed." Abraham was satisfied he had closed the final door on René's interest in her.

"Believe it if you will, those words are a song to my ears. Yvette deserves a good husband and a happy life. Amazing that we should meet this way." François meant it, anything to keep Yvette away from René.

"Yes, it is, sir—quite a coincidence," replied Abraham. He forced a smile.

"Hmph, you learned French so well just working in Brest?" the Governor de Conflans said, doubtful. "You could pass as a Frenchman."

"Since you mention that, sir, I did pass as a Frenchman when I escaped from the captured *Northumberland*."

"Then, Mister Robinson," began Washington, smiling at the coincidence, "Governor de Conflans and you have something in common, too. He was the captain of *le Content* when it captured the *Northumberland*."

"Governor, that was sharp action your ships took that night."

De Conflans, still in much pain from his wound, looked away and remained silent. Humiliation filled his veins at having an enemy carpenter now compliment him on his old victory.

"Governor de Conflans, I noticed *lignum vitae* in the cargo manifest. Is there that big a market for the cure in Saint-Domingue? It's usual to ship the other way, to France." Washington, chuckling, wanted the governor to relax.

"The increase of English patrols depleted our supplies, and we need that medicine with so many men from the war passing through the islands. Too much syphilis and too few remedies." De Conflans shrugged. The man wore his wig longer than the norm for most Frenchmen, perhaps because he preferred the older fashion. He was senior to the others in the cabin, in his mid-sixties; this contributed to his embarrassment. "Many men will be sorry when our cargo doesn't arrive, also many women," he said with a weak smile. A hand rubbed his bandaged leg.

"You mean *our* cargo," Washington reminded him.

"Ah, forgive me, it will take time to realize our capture."

Washington reached to pick up a book. "Here's the book I mentioned, Mister Robinson, Halley's. It's a collection of his discoveries and theories on the movements of astronomical objects. It includes a bit of trade wind facts and geology as well."

"Thank you, sir." Abraham took the book, thumbing the pages. "You mentioned you met him once. What was he like in person?"

"Halley was very common in most respects." Washington tapped his fingertips together. "He also was a naval man in addition to his other accomplishments. When I met him he was old; but his ideas, they were new!"

"Such a loss of so gifted an intellect," added François, who had followed the scientist's discoveries in newspapers.

"Yes, indeed." Washington leaned forward. "Like most of us at sea, I had the most wonderful experience of observing the extraordinary displays of the northern lights. Halley propounded that they're sun particles following our Earth's magnetic lines and interacting to glow." Washington looked up, recalling the incident. "And his mind was so quick, he grasped everyone's attention at the table and could expound on any question asked. He was still sensible after quite a few glasses of sherry. We'd think the Astronomer Royal should be a stuffy old man, but Halley was nothing of the sort. He was a man who spoke his mind and even swore like a wharf man to emphasize a point." Washington laughed.

"More wine, gentlemen?" He reached for the bottle. "Join us, Mister Robinson." Without waiting for a reply, he poured a glass of wine for Abraham and another for the French guests and the marine lieutenant. More wine, he thought, could reveal more military information.

"Halley's brilliance extended far beyond the sciences though. A genius in many disciplines, Halley excelled in construction and fortifications, too. Lest I do all the talking, were either of you ever at Louisbourg?"

François eyed Washington, "Yes, of course." Even through the wine, he knew Washington's intentions. "Surely you're aware that it's impregnable!" They laughed harder than the joke deserved thanks to the alcohol, but De Conflans did not break a smile.

"Sir," Washington said to him, "you should be thankful you were not governor there."

"Little difference, Captain Shirley. I would still have become a prisoner in either case," he said glumly.

"Perhaps, or not. If you had been the governor, Louisbourg may not have fallen." Disappointed in getting nothing on the subject, Washington hoped de Conflans would remark on his new duties. "When you arrive at Saint-Domingue, what challenges face you there?"

De Conflans, still shocked and irritated by a common carpenter invited to the conversation, and aghast that such a carpenter's fiancée had once been courted by an officer, said nothing. He turned only to Washington.

"Gentlemen, I must retire. My wound is bothering me. Captain Shirley, I have enjoyed your hospitality."

"We've enjoyed your company, Governor de Conflans and Captain de Saint-Alouarn. I hope your first night on a British warship goes without incident and you can sleep without nightmares of the battle. Perhaps we can discuss more enjoyable topics on another night."

Washington motioned to the lieutenant. "Accompany the gentlemen to their quarters."

Washington turned to Abraham with a more serious expression. "I'm glad you were here. Three pairs of ears listening to Frenchmen are better than two. Who knows what we might have learned or may yet learn from them? The governor might divulge more on the defenses of Saint-Domingue if we could get him to speak freely. He's a tight-lipped man. You may go now, Mister Robinson."

"Aye, aye, sir. The evening was enlightening. Thank you."

For over two weeks, the *Dover* struggled to tow *la Renommée* toward Ireland, even after attaching new yards to carry sail on the French frigate's foremast. When the winds became contrary, the *Dover* changed its heading first for Portugal and then for Plymouth and landed there over two weeks after *la Renommée's* capture. They shipped the prisoners ashore and sent François and de Conflans to the port commander for interrogation and disposition.

Washington learned the *Amazon*, much mangled from her engagement with *la Renommée,* had sailed into Plymouth for repairs soon after the battle. Captain Faulknor of the *Amazon* had lost twenty men with thirty wounded, including every officer, and had many hits at the waterline. Moreover, the fire from cannon cinders had threatened his ship until they brought the blaze under control. The *Dover,* too, needed repairs Abraham couldn't make at sea, as he lacked enough wood. After docking, he busied himself by requesting lumber and parts to finish up the damage from the combat, while the officers and other masters were free to go on leave.

CHAPTER SEVEN

The Chivaree

Washington left the ship two days after arriving and put command in the first lieutenant's hands. Happy with his safe return, Anne asked about the recent voyage, and he described the capture of *la Renommée* as they walked along the seaside in Plymouth.

"What value is a French frigate so damaged?" she inquired.

"The damages weren't ruinous, only severe," he said. "We destroyed her masts, which we shall replace, and she took shots below her waterline. Those we can fix, too. Not vast damage, just leaks that threatened to sink her. If they take her into our navy, the capture will be worth a great deal. The *Renommée* is barely three years old, and she's famous for her speed. That's what we need to catch other French ships. If the navy takes her and doesn't sell her to a privateer, the prize share might be more for the *Dover* crew.

"I'm hoping they deem her suitable for commissioning," he added. "I'd love to command her. The *Dover* is a good ship, but the *Renommée* would let me capture more of the enemy. They'll have a survey finished by the time I return from leave, and I'll find out if they're acquiring her. If so, I've already asked to captain her."

"More captures means more fighting, which means more chance of you getting injured or captured yourself," Anne said.

"It also means the Admiralty will speed my promotions. If I'm to make a name for myself, it's the chance I'll have to take."

"Ah, sailors." She chuckled, trying to lighten her lingering worry. "Sometimes I wish I'd met a blacksmith instead of a sea captain. At least I'd know where he was each night, and horseshoes don't fight back."

Washington paused. "I'm sure, my dear, you see blacksmiths weekly, along with bakers and liverymen. If you'd sooner be with them..."

"Oh, humor? You're who I want. I only wonder if being a belle and not a bride is worth the effort," Anne replied.

"If I could change that, I'd do it," Washington answered, somewhat irritated.

Anne sighed. "I'm aware of your feelings toward me, Washington. I wish you'd commit to them."

This truth suddenly struck Washington as though for the first time, crystallizing: it took full commitment, not just fleeting affection, to have a life with someone. He had postponed any prospect of marriage for the sake of his career, but he realized that what he wanted to commit to was Anne. Their relationship was a drifting ship and he needed to fill the mainsails. His frustrations had peaked.

"Anne," he breathed, "you're right. I've wavered on dedicating myself. That's not proper behavior for an honorable gentleman." He turned to her, stopping the walk and taking her hands. "Anne, will you marry me? I swear that I will cherish you and forever be faithful to our love if you accept my proposal."

Shocked, Anne wondered if she hadn't slipped into a dream in the daytime. "Washington, I'm so surprised," she stammered. "I love you so much and have waited for so long for you to ask me. Yes, of course, I will marry you. It's all I've wanted."

They spent the rest of the day planning how he should ask for her father's blessing and when the wedding should be. For Washington, the burden of a self-restricted naval life had ended. Bold and determined, he wanted his family to know of his resolve as soon as possible.

* * *

The patrol along the French coast remained stormy, keeping Abraham seasick for weeks. Around the middle of October, the *Dover* attacked a privateer from Saint-Malo, the *Jean Frédéric*, a 22-gun corvette. After a three-hour fight with both ships mounting damage, the French ship struck. Washington again escorted his capture back to Plymouth. Unlikely to be a candidate for commission into the navy, they could sell her for a sizable prize share.

"Well, Mister Robinson," said Washington to Abraham, "it looks as if your work in France benefited our navy."

"Sir?"

"The Admiralty surveyed *la Renommée* and decided she's fit for service and will commission her."

"So, sir, I guess an English shipwright in France made a French warship for the British navy?"

"Strange, but true. It's one I hope to command."

"Sir, you want to captain *la Renommée?*"

"I wrote to the Admiralty for her command before they considered taking her. Since I captured the ship, they'll honor my request before others. Time to see what a British captain can do with the fastest frigate."

The crew rejoiced when they heard that the prize shares for both *la Renommée* and *le Jean Frédéric* could be worth years of wages; Abraham's share could be hundreds of pounds.

The navy soon confirmed Washington as commander of the frigate. They also ordered the transfer of the crew to the accommodation sloop, *Swift,* while they made *la Renommée* ready for sailing.

When Washington told Anne about the new command, he also mentioned that his brother, Laurence, was not to attend their upcoming wedding. "Because of manor business, Laurence can't come. Although he's invited us to the manor afterward for a marriage celebration at Staunton Harold."

"I never imagined as a young girl I'd be getting married in cold December. My dream was it would be in June or July; a nice warm month with hundreds of flowers everywhere."

"Well, we can put it off, if you..."

"Oh, no! You won't get out of it that easily," she laughed. "I'll take December. Even in the bitterest winter storm is fine, the sooner the better."

The wedding was to take place in the old Saint George's Church in East Stonehouse. Planned for the 1st of December, they'd live in Anne's father's home until the newlyweds found a suitable house near Plymouth.

* * *

Abraham left for London after the purser gave the crew an estimate of their prize rewards, though they would have to endure a probation period. The Spanish prize previously taken aboard the *Lark* was still in litigation.

Yvette was overjoyed when he arrived, ignoring her dinner preparations to throw her arms around him. "Darling," she greeted. She studied his eyes; they always told a great deal.

"Hello," he said smiling, bending to kiss her. They squeezed through the doorway and he dropped his leather bag just inside the room.

"Here, sit and I'll cook dinner. Did you eat tonight?"

"No, but don't cook yet, there's good news to tell you. After my commission ends, we should receive share prizes from the captures of the two frigates, almost 275 pounds. That's more than seven years of pay!"

"Incredible! We could buy a small cottage." Yvette's hands clapped at the thought. "This is so exciting. Just like a pirate returning from the sea with his booty. I have my own Blackbeard."

Abraham laughed but added a word of caution. "Remember, those two may be the only extra income we get. I heard the company that shipped the gold on the Spanish treasure ship has appealed the prize court's verdict. It's asking us to return the treasure because the cargo belonged to a neutral country and not Spain. I warned the *Lark's* crew such things happen and Lieutenant Burston got mad at me for saying it. I was right, though."

"Oh, too bad! If you received so much for the warships, imagine what you could have got for a treasure ship."

"And that's what the crew was doing, imagining. That's not reality. We must be realistic."

Days later, he reported back to the *Swift,* learning on arrival that *la Renommée* had been renamed its English definition, the

Renown. Upon returning one of Washington's many loaned books, the two discussed their upcoming nuptials.

"Mister Robinson, have you set a wedding date? I've just announced mine to my relatives. We're to marry in December."

"Congratulations, sir. Our plan is to wed as soon as we can get back to France after the war ends. Yvette wants her family to be present. We must save for it, and maybe we'll buy a small cottage. I'd like to invest my prize money, but so far we've had no luck in finding anyone trustworthy enough."

"Well, I can suggest an honest broker whom I know through my younger brother, Robert; he's handled our family's investments for years. I'll write a letter of introduction if you wish, although investing is a tricky business."

"Sir, I'd like the introduction." Abraham felt privileged. The Shirley family name was synonymous with wealth. Before the captain left to get married, he arranged a transfer of Abraham's prize shares into an account with one of his investment brokers.

* * *

In East Stonehouse, the church bells of Saint George rang as Washington and Anne descended the worn stone steps as husband and wife. They traveled to Staunton Harold in Leicestershire and, upon arrival, Laurence greeted and welcomed them, easing Anne's apprehensions. Though Washington had not spoken highly of him, in the flesh, Laurence behaved as an impeccable gentleman.

Staunton Harold Hall was a large manor, the lands encompassing thousands of acres of rich pasture, trout-filled streams, and beech woods. The main estate hall and chapel, in a long sylvan valley, captured the heart at first sight. The estate contained many buildings and stood amidst immense formal gardens and wooded lots held by the Shirleys since the early 1400s. Their family had prospered from lucrative agriculture and successful cattle breeding. In addition, lead and iron mines, seams of coal, and quarries of limestone peppered the land—a cornucopia of wealth passing from generation to generation of Shirleys.

On their third day, arriving back from a meadow ride in the late afternoon, Anne and Washington met his brother at the front entrance. His waistcoat was half unbuttoned and his wigless head bobbed from one shoulder to the other, with no regard for Anne as a guest. Laurence, drunk, harangued Washington over a trivial comment he'd made about a horse sale.

Though Washington remained calm, Laurence only got angrier; the only thing to do was walk away as his brother shouted vulgarities after him.

"Washington, I see now what you meant. Laurence shouldn't drink," Anne said as they walked up the staircase to their room. Laurence's mumbled tirade still echoed behind them.

"Well, now you've seen him as he often is. It doesn't always take a drink to set off his anger. He at times infers insults. When he acts like this, I just leave."

"It's so strange. Laurence has behaved so polished and proper since we arrived. First, I thought you vilified him for an old childhood wound. I was beginning to enjoy him. What a shame he can't control himself."

"He always turns into a beast of a man whenever he gets offended." Washington threw his hands up in exasperation. "A contemptible phantom rises within him and takes control. We mustn't allow him to spoil things. Let's hope he doesn't turn belligerent and ruin our marriage celebration."

During the festivities, Laurence acted respectably, escorting Margaret Clifford and their two daughters. Anne noticed his mistress was pregnant again and wondered if she clung to a secret and impossible dream he might someday marry her. The thought branded Laurence's knavery in her brain. At least, however, the rest of Washington's family received her well.

Once the relatives retired to their rooms for the evening, Laurence and the newlyweds rested in the dining hall.

"You are so lucky to discover each other. I hope you will live a happy life." Laurence was in a good mood and hadn't drunk too much after gorging himself on the food spreads. "Washington, you have every freedom one could imagine. As a sea captain, you go where the wind blows. Now you've wed a beautiful wife. You're not the Earl Ferrers. I'm chained by it, performing for our dead ancestors. When Father lived, he expected me to make good as the eldest."

"You did, Laurence. The family mills, farms, and mines are producing well."

"The businesses run fine but I still must watch to make sure the managers don't rob me blind. Those buggers would cheat me of every bushel, barrel, or wagon load if they could."

"Oh, you don't think that. Most are honest, happy to work and earn money. If they steal anything, it's likely so little it'd not disadvantage you. At sea, I allow a sailor to get away with a little chicanery. To demand total obedience is to invite mutiny. They need to believe they bested authority once in a while."

"First, they'd take a horseshoe and then the horse." Laurence wagged his finger at Washington and thumped his fist on the chair arm. "Come down hard on them before it gets worse."

"That philosophy leads to disaster. On the empty seas there must be leeway," Washington said.

When Washington returned for duty, the *Renown* was ready to receive her new crew. One week later, as scheduled, they set sail.

* * *

François, now a captive officer, was living with the family of a livery manager within Plymouth. As he was an officer prisoner of war, the British navy gave him an allotment and freedom to roam the parish at will during the day. Many French officers even returned to their civilian trades during their internments. Others made an effort to acquaint themselves with their captors' lifestyle. François spent the first weeks of September drinking wine and pining for his family.

He'd never been to England and didn't like English customs: he found the food unusual and bland, and the lack of social activities for prisoners boring. Since Governor de Conflans had diplomatic status and an injury, the navy sent him back to France days after *la Renommée's* arrival in Plymouth. François, though, was a military prisoner and bound by his word to stay until the end of the war.

When Marie learned of his capture, she found herself unsurprised; she'd been preparing years for it. She didn't tell the children, and although Louis found out at school, he kept it to himself. Marie wondered if Governor de Conflans, freed himself, might vouch for François's early release, so she wrote to him. With his influence, François was set free the first week of the New Year.

François returned home looking no worse for his brief imprisonment. A condition of his release was an oath to not return to sea during the rest of the war. Such promises were common and seldom upheld, but François kept his for Marie's sake.

* * *

Yvette beat Mister Willocks to the bookshop, eager to start the day's work. He tottered along moments later, books under his arm, keys jingling in his hand.

"Good morning," she said with a happy lilt to her voice.

"Good morning to you. It's a cool morning with this breeze—a fine day. Spring is almost here, I can sense it!"

"And it will be a wonderful spring," she chirped.

Mister Willocks turned the key in the old lock with a squeak. "Let's go inside out of this chilly wind."

Mister Willocks fussed with books in the window. Yvette tore pages from an old damaged book, using them to start a coal fire in the iron parlor stove. As she had become very familiar with the business, he had recently given her a penny raise. For a treat, one she often enjoyed, Yvette hurried to Garraway's coffeehouse for fresh coffee. She and Mister Willocks sipped their beverages as they set up the shop until the typical morning sounds outside grew into alarmed shouts.

"What is happening out there?" Mister Willocks raised his head from his work.

Yvette peered out the window, but she couldn't tell from where the hubbub came.

"I don't see anyone. I hope it's not anti-Catholic or anti-Methodist mobs like last month," she said, knitting her brow.

"Well, many know you're French Catholic. You hide in the storage closet. No sense in taking a risk. I'll tell you when to come out." He scurried out to investigate.

Yvette settled in the little room at the shop's rear, which served as a storeroom for books too old or unpopular to sell. She still held her cup of coffee and sipped it, not particularly worried about the outside disturbance.

As time passed and the shouting got louder, she grew worried. Peeking into the bookshop, she noticed that a fog had rolled in. But this fog was a dense, gray smoke with bits of swirling cinders. She could smell it. She ran to the front of the store.

"Mister Willocks!" she cried hoarsely through the smoke. "Mister Willocks!"

Yvette flew out the door and saw a black pillar of smoke rising from nearby buildings. A fire blazed a block away. Yvette gaped.

After a minute, a man ran by, yelling the fire was spreading on Exchange Alley. A family had perished. As he spoke, bells tolled, and she heard the alarms of horns and shouts everywhere in Cornhill. Soon after, Mister Willocks came rushing along the street.

"My word—oh, my word," he was muttering as he approached. "Oh," he cried, "at least three buildings are ablaze on Exchange Alley! The men can't extinguish it. They can't even get near the flames. A fire machine is there, but the water reaches the outer walls, not the interiors. I'm afraid we may lose everything it's spreading so fast."

"Let's put the books in the street; the fire can't burn that." She pointed across the road.

"Good, good. Stack the most expensive ones first and…"

"No, no. Water will cover the streets by the time they finish. We'll put books from the storeroom on the bottom and better books on top. I'll run home for blankets. We can wet them and use them for cover."

Both frantically carted out the books, placing them upon the roadway on the far side of Cornhill Street. Soon other shop workers did the same. Before long, the street was like a flea market with merchandise of every kind piled in disorderly heaps. The old buildings behind the bookstore ignited one by one as orange tongues caught adjacent buildings. Lead soldering from the rainspouts and roofing dripped onto the streets. The roar of flames, collapsing walls, and breaking glass reverberated along the alleys. Embers settling on more distant buildings began new fires in the neighborhood.

Mister Willocks and Yvette rushed in and out of the store, stacking hundreds of books in columns chest-high. Two hours later, with their goods outside like the other merchants, they tried to save shelving, display furniture, and whatever else they could move onto the wide thoroughfare.

Soldiers in bright red uniforms, living flames themselves, marched from the barracks at the Tower of London. Officers ordered them into lines around the stacks of merchandise to prevent theft.

Yvette rushed toward her home to get blankets to cover the bookstore's goods, but soldiers forbade her from entering her street, fearing looting. Back at the bookstore, the fire was spreading faster and faster. The flames now reached seventy feet high. Walls tumbled to the ground and screams echoed along the streets.

Yvette spotted a cloth merchant nearby and darted toward his piles of fabric bolts.

"Sir, can we buy on credit a few bolts of your thickest fabric? We must cover the books from our store or they will burn for sure," Yvette pleaded.

"Here take these two. Go," the merchant said, loading up her arms without asking for compensation.

Yvette, carrying the bolts of canvas weave, dashed back to the books. She and Mister Willocks wrapped the heavy cloth swag around their stacks, covering the entire literary mountain. Yvette took a bucket from the pile, filled it at a horse trough, and wet the mound. Just thirty feet separated the books from the building; she prayed the distance could keep them from igniting.

The fire, now into its fifth hour, spread from Exchange Alley, a zigzag street behind the bookstore. It jumped the alley, spreading south and west, but moved northeast and east faster with the light winds. Soot covered everything, including a downcast Mister Willocks, and Yvette knew she must look the same.

When the fire reached the back of their building, the back wall, visible through the window, began to glow. Poor Mister Willocks turned away. His soot-smudged cheeks showed tracks of tears as glowing cinders fell in front of the store, covering the walkway and street. After pouring one last bucket of water upon the side that faced the store, she guided the old man away from their hoard and watched from the Royal Exchange.

The bookstore blazed within minutes while parish firefighters and insurance firemen battled with hand pumps. The flames won every building.

Gathered around Yvette and Mister Willocks were hundreds of dumbfounded people. Most were untouched; many, like herself, coated in soot, had small burns and smoldering hair. She checked herself. Burn holes spotted her dress, too far gone to wear again. Yvette's flat on Castle Court, just east of the conflagration, lay hidden in a thick smoke. Suddenly, she wondered what she'd do without a job.

"How will I live?" she whispered to herself. Her workplace had disappeared, and poor Mister Willocks had lost his store. Her eyes searched his sooty face.

"Mister Willocks, do you think you'll open another store?"

"If the fire hasn't ruined the merchandise, I may. If it has, well, I don't know what I shall do."

Their futures dispersed like the smoke on the wind.

Every so often, someone brought news about the latest destroyed building. The famous coffeehouses burned. The flames had reached Castle Court Street, just doors away from her flat. She wept without a sound, thinking of her and Abraham's belongings going up in the blaze. Tears now streaked her face, too, painting a ghoulish mask.

Ten hours passed, and she hadn't eaten the entire day. Mister Willocks told her to go home and then remembered where she lived.

"Oh, I'm sorry. Do you have anywhere you can stay?"

"A friend living nearby may help me. But let's wait longer and see if we can check on the books."

As the fiery pillars dwindled, officers repositioned soldiers back onto Cornhill Street by the goods across the ruined storefronts. Much merchandise made it through the fire unscathed, mostly wares made of metal, porcelain, and hardened materials. Others such as leather goods cracked under the heat. Expensive materials like feathers, silks, and those with fine varnished wood, became withered, blistered, or brittle.

Yvette and Mister Willocks found their steaming hoard; the canvas dry and hot to the touch. They grabbed a cool end and unwound the fabric. Beneath, the outer books on the storefront side had absorbed the steam from the canvas; the baking ruined them. The pages warped, stuck together. The entire layer would have to be thrown away. On the opposite side of the mound, the covers of the books felt damp, yet the pages remained dry with no damage. Inside the middle of the stacks, the warm books survived undamaged. By far, most of the books appeared fine and salable.

The army officers promised that soldiers would guard their merchandise until they arranged transport to a new location. Mister Willocks, elated with salvaging his inventory, now wept thankful tears. Yvette told Mister Willocks she'd return to help him the next day and headed toward her flat to see if anything had escaped the firestorm.

By the time she got to her neighborhood, taking a route that avoided fallen remains, dusk had arrived. It was a color-drained scene. Still-smoldering ruins surrounded her with blackened brick walls half-crumbled, burnt timbers, and glassless holes in charred window frames. It was hard to tell where she lived, since the landmarks she knew had fallen to rubble. It was clear the flames had consumed the building, including her flat, her clothes, their books, and Abraham's excellently crafted furniture. Debris continued to flicker and crackle and the foundation of her home held only cinders and ashes. The blaze had left nothing to salvage.

Madame Goubert was Yvette's closest friend in London, so she set off toward her home, ignoring the stares of passersby. Though she had nowhere to sleep and no money for food or rent, Madame Goubert graciously opened her home and offered for her to stay. Yvette didn't know when, or if, Mister Willocks could reopen the bookstore, but all she needed right now was Abraham.

News covering the inferno came the next day in newspapers. It took twelve hours to stop its progress through the efforts of men fighting it or by large open parks and wider streets, containing it to Cornhill. Rumors had circulated that Jacobites, Catholics, or French started the fire until the broadsheets confirmed it to have begun in Mister Eldridge's wig shop on Exchange Alley. It destroyed everything for five hundred feet between Cornhill and Exchange Alley, and east beyond Birchin Lane to Saint Michael's Alley. The calamity had leveled over one hundred businesses and homes and killed whole families. The famous stock and wine traders' coffeehouse, Garraway's, where Yvette got their morning coffee, burned, as did many other popular gathering places for London high society.

Mister Willocks arrived the next day at the shop remains, with a rented cart to haul his wares. Yvette was there to help him all morning. With the help of workmen, it took four cartloads to transport their store goods.

"Yvette, things will be a little difficult for me before I can pay you the money I owe you. I hope you can be patient. If I find a place to start a new store, I'm hoping you'll work for me again."

"I would be angry if you didn't hire me back in a new shop," Yvette teased, trying to smile. "If nothing else, I am just grateful we survived and saved so many books. The shillings you owe me are nothing."

That evening, Abraham arrived by coach from Plymouth and ran most of the way to Castle Court Street when he heard of the fire. Learning of the deaths and seeing their flat gutted, his heart pounded. Frantic, he sped to the nearest constable's office and inquired after Yvette's name. When he learned she wasn't on the list of the perished, he found her at Madame Goubert's house.

Yvette rushed to the door and flung herself into Abraham's arms.

"Oh, my poor, poor dear," said Abraham. "Thank God, you're all right. You can't know how worried I was when I arrived in London and talk of the Cornhill fire was all I heard."

"I'm safe and so is Mister Willocks. It was awful—just awful," Yvette said, hugging him. "Everything is gone, the furniture, too."

"To hell with the furniture, I worried over you."

Madame Goubert invited Yvette and Abraham to stay with her until they found a place and got established again. "I don't mean to sound indelicate, but do you need money?" she asked.

"No, thank you. The navy paid my salary into my account. We'll be fine."

The highest priority the next day was finding clothing for Yvette. Since Abraham had never purchased nice apparel for her, they visited the finer clothiers and bought expensive dresses and accessories. He wanted her, at least once in her life, to own quality garments. They returned to Madame Goubert's with armfuls of packages.

The next order of business was finding a new home. In Bell Alley, they found a decent, inexpensive flat. By the time Abraham departed for the *Renown,* they had replaced enough necessities that Yvette could live on her own. Unfortunately, Mister Willocks, having limited funds, had no success reopening the bookshop. Abraham's salary, however, would be enough to support Yvette to the end of the year.

But peace arrived. In mid-October of 1748, the bells rang and cannons fired as the population of London turned out to celebrate the end of the war. All countries involved had agreed to a treaty at Aix-la-Chapelle. With the treaty came the Admiralty's announcement of the discharge of sailors who were beyond their enlistment time. This included Abraham, who had served six months beyond his four-year contract.

"Are you sure you want to leave?" laughed Washington. "We need good carpenters. The *Renown* will miss you a great deal and I a bit more."

"Thank you for the compliment, but Yvette and I have put off our marriage far too long. It's a shame I won't be going with you to the West Indies though; I've always wanted to see them."

"They are a wondrous sight, Abraham. If I can't persuade you to come along, then I wish you the best in your marriage and future. If you ever return to sea, be sure to find me. I'll sign you up for a tour."

Abraham said his goodbyes to his friends and departed the *Renown*. As soon as he returned to London, he and Yvette planned their trip to Brest for their wedding.

* * *

Late summer in Staunton Harold Hall transformed the immense gardens into vivid patterns of colors. Lakes reflected the display and Anne loved awakening to such a sight. Whenever visiting Washington's brother, witnessing his mistreatment of others, the blossoming gardens comforted her.

Washington had noticed his brother's emotional disturbances were occurring more often. The horses on the property, which were raced for sport and bred for profit, were Laurence's greatest joy, his greatest skill. Washington found him one day in the stables, shouting at a groom.

He entered just as Laurence's riding crop struck the side of the old groom's neck, causing him to stumble into a stall gate. "What is this commotion, Laurence?"

"I've told him fifty times to take care saddling that mare. She bloats her belly when he's cinching her and makes it too loose every time. Perhaps he'll remember next time."

"Or maybe you could use a different groom who has a feel for it," suggested Washington.

"The bastard does it to spite me."

"Is it worth the aggravation? Just have a different groom do the saddling. You'll keep from getting upset."

"If I spared the whip on this offense, the offenses will continue. I shouldn't have to change a thing; it should be he that changes," spat Laurence. That was the very problem: emotion, not logic, dictated his reactions.

"Why don't we go in for breakfast; I'm starved," Washington suggested, trying to cool Laurence's temper.

"I ate earlier and have to go to Shepshed," he replied, less irritated after having taken his ire out on the poor groom.

"If you want, I can accompany you."

"Why? So you can spy on the way I run my affairs?"

"No, I just wondered if you wanted company."

"No, I don't. I've business to handle. It's no one's concern but my own. Go back to the house and have your breakfast," Laurence ordered.

Washington was familiar with this type of reaction from his brother. Laurence was sensitive to criticism, imagined or not, and easily became agitated.

Their Uncle Henry, the Earl Ferrers before Laurence, had exhibited an unstable personality that most claimed was insanity. Laurence wasn't as unpredictable as their uncle but he had a similar flaw. As the second consecutive Earl Ferrers with such a trait, it seemed madness might be inherited along with the title. Washington was fortunate he didn't share such a feature.

As Anne and Washington ate breakfast, he mentioned Laurence's behavior in the stables. The love of his brother weighed against his brother's uncivil actions. Anne sensed this conflict and encouraged Washington to avoid his brother's company.

"If he's gone for the day, then it'll be peaceful," Anne suggested.

"I wish we could visit him when his combative attitude wasn't ruining everything. His suspicion of others is beyond rational," lamented Washington.

"Maybe someday he'll get married and stop." She doubted it though.

He sighed. "If only he would marry. But who'd marry him? As for his temper and drinking, even he knows what it does to him."

Anne and Washington left for their new home on Emma Place in East Stonehouse a few days later. It was a modest house by Shirley standards, but Washington was happy enough with his library full of mathematics and natural science books. On occasion, he remembered his ship's carpenter who had shared this interest.

Months after the treaty of Aix-la-Chapelle, Washington asked for a permanent sea duty assignment aboard the *Renown* with his younger brother, Thomas, as his midshipman.

Anne braced herself for this next tour and the long, lonely months, but would never prevent Washington's admirable drive to uphold his family's loyalty to serve the king. Even Shakespeare paid them tribute in *Henry IV: "The spirits of valiant Shirley, Stafford, Blunt are in my arms now."* With the peace, Anne was less fearful for his safety.

She also now looked forward to a child. At first, Anne speculated on bearing a son who might become the next Earl Ferrers if Laurence went without a legitimate heir. Now that Laurence was even more set on marriage, that fantasy faded away.

* * *

Abraham and Yvette braved a wicked trip across the Channel. Yvette, excited that she would see her parents again, wanted to marry in the small Church of Seven Saints in the oldest part of Brest. Its tall steeple rose north of the city, and it was where she had attended mass for years.

Abraham's first glimpse of the high walls around Brest represented so many different things: a home, his work, a love, friends, a prison, and an escape. Above all, it reminded him of his evolving fate. He mused that returning to Brest might redirect his life in yet another extreme fashion.

At home, Yvette expected a cold reception from her mother but, instead, was greeted by a squeal and a hug so tight it made her gasp. "Mama, I've missed you so much," Yvette cried.

"Oh, come in, my darling. You, too, Abraham," Louise ordered.

"Mama, Abraham and I are getting married as soon as we can at Seven Saints," Yvette began.

"Oh, wonderful, wonderful!" Louise shouted. "We must tell André and Gaëlle at once. They'll be so thrilled. We prayed you'd return after the end of the war to marry in Brest. God answered."

Louise was no longer concerned her beloved daughter planned to marry an Englishman or Anglican. With years to consider her actions, she'd realized how her religious intolerance and patriotic prejudice had almost fractured the crystal thread of love between her and her daughter.

Later, when Anton arrived, chaos erupted with loud shouts and laughter. He grabbed Yvette, holding her hands, dancing in a circle with joy. He then rushed to Abraham and clapped him on the back, kissing his cheeks.

"You look good, Abraham! Oh, what a wondrous day!" Anton exclaimed.

Abraham and Yvette filled them in on their adventures since departing Brest and, that evening, André, Gaëlle, and their children arrived. After catching up, the women planned the wedding and the men discussed politics and work.

"Things are slowing, but we will have to build ships for the next war," Anton answered Abraham's question. "This peace is just temporary. We'll be fighting the British again."

"I agree, Anton. The kings just prolonged the war for the future to fight. Both governments should have agreed on how to divide the territories they want to colonize. But at least Louisbourg is French again." Abraham smiled over the singular accomplishment.

"King Louis is, like they say, as stupid as the peace. His only interests are virgins and bedding Madame de Pompadour. He's a weak king and ineffectual," André replied.

"André, that's unfair," Anton hit back. "He's far more intelligent and respectful of the people than Louis XIV was. We can't judge him unless we're aware of what his options were every time he made a decision. No doubt he had to make compromises at Aix-la-Chapelle. Politics have wheels within wheels like a pocket watch, each intricately meshed and moving others. Simple solutions to complex problems only create more problems than they solve. We are at peace now. That's what we wanted."

"In London," added Abraham, "the people blamed King George for starting the war to protect Hanover, his homeland, more than Great Britain. The war ended with the people of both countries mad at their kings and neither king solved any of the issues that started the war."

Yvette visited her friends the next day and invited them to the marriage ceremony. Abraham looked into converting to Catholicism and wanted to visit his old shipwright colleagues at their noon break.

The dockyard looked no different from when he had last seen it as an escaped prisoner. When he neared the workshop, he recognized a few of the faces of the workers and waved to them as he went into the shop.

"Ah, Abraham, come see," laughed Anton, heading toward the front of the shop. He reached down into a tool chest and unwrapped the cloth from an adze, holding it up before Abraham.

"Oh, my God! How did you get them off the ship?" exclaimed Abraham. They were his old tools.

"When we repaired the *Northumberland,* there in the tool locker were your tools. I knew them right away from the engraved initials *AR* on the blades. I carried them back and hid them with my own. They're all here. I've kept them oiled and sharp. Though, when I brought them back, Caffieri asked me about them. He was going to accuse me of theft until I showed him your initials. I told him the story of your escape." Anton handed the adze to Abraham and reached for the others.

"That's quite a surprise wedding gift you've prepared for me, Anton. I bought new tools though they aren't as good as these." He hefted the adze and felt the weight he'd missed. "Thank you so much."

"Call out the guard, there's an Englishman stealing tools in the shop!" someone called.

"Master Caffieri! How are you?" Abraham shouted back.

"The question is, how's your adventurous life?"

"Still alive after dodging French cannon balls and surviving storms at sea."

"Good to see you. Unfortunately, I've had to fill your position with another man," laughed Caffieri.

"That's all right, Master Caffieri, I make twice as much in England," Abraham rejoined.

"Too bad. If they allowed me to hire you, I'd do it in a blink. Even though the war is over, we still have lots of work. Did you notice the ships in the dockyard? We're working on two big ones."

"I saw a 64-gun near here."

"That's *la Protée*. She's almost done but not the biggest. Further along is the keel for an 80-gun, *le Soleil Royal*. You'd love to work on that one, I bet."

"Of course, but attending my marriage comes first. Then we're off for London."

After the carpenters returned to work, Abraham wandered over to look at the long thick keel of the 80-gun ship. He inspected the scarfs joining the huge timbers. One scarf wasn't as exact as he'd have cut it. Caffieri was correct; he'd have loved to build the warship.

On the morning of the wedding, Yvette dressed in her bridal gown and Abraham donned his best clothes. It was a traditional wedding and friends, who thought the day might never come for Yvette, shared in the joyous celebration at the church and later at their home. The customary sharing of wine and bread, a pyramid of pastries, and dancing lasted much of the day into the evening.

When the last of the guests had left, Abraham, with Yvette sitting on his lap, rested on a chair in their usual place before the fireplace.

"It's late. I'm so tired from the partying. Ah, perhaps we can sneak upstairs and consummate our marriage?" he whispered with a raised eyebrow.

"Oh, as if our union needs more. We've been consummating for years," she laughed. "However, it's tradition, and we must honor the past." She grabbed his hand, giggled, and led him upstairs to her room.

Half an hour later, a loud clatter of bangs and shouts sounded down the road: it was a crowd of well-wishers pounding on pots, carrying torches, whistling, and shouting.

"Anton," said Louise, "you better go get them. It's a chivaree."

"Oh, my Lord, don't these people ever get enough?" Anton grumbled.

"I don't believe what I'm hearing. First, you complain for years about getting her married, and now you complain about the wedding. Just go and get them," Louise demanded.

The two were already coming. "I'll get the cider and the left-over dessert," Anton offered.

Abraham and Yvette waited by the door as the mob, bent on embarrassing them and interrupting their nuptial evening, drew closer. In time, they surrounded the front of the house hollering and howling while creating a cacophonous racket banging spoons on their pots and tins. The entire neighborhood was at their windows, laughing, watching the merry throng demand an audience with the newlyweds.

Rather than give in to the boisterous crowd, the couple waited in front of the window in full sight until the din of battered pans grew to full force. Then Yvette opened the door and, laughing, poured cider into the neighbors' pots, cups, and mugs. Abraham handed out the last of the pastries as the group saluted them one last time. Then they tromped away up the street, still yelling and banging until they were out of earshot.

"Well, I hope that's enough celebrating for one day," said Anton as they all climbed up the stairs for bed.

When Anton returned from work the next evening, he told Abraham that Caffieri needed to hire more shipbuilders. The Admiralty wanted more ships built instead of stopping production since France had suffered on the seas from British ship superiority. They wanted to boost the number of warships. Caffieri urged Abraham to work again at the yard.

"It's hard to imagine," said Abraham. "We planned to return to London and hunt for jobs. But I have work guaranteed if we stay in Brest."

He and Yvette discussed the benefits of staying and concluded it was foolish to ignore the possibility of finding no work in England. Likewise, the British wouldn't reverse their practices and begin tolerating Catholics, a difficulty for Yvette. The newlyweds decided to stay in France.

They still had over two hundred and twenty pounds to buy a home of their own but became discouraged after a few days. "They're all so small," Yvette pouted. "The only one I liked was near the river which stinks of fish and sewage."

"Perhaps we should look over in Recouvrance?"

"No, they're not...not French enough. Half of them don't speak French, just Breton. I'm used to living on this side of the

Penfeld. It's a nice mix between old Brittany and modern France. Even the farmers up the river speak more French than fishermen in Recouvrance."

"There's a thought. Why not live outside the walls? A cottage in the countryside might be nice. I could fix up an old one. They're cheaper out of town."

"You'd walk so far to the navy dock. I'd have to trudge those roads into the city to the market. No, that's not a good idea," argued Yvette.

"Well, you put the idea in my head. Perhaps it's a good one. We could afford a bigger place in the country than in town—and no smelly port! Besides, I can catch a boat into town if we lived near the river."

"Hmm, living in the countryside has never occurred to me," she admitted, smiling.

Abraham accepted Caffieri's job offer and immediately set to work on *le Soleil Royal*. He worked on her throughout the colder months of November and December, loving his job but growing discouraged in searching for a new home.

"Abraham," Yvette said one day after work. "I've found it! Wait until you see."

"So tell me!"

"I've found a cottage for us. It's just outside the walls and down near the river. The land is still wooded, so if we want to plant we'll have to clear it, well, you'd have to clear it. But the scenery is unbelievable. Plus we can get the cottage cheap."

Knowing Yvette, the consummate haggler, no one could get it at a better price. "Then we'll visit it on Sunday," he agreed.

The thatched-roof cottage was sheltered from the view of the road by a strand of apple trees. Made of stone, it faced the river, and a dirt path led to the road. There was a well and a large field.

"See. Isn't it wonderful," Yvette squealed, spinning around with her arms out as they reached the front of the cottage.

"I like it. Let's inspect it to see if it's sound," Abraham cautioned.

They examined the exterior, checking the masonry walls, foundation, and thick thatched roof. The window frames were rotting on the south side, and they'd have to replace the door but the cottage had six windows, unusual for one so small, and both a front and back door.

"We'll have to expand it for another bedroom and a kitchen. But the house is sound and the stone floor is level and won't puddle," Abraham admitted.

"The owner's starting price is two hundred and ten livres. But I know we could knock off money during the bargaining," Yvette said.

"We'll need money for repairs and to expand the living area. I'll want to replace the roof with slate and put up a ceiling. If we garden, then we'll need a shed or even a barn for a horse.

"I can make money, too," she added. "Until our first child comes, I'll have plenty of time to work."

"Well, I guess nothing should stop us from getting it. It's only an extra twenty minutes or so of walking to work. Let's do it."

The owner, a merchant who lived in Brest, was as good at haggling as Yvette and didn't budge below two hundred livres. Abraham and Yvette agreed to the price, now infatuated with the thought of living in the remote cottage.

Until spring, they continued to live at home while they made the dwelling suitable. Then, with flowers in bloom and the warmer breezes blowing off the sea, they settled into their little cottage in the woods.

D.E. Stockman

Abraham still loved his work at the shipyard, and Yvette created tambour lace to sell to local shops and merchants. The extra money she made helped ease their financial burden. Together, they filled their home with all the necessities for a comfortable country life.

CHAPTER EIGHT

The Pirates

The vibrant-hued waters lapping upon Jamaica's tan sands relieved the stresses of the crossing. Exotic fragrances and the beauty of the isle cleansed Washington's weariness after weeks at sea. As he caught sight of the emerald-green island of Jamaica, the unique, diverse vegetation and animal life ignited his scientific curiosity.

The *Renown* had sailed to Port Royal for patrol duty, carrying military supplies and a few government men. Once the notorious home to Caribbean pirates like Mary Read and Anne Bonny, Edward "Blackbeard" Teach, Calico Jack Rackham, and Captain Kidd, the quiet Port Royal was now the British Navy's best defense against smugglers. The harbor offered safe anchorage from frequent hurricanes and the breezes kept away most insects carrying diseases.

With the war at an end, the likelihood of career advancement grew slim. A Caribbean assignment, however, offered action against smugglers and occasional pirates, and a chance of commendation. The *Renown's* speed provided an advantage over other frigates, and Washington's orders read to remain on station in Jamaica for an indefinite period.

When ashore, he explored the tropical wooded beaches as often as he could. The unusual plants and animals such as crocodiles, iguanas, snakes, flamingos, and parrots, which he recognized from books he pored over as a child, sated his curiosity in biology. Now Washington had much time to devote to science; the occasional smuggler seldom interfered with his naturalist pursuits. His *Renown* often cruised with a sloop or other smaller warship for more protection, but the rum runners they encountered were out to make a fast profit and usually surrendered with little effort or bloodshed.

Soon after arriving, he met with Commodore Townsend, the station commander in Jamaica.

"Captain Shirley, I'd like you to sail on patrol accompanying Captain Smelt of the sloop *Viper*. After the peace treaty, Captain Smelt brought the orders from London to Louisbourg to evacuate our troops. He's just arrived from the New England colonies and Louisbourg. Such a pity we had to return it to the French."

"I'll enjoy meeting him, sir," answered Washington. Acadia interested him. He had learned the colonial settlers and militiamen in Louisbourg were relocating to Chebucto in Acadia to establish a new English settlement there and wondered how it was progressing.

The two officers met the next day, and Smelt's appearance startled him. He was much older than Washington imagined, about fifty, and didn't look fit. Still, he had a rough, weathered look like many captains, and his face was more angular with prominent cheekbones and a large brow.

"Captain Smelt, nice to have you in Port Royal," Washington said, smiling as the stranger came aboard the *Renown*.

"My pleasure," replied Captain Smelt. "Have you been in these waters long?"

"We've been here since late winter and nabbed just a few smugglers. A pirate sailed near the Leeward Islands two months ago. We haven't heard more of him since then."

"I looked forward to Jamaica. I've had terrible health and need the tropics to rid me of the cold air ills. Has fever attacked Port Royal?"

"No, not here. The breezes keep the foul airs away. You'll be fit again in little time. Let us go to my cabin." Washington headed for the stairs.

"Perhaps you can fill me in on the latest from London. I left over a year ago," said Smelt, following.

In the cabin, Washington informed him of the political gossip in London and then asked about Louisbourg.

"Admiral Townsend told me you delivered the evacuation orders to Louisbourg. Wasn't that mandate difficult for the colonials?"

"Well, the officers and businessmen threw fits over the news of the treaty and returning the citadel to the French, but it relieved the troops and families until the plans announced building Halifax."

"Halifax? After the Earl Halifax? Is that what they're calling Chebucto now?"

"Yes, they've renamed it, though I liked Chebucto. With Cornwallis as governor of the colony, it wasn't appropriate to continue using the Mi'kmaq name."

"Is he intolerant of the natives?"

"No, more prejudiced as a necessity to secure the lands for settlement and maintain peace. He's placed a bounty of ten guineas for each Mi'kmaq scalp whether man, woman, or child. Of course, the scalps won't come from just Mi'kmaq heads. A scalp is a scalp. If they are from an enemy, who cares if from Mi'kmaq, Acadian, or French heads? The more taken, the sooner we can take over their territory."

"I thought the treaty ended the war."

"That didn't appease the Mi'kmaqs when General Cornwallis cleared their land and built a fort to protect the new settlement in violation of earlier treaties. A few Mi'kmaqs attacked his soldiers. He retaliated by declaring all of them enemies of the Crown. Once we take scalps, the Mi'kmaq will flee the area. But what a harbor Halifax is. It's enormous, with deep water to the shoreline. Every soldier in Louisbourg received fifty acres, officers even more. It'll become the shipping center of Acadia."

"I'd think the remaining Acadians and French living there would migrate back to Cape Breton and Acadia." Washington doubted an easy transition for English expansion.

"Not with the laws he's imposing with fines and arrest to discourage trading with the French. If Acadians return to the region, they won't be purchasing tools or food in British settlements. The treaty did nothing to stop hostilities."

"It's quieter here in the Caribbean, I can assure you. At least so far," Washington said. "The French have stayed in Saint-Domingue. We've stayed in Jamaica. The sugarcane planters complain of smuggling from the French West Indies to the English colonies and that's what we're here to stop."

Within a week they were patrolling together along the coasts of Jamaica and the islands. Although the weather was fair, Captain Smelt's poor health continued to suffer from occasional fevers and a weak appetite. The *Viper's* cramped cabin provided little room for the ailing old captain. At the end of April, Washington received disturbing orders.

"Lieutenant Griffith," Washington said, aghast. "Admiral Townsend ordered our transfer to the *Viper*. Captain Smelt is to take command of the *Renown*."

"Sir? We've only been on station for a short time. I expected to be aboard the *Renown* for at least another year. She's an excellent sailor."

"I regret leaving her, too, yet those are our orders. We'll take half our men since the *Viper* crews just ninety. The rest will have to remain on the *Renown*." Washington, frowning, did not appreciate the move to the smaller vessel.

"Sir, I talked to an officer two nights ago from the *Viper*. He told me Captain Smelt requested a transfer to a larger ship," the lieutenant informed Washington.

"Bad health likely urged his request for the *Renown*." Washington surmised that Captain Smelt, familiar with Admiral Townsend, had asked the admiral to assign him to the frigate.

It angered Washington since he, not Smelt, had captured the *Renown*. He sent a letter off to a family friend, a senior official at the Admiralty but, the next week, Washington and his crew transferred to the *Viper*, sailing out alone in chase of a reported smuggler carrying rum to the colonies. Although the *Viper*, a sloop of war of 14 guns, was seaworthy enough, she hadn't the speed or firepower of the *Renown*.

In the Caribbean, his French-built frigate could overtake most vessels Washington encountered; the *Viper* couldn't. Many of the smugglers used the faster, ingenious Jamaican sloop, a design that outran the *Viper*. This would handicap his career plans.

In August, after hurricanes wrecked the western half of Jamaica, though hardly damaging Port Royal, the Admiralty reversed Townsend's order and placed Washington back on the *Renown*. Townsend was not pleased, but it made him aware of Washington's substantial pull.

It didn't take long for Washington to notice how much the *Renown* had slowed due to growths on her hull. The warmer waters teemed with wood-gripping and wood-eating parasites. Repairs were necessary, so slaves careened the ships by burning and scraping as Washington supervised from the wharf. After cleaning her, they refit the *Renown* with new rigging and replaced her contents. Once Washington had inspected her, he and his men went back on patrol.

Soon after, Captain George Mackenzie, commanding the *Amazon,* joined the *Renown* on patrols. This captain was younger than Washington and a stickler for naval regulations; Washington liked the man and helped him adapt to the tropics.

In early March of the next year, the *Renown* shipped out for England. When they had assigned the *Renown* to Jamaica after the war ended, Washington had assumed the Admiralty intended to keep her active. A few weeks after arriving in Plymouth, however, the navy paid off his crew and laid up the ship in ordinary, anchored for future use.

"I'll be receiving a new assignment soon," Washington told Anne. "Too bad they want to take me off the *Renown;* they should have continued using her in the West Indies. She out-sails every ship there and handles well in those waters."

Within a month, he learned the Admiralty considered selling or breaking up the *Renown*. Since she did not conform to the Admiralty's Establishment shipbuilding codes, they planned to strike her from the Navy's list. Washington sent a personal petition in favor of keeping the ship, claiming the ship's shallow draft and speed were ideal for catching the fast Caribbean smugglers.

The positive report and her superb reputation influenced them to reconsider. In July, after a close inspection, they again ordered her to lay up in ordinary. The captain's sheet of paper and ink was as effective a defense as her cannons in battle, saving her from being demolished and sold off for pier and barn timbers. The ship sailed to Deptford a few miles downriver from London. With just a few crewmen: the gunner, the boatswain, a carpenter, an officer, and the cook remaining on her, they fastened her to the mooring cable. *Renown* joined a long line of other ships, moved like buoys by wakes instead of the winds in their sails.

"Well, I never could have thought!" Washington blurted when he finished reading the letter from Laurence. "My brother will wed Mary Meredith. The letter says she's the granddaughter of Sir William Meredith. Just a moment, I know him, from Henbury in Cheshire. They're to wed in September.

"I don't remember him ever mentioning her earlier." He frowned, trying to recall the name.

"Let me think...Mary...Mary...my goodness. She was at a social and was a young thing, only sixteen or so."

"Oh, my, he's twice her age. Oh, how I pity the poor girl. She's ignorant of what is in store for her." Anne placed her hand on her cheek.

"Dear, I feel sorry for the young woman, too. Perhaps though, this may transform Laurence. Maybe this is what he needs."

In September, they attended the wedding, and Laurence spared no expense. The groom was resplendent in a white silk coat, waistcoat, and breeches, while his bride dressed to match with pearls sewn onto a white silk gown.

"Laurence, you're very lucky. Such a fine young lady you've found," complimented Washington.

"Washington, she is as pure as a spring rain," Laurence replied in an uncommonly good mood.

"Not to pry, but I can help resettle your mistress Margaret if you'd like," offered Washington, smiling.

Laurence bristled at the suggestion. "Margaret isn't moving."

"Well, I assume now that you're married, she and the girls will move off the manor. I wondered if I could help take the task off your hands."

"Are you mad?" Laurence bellowed, drawing the attention of the few guests still in the room. "She'll continue to live here, of course."

"Might that upset your new bride?" whispered Washington, not wanting to create a disturbance.

"I could not care a whit if she's upset. Margaret is my lover. Mary is my wife, a difference a fool can see. They'll both live at the estate."

"Ah...there might be talk," Washington sheepishly suggested.

"I don't have to explain myself or my private affairs to you or anyone. Dare you question what I do on my land? You sail away from your wife for months—no, years at a time. And you question me?" He grew red in his face.

"Well, now, I meant no harm," pleaded Washington, forcing a smile.

"You never do, yet you stick your nose like a sniffing dog into my affairs every time you come here."

It was late, almost one o'clock in the morning, and the guests moved to get their cloaks. Most had seen him in his rants and wanted to leave quickly.

"You're correct, Laurence, I had no right to question," Washington added.

"There are businesses to attend to and manors to run, let alone responsibilities you couldn't understand! There's more than a ship to sail with the navy taking care of bills and needs. What happens on my estates can change the lives of hundreds, thousands, and..."

Washington knew to clear off before it got worse. He headed for the parlor.

"Don't you walk away after insulting me. Come back here, you'll listen to me!" His ears crimson with anger, Laurence pulled out a folding knife from his coat pocket. He rushed toward his brother, paused, and then climbed the stairs, and raced along the hallway.

A servant, who'd heard the commotion, stepped innocently into the hall. "Where's my wife?" screeched Laurence at the man.

"She's in her room, sir," replied the frightened servant.

"Follow me!" he commanded. He went into his new wife's chamber, where he kept a pair of pistols.

"Load them," he ordered the servant as the countess woke in bed, stunned.

The servant took the guns and put gunpowder into the barrels and then rammed wads and balls into them, giving them back to the earl without priming the pans. Laurence noticed the unprimed pistols at once.

"You bastard. Give me the powder," Laurence said. He called another servant, shouting, "Take these, go downstairs, and shoot my brother, the captain, or I will blow out your brains. Someone will die this night!"

"Sir, I cannot. He has harmed no one."

"Then you shall die now!" threatened Laurence as he placed a pistol on the servant's chest. He pulled the trigger, however, the pistol misfired. The crazed earl cocked the other to repeat the lunacy.

"No—my, darling!" cried the countess, as she rushed to her knees in front of her new husband and pulled at his vest. "This is madness. Think of what you are doing. They mean you no wrong. We love you. Put the weapons back in the cabinet."

"Away, bitch! Stop me again and I'll shoot you first," he threatened, pushing his pistol against her head.

The servants rushed from the bedroom, fearing for the countess's life. One ran to Washington downstairs.

"Captain Shirley." He rapped at the locked parlor door. "Please, open! The earl just now threatened me and the countess with a brace of pistols and wishes to kill you, too."

Washington ordered a carriage readied when realizing he was the source of Laurence's wrath, and decided to leave for everyone's safety. From upstairs he overheard the countess begging as she sought to mollify Laurence.

Running to his bedroom, Washington shouted, "Wake up, Anne, we're leaving right away! That fool brother of mine wanted to kill me, a servant, and his bride just now. I can't stand it anymore. The devil take him, he's insane!"

"What?" Anne said, waking. "We're leaving? Oh, no, not you and your brother again."

"Laurence exploded and came chasing me with a knife in his hand. If it hadn't been for a servant, he'd have shot me. We're not safe here and must leave!"

Within an hour, servants harnessed horses to the carriage and packed their baggage. Washington and Anne left the Shirley manor without a word to Laurence, who calmed after his appalled new wife coaxed him into bed with a hot brandy.

* * *

The unsettled affairs in Acadia and Cape Breton, and the rivalry between the British East India Company and the French East India Company had increased. All were aware the treaty had only delayed war and its financial pressures for a short time. The two kings had previewed the other's weaknesses during the earlier conflict and were already planning strategies for the next.

In France, the king authorized more ships built. For Abraham, this meant a steady job and a permanent promotion to crew supervisor. He added another bedroom to the cottage and also enclosed the outside oven as a small kitchen. None considered the building a cottage anymore; with that many rooms, it was a good-sized country home.

Abraham had settled into a comfortable routine and built himself a small sailboat he used to get to work that he could pole or row when the winds were calm. During lazy summer days off, he used the boat to fish in the river or sail out into the bay, taking along friends and relatives. For the first time, his shipwright's life was satisfying and worry-free.

Although Yvette was happy doing lacework, the fact that she was still without child after five years of marriage hampered her life satisfaction. The countless candles she burned to St. Gérard in church did nothing to ease the pains of their childless union. She and Abraham sought medical advice from midwives and doctors. They even tried the many traditional remedies, including quantities of chocolate for Yvette and coffee for Abraham.

To Yvette, the refusal of her most ardent desire was God's punishment for past sins. An unknown transgression hung from her spiritual neck like a tether of shame. Abraham, on the other hand, was confident Yvette would someday get pregnant.

Money-wise, they were doing well. Abraham's new position paid more and Yvette saved the earnings she took in for her needlework. For the first time, it seemed life's fair winds filled their sails.

* * *

Washington Shirley received command of the *Mermaid,* a small 24-gun frigate. No longer on Channel duty, he sailed to the American colonies for patrols against French pirates and smugglers, most of whom sought shelter in Louisbourg. Peninsular Acadia in 1755 was inhabited by ten thousand Acadians who refused to swear unconditional allegiance to the British and outnumbered the English settlers two-to-one. The colonial governors saw the French-speaking menfolk as a possible threat if another war began.

Widespread military garrisons had done little to encourage the peopling, or *Englishification,* of the peninsula that Cornwallis envisaged. A few non-English settlements thrived, at peace with the Mi'kmaqs. However, the Mi'kmaq natives detested the British settlers, forcing them to hide in their forts.

Tensions rose as the French and British alike built military strongholds in preparation for the next war.

Through all of this, the two great rivals forced the Acadians from their lands. Although lawful citizens, the policies treated them as enemies. The misfortune of the British government in Acadia was that the majority of its subjects were French! They deemed Acadians, who refused to take up arms in war or to surrender their private weapons, as bad subjects of the Crown. In early 1755, the colonial governors initiated a secret grand scheme to solve this problem altogether with the support of Parliament: a full-scale removal of Acadians and French settlers from Acadia.

The Admiralty ordered fourteen warships to the coasts of Acadia to block any French reinforcements. Although neither king had declared war, the directives created a British naval barrier extending around the French territories. In mid-March, Washington put into Boston for supplies and more crew. He had rented a small house earlier in the year and placed ads in the newspapers requesting seamen to enlist in His Majesty's Navy at his home.

To Washington's satisfaction, he received orders to convoy troopships for the proposed attack on Forts Beausejour and Gaspereau in northern Nova Scotia. Boston became the staging point of the expedition and, by May, there were two full battalions of men ready to embark. The first phase against the French possessions in the northern colonies was set to begin.

The *Mermaid* was one of three frigates to protect the transports in a convoy of forty sloops and schooners. Washington departed, guarding almost two thousand New England militia up the Bay of Fundy to Fort Laurence, and in days, they attacked. Overwhelmed, the two French garrisons capitulated.

The sieges, which lasted only a few weeks, marked the expulsion of French control over most of Acadia. The first of the four goals was a success. Fort Beausejour's capture severed the land route from Canada to Acadia and New Breton, and in particular to Louisbourg.

"Lieutenant, we'll board the French infantry from Fort Beausejour and transport them to Louisbourg per the surrender agreement. The frigates, *Success* and *Siren,* and a sloop will sail with us," Washington directed.

"Are we going straight to Louisbourg, sir?" the lieutenant asked.

"No, first, we're sailing to the mouth of the St. John River on the northern shore of the Bay of Fundy to investigate reports of two 36-gun warships. If the enemy reinforces the small outpost there, it'll become the dominant French position on the bay and within quick striking distance of our Annapolis Royal."

When they arrived at the estuary of the St. John River, they saw no ships but soon heard explosions at the fort. The few French soldiers there had assumed they were under attack and blew up their powder magazine; then they retreated into the woods.

The four ships, having accomplished by chance another victory, continued on their way to Louisbourg to disembark the surrendered French troops.

These successive victories bolstered the colonial governors but their luck turned: General Braddock, in command of two thousand men marching on French Fort Duquesne, lost his life in the failed and bloody raid. A battle on Lake George was a British victory, but they didn't press the additional attack for the real goal, Crown Point. Lastly, the pretentious Massachusetts Governor William Shirley led an army against Fort Niagara but returned home in failure. British attacks on land ended up lacking after their initial successes. The navy succeeded in capturing French warships and privateers in the waters off North America in the de facto blockade.

In every way, the war in North America had already begun for Great Britain. Yet France lagged in countering these intrusions. The pressure on Versailles grew, and they devised a strategy to send an army to capture Halifax and Annapolis Royal, aiming to secure all of Acadia for France.

In early 1755 France prepared eighteen ships of the line and nine frigates to carry six battalions of French regular infantry on transports totaling forty-three ships. Half of these were to sail to Québec and half to Louisbourg. To convey such a load of human cargo and their supplies, they armed most of the warships *en flute*. That is, the ships were sailing as transports without all of their cannons to compensate for the added weight and space for the troops.

The first division of the fleet had old Admiral la Motte as commander; he fired a cannon signaling the expedition to sail from Brest.

* * *

"No, no—never!" Marie shouted, eyes flashing. "Louis has just finished the *Garde de la Marine*. He mustn't go with René!"

François fretted. She hated for her son to go off with René, in whom she had no confidence. Louis, however, was his own man now. He had chosen to train at sea with his uncle. Over the years, René's influence on Louis had grown. Louis lived to hear his uncle's adventurous tales, and much to François's chagrin, he requested to board René's ship for training instead of François's.

Marie was beside herself. Of the paths he might have taken, none could have distressed her more than Louis choosing René over his father. Not only had it hurt François's pride, but the danger it put Louis in was more than she could imagine. She was distraught and had wailed over the situation for days.

François, likewise depressed, tried to persuade her that René was capable and had proven credibility as a naval officer. He was second in command under Captain de Bouville. Yet, this gave Marie no relief.

For the first time in his life, François was at odds with his brother, although René did not know, and it was not his fault.

"I'll talk to him in Brest when I go. If he can't do anything to change Louis's mind, then I shall speak to Louis myself," François suggested to give Marie hope.

"Oh, I never wanted to force Louis to go against his wishes— but to be sailing with René!"

"I'm sure Louis will either reconsider or René will fix things."

Two days later, François tracked down his brother in mid-morning aboard his ship, *l'Esperance*. René hadn't realized the pair was upset.

"Don't worry, François. I'll talk to Louis and tell him he should train with his father. Had I known you were unhappy, believe me, I'd have settled the matter right away. Let's call Louis to my cabin. We'll talk to him."

"No, then he'll assume I forced you into rejecting him. I want it to appear as if it were your idea. You know Louis; he can be headstrong, even more so if he thinks someone is against him, in particular, me." François stood with eyes closed, shaking his head.

"All right, I'll discuss it with him. Hope the winds don't shift; we've been wind-bound for two days."

Louis had chosen *l'Esperance* with the hopes of adventure and glory, the oft-illusive aspiration of young manhood. Although he respected his father's skills at commanding a ship, he preferred René's exploits, or at least René's telling of them.

With the simplicity of youthful hopes and decisions, he was sure his fame was more quickly to come on René's ship.

"Captain, you requested to see me," Louis addressed his uncle.

"Sit, please, Louis," said René. "I want to ask if you might reconsider sailing on *l'Esperance*. Think of the benefits you'd gain by going with your father."

"Sir, I thought long about which ship I should complete my training on. I chose *l'Esperance* for several reasons. Foremost was my admiration of your skills. Not to say my father's are any less, but I've learned more over the years through your descriptions than his. I decided that to learn the mariner's way best, I should sail with the tutor more suited to me."

"Well-spoken, Louis." René was impressed, but he added, "I wonder if you might be forgetting this mission is just a convoy to Louisbourg, whereas your father will patrol the coast or the Channel. There would be far more to learn. It'd be much more useful for you to be on an active cruise where anything can happen. You'd put into new ports along our coast where you'll master how to identify and navigate them."

"I see your point, sir. What you say makes sense for my education as well." Louis was searching for the proper rebuttal to stay on his uncle's ship. "It's something I must contemplate. Need I transfer right away or wait until we return to Brest?"

"I'd prefer you decide before we weigh. If the wind turns, we may not have any time for you to switch. In that case, I suppose one mission on this ship could be a good experience, too. Regardless, settle on an answer for me by day's end." René saw no harm in allowing his nephew at least one voyage to Louisbourg if they were forced to put to sea.

"Thank you, sir," replied Louis, stifling a smile. He got up, saluted, and left the cabin feeling he had avoided a sentence of drudgery under his father's serious nature.

The wind shifted later in the day, abetting Louis's little triumph in putting off the decision. Admiral la Motte ordered the fleet underway as soon as possible to reassemble beyond the Raz de Sein in the ocean. In hours, pilots guided the ships out of the Road of Brest through the Goulet, and they entered the open sea. *L'Esperance* departed, too, assembling with the rest of the fleet.

As *l'Esperance* and the fleet progressed southwestward, René was happy everything was going according to plan after a week of sailing.

"The calm yesterday held us up but we should make up for it today. Correct, sir?" Louis said to his uncle on deck. "We've made good time."

René was leaning with his back against the windlass in the waist. He chuckled. The young man was too premature in his optimism. The seas were calm and the sky hosted high brush-stroked clouds. Most of the fleet surrounded them with a light wind billowing their sails.

"So far," René emphasized. "In two weeks, we'll be hitting the fogs along the Banks. Those ships that have never navigated them must beware of shoals and ice floes, slowing us."

As he said this, they heard a low snapping sound from aloft.

"Damn!" cursed René. "Send someone up there and go to hull." Topmen took the sails in as carpenter's mates and the carpenter climbed the shrouds to check on the yards and masts. After a few minutes, they had found the problem.

René shook his head and ordered flags raised to inform the fleet they must stop for repairs. Then he headed for the great cabin to tell Captain de Bouville that *l'Esperance* would hold up the trip.

Throughout the fleet, other ships came to a stop, passing signals from one to another until the entire group had halted. On the poop deck, Captain de Bouville watched the repairs as the mass of troops midships craned their necks and heads upward. Each wondered whether any of the carpenters aloft might fall from their precarious height as they hoisted new lumber to fix the crosstree. The ship was carrying hundreds of soldiers, with only half a crew onboard.

By dusk, the repairs ended. Captain de Bouville informed the others they could raise anchors and proceed. For the next week and a half, they experienced good sailing weather with only one becalmed day.

When they reached the Grand Banks, Admiral la Motte had the ships stop and hold their positions while captains from each ship gathered. It was time for the admiral to open and read the navy's sealed orders to assign destinations for each ship. René's *l'Esperance,* three ships of the line, and a frigate were to steer for Louisbourg while the rest were to sail on to Québec.

By the end of May, dense fog on the Banks enshrouded the ships and limited their vision to a hundred feet. In the gray mists, they separated from one another. After four days of blind traveling without meeting others, each captain opened and read new orders for such conditions. The instructions told them to rendezvous in the Gulf of St. Laurence. Once there, French colonial frigates and pilots would guide them the rest of the way. As they made for the coast, they met and joined other fleet warships, until little squadrons formed, making their way westward.

"Listen," René said to Louis as he and the crewmen leaned over the port rail to make out the sound better.

"What do you hear, sir?" Louis asked.

"Breakers," replied René, hearing the waves crash and straining to see through the gray curtain of fog. "The sea bottom is too deep for a shore."

He knew the sound meant they were near an iceberg off to their port and not too distant. "Tell me if you feel the chill of a berg," René called to the crewmen standing on the main deck.

All eyes fixed on the grayness when moments later they saw the swirl of air currents in the fog and felt the temperature drop at least twenty degrees.

"Keep a keen watch, men," René called. "Helmsman, sag to leeward," he ordered as a precaution. In the distance to starboard, they heard the other ships in the murky air. René called out and warned them of the iceberg on their port side. Just as he did, the giant glowing ice mountain appeared not fifty feet off; the crew ran to the railing to watch as the ship passed the monstrous peril.

"We're too close—hard to starboard!" René shouted just as a scraping sound shuddered along the hull's side.

"Carpenters below!" he ordered. Within minutes the carpenters returned to report no leakage or damage to the hull.

A strange white glow formed a halo around the berg's silhouette. The men had seen many since entering the Grand Banks, yet this berg was spectacular for its height and eerie nimbus in the fog. The strangeness of the scene provoked both fear and awe in Louis.

They cut through the fog, leaving it behind, but then spotted sails approaching a few miles away. The vessels were British; René shouted to return to the fog to avoid confrontation.

The British warships had spotted them and fired a signal cannon, intending they haul up for them to board. The approaching craft headed straight for the French, who slipped into their cloudy cover and continued. For the next five hours, they remained ahead and lost their pursuers.

"Sir, I don't understand why they signaled us for boarding, this isn't their territory. Shouldn't we stop them and demand what they are doing in our waters?" said Louis on deck, keeping a lookout for the British.

"We might be at war is my guess. Our squadron played it well withdrawing into the fog. We won't stand a chance with most of us armed *en flute*. What I find more interesting is they must know we're in these seas. Why else were they so far east of Acadia?" René suspected the British were patrolling to intercept. He wondered how the rest of the separated ships could get through to Québec and Louisbourg past them. "I don't think we will get to either Québec or Louisbourg if they're searching our usual routes in force. There's a chance we'd get by them on another route, though, if the waters are free enough from ice floes.

"We could try sailing east of Newfoundland to the north and head west at Belle Isle. The British expect us to go south and reach Louisbourg by passing through them, not north around Newfoundland."

"Aha, clever, sir! In June, aren't there floes and icebergs to the north? Has anyone tried sailing it so early in the year?" countered Louis.

"No. But all we need is a little luck and open water," René said, smiling. "We can face ice floes or British ships of the line. I'd say the floes are the safer adversary, they don't shoot."

René mentioned his idea to the captain, who then ordered the *l'Esperance* to pull abreast *l'Aquilon* and signaled the other ships to converge. When the captains came aboard *l'Esperance,* Captain de Bouville suggested René's plan for their consideration. They agreed and sailed north.

The French vessels passed safely around Newfoundland. They split up then according to orders and arrived at Québec and Louisbourg where other ships of the fleet made their way to port. There they learned that the British had captured *le Lys* and *l'Alcide,* both having taken the usual route. The British had seized eight companies of infantry, officers, engineers, and 76,000 pounds sterling. Although the majority of the fleet made it through.

Since Great Britain and France were still at peace, it incensed René when he learned of the unprovoked attacks, especially when learning that an English warship had hailed *l'Alcide,* claimed the countries were not at war, and then fired a broadside into the French ship.

When news of these encounters reached Paris, the king was outraged and each country recalled their ambassadors. Versailles hesitated in declaring war against Great Britain because of internal political strife but King Louis ordered preparations for war. Dispatch ships arrived at Cape Breton and Québec with urgent orders for defense against possible invasion. René's *l'Esperance* sailed the coast of Cape Breton to the St. Laurence River, looking for the British. With fogs and mists hampering visibility, they saw few enemy ships and were soon ordered to return to Brest, but the six months at sea gave Louis the experience he desired and the ability to postpone service on his father's ship.

"Sir," Louis began, "when we arrive in Brest I'd like to speak with my father about not transferring to his ship. I hope to convince him of how important it is to remain on *l'Esperance* with you for more training. Do you mind, sir?"

But René was impatient over Louis's obstinacy and uneasy over being caught between a father and his son.

"Louis, your father has had only the best intentions for your education. Perhaps he'd allow you to sail with me. However, Louis, you owe him respect. He shouldn't have to ask you to sail with him. You should want to do it because you know he wants it so."

Louis paused and answered in a weak voice, "Yes, sir." The sharp criticism was the first he'd ever heard from René. His face flushed. He felt ashamed he needed to be reminded to respect his father's desires.

As he walked amidships in the heavy misty seas, his legs now accustomed to the rolling of the deck, a cry above startled him from his self-rebuke.

"Sails and flags, afore!"

"What flag and distance?" called a lieutenant from the poop deck, with large waves blocking any view of the horizon.

"British at three leagues!" came the reply.

"To quarters! Prepare for action! Two points to starboard—cut the topsails—under all courses!"

In seconds, the ship thundered with feet pounding upon decks, blocks squealing as porthole covers raised, gratings opening to allow storage, and other sounds of the preparation for action.

Every crewman rushed before the warships closed. René ran to the poop deck. "Lieutenant—speak!" René shouted as he stood near the mizzenmast.

"Sir, three warships bearing upon us with the wind!"

"Then bring her about and we'll run with it, too."

Captain de Bouville arrived on deck. "Sir, British coming on fast. It'll be a day for us, I'm afraid," René informed, catching sight of the ships' topmasts close by.

"Much so," was all the captain responded. Then after assessing the situation, he added, "Have the dispatches at the ready to cast overboard and prepare the pumps if we flood through our gun ports."

Louis, assigned to the marine lieutenant, carried his musket forward as his nerves tingled with the fear of combat. All his life he'd heard René and his father tell of the battles they fought at sea. He was now being given a role in that drama. His hand once more grabbed the hilt of his sword to check he had it. He felt brave, yet uncertain how to be brave. More than anything, he didn't want to be ashamed of his actions.

Before long, the warships closed enough to hurl their cannonballs and the fight for survival began with wood splinters flying, lines falling, and deafening roars.

After firing and running out of powder, Louis ran to get more and suddenly fell onto an iron tackle ring. The pain took his breath away, paralyzing his chest, and it took a moment for his lungs to work again.

Breathing allowed him to feel new pain, dull, growing more severe by the second. He fingered the wound that caused his fall, a gash in his scalp four inches long. His first instinct was to run to the gun deck for medical treatment, yet he realized the marines needed him. Louis grabbed his powder and musket and returned to the forecastle and continued firing.

"Cadet de Saint-Alouarn," the marine lieutenant roared. "You're wounded. Go below!"

"Sir, I'm fine. It's slight and I can shoot."

"They shot you. Get below—*now!*"

Louis obeyed and ran to the gun deck where others lay covered in blood and bandages as the surgeon's men worked on them.

The pain increased as the blow's numbness wore off, replaced by the hot sear of torn flesh. Louis sat still while a surgeon's aide wrapped a tight bandage around his head to stop the bleeding and made Louis lean against a partition.

The surgeon, after spending half an hour working on patients with serious injuries, came to Louis and inspected the wound. "You're lucky; the musket ball grazed your scalp and took no bone with it. I'll stitch you up later. Are you in great pain?" he asked.

"Yes," was all Louis answered. He had been grunting as the beating of his heart sent sharp pains to the laceration. He wanted to just moan as the others near him.

"Give him laudanum," the surgeon said to his assistant, "two drams in half a mug of brandy, no more."

The opium-based drug tempered the burning. Still, he couldn't keep from focusing on the throbbing wound.

L'Esperance could do nothing to stop the onslaught as the British warships took turns beating on her. Yards fell and canvas and cable littered her decks as the battle continued. Out-gunned and outnumbered, she fought on with the crew determined to do their best. Captain de Bouville was not of the ilk to capitulate without a stiff fight.

The steady bombardment of the warships made sailing progress almost impossible. Yet they managed to maneuver the ship, carrying less than one-third of its full complement of guns, into positions that fended off the nipping hounds. After three hours of deadly action, *l'Esperance* forced the *Orford*, a 70-gun English ship of the line, to withdraw for repairs. The respite was a brief one as the warship soon returned, leading others to renew the assault. By now *l'Esperance* was without her top mainmast and the mizzenmast had split.

René on the poop deck, and target of many muskets, felt the hot sting of metal strike his left arm. Looking downward, his uniform darkened with blood. He grabbed the spot even though the pain increased when he put pressure on the hole. René ran below for the surgeon, who bandaged the injury. He went back above, his limb in a sling and aching. A small pistol shot had passed through his biceps, just missing the bone.

The *Revenge,* a 28-gun frigate, closed to offer more destruction from her guns. In a serious, though short engagement, the British warship dismasted the split mizzen of the French vessel. Now, with nothing except her foremast and damaged mainmast standing, the French ship attempted to flee before the larger warships could overtake her.

The waves, still rough and getting rougher, were no friend to the French ship as she tried in vain to drive through the troughs and peaks. Those high seas, once their ally during the attacks, now became her curse as water poured over the ship, seeping into the damaged hull and retarding her escape.

René held onto a line on the poop deck to keep from being washed overboard and waited for the weather to improve. His huge warship was a hulk of rigging, sail, and broken yards.

The carpenter and a lieutenant rushed to René. "Sir, we have severe leaking. I doubt we can stop it. She's done for unless it calms," the carpenter reported. However, the storm's intensity wasn't subsiding.

Captain de Bouville overheard the damning sentence and stared at the flag overhead. Then in one word sealed their fate. He laid his hand on René's shoulder and ordered in a firm voice: "Strike."

René could think of no other alternative. He ordered the French flag lowered and fired a single signal cannon to draw the attention of the enemy, now distant and lost in the swollen mounds of the sea. *L'Esperance* was now much in danger of going under, riding lower and lower with each gray-green swell as dusk closed around them. René even lost sight of the enemy ships, their potential salvation.

Throughout the night, the ship now battled the flood as crewmen working the pumps reduced the water in the hold. Their damaged ship creaked and groaned as the battering continued upon its hull. The sea was leaking into the hold, though the ship had reached a dangerous equilibrium between sinking and remaining afloat.

The head wound and the betrayal of war's glory had shaken Louis. Together with the fear of the ship sinking, he came to a new respect for the fragile tipping of life's scales and for the power of the impartial sea to carry one to new lands or into the abyss.

The next day, in quieter seas, René spotted the *Orford* and *Revenge* in the distance. The *Orford* drew closer, staying off the port side of the distressed ship, and waited to see if they could assist or only watch the destruction of the French ship. Eventually, enemy longboats carried the French officers to the *Orford* and split the remaining three hundred crewmen between the two warships.

The British inspected *l'Esperance,* too old and damaged to be worth salvaging, and set her afire. As the squadron sailed away, Louis's first ship burned and sank below the rough waves.

Onboard the *Orford,* Captain de Bouville and René sat in the captain's cabin. The British questioned them on their mission and destination.

"Pardon me," said Captain de Bouville, "you are questioning me as if I were a prisoner of war. How so? What right did you have in attacking and sinking *l'Esperance?* Were we on the coasts of England or one of your colonies? No. We were far at sea. When we left Louisbourg, we were not at war with the British. Do you have news we are? When did our king declare war on Great Britain? You've no authority to attack a French ship. Sir, you are a pirate!"

The British Admiral never enjoyed the company of Frenchmen and answered, "We are not pirates. We are following the orders of our Admiralty under the command of our king. As you say, your king hasn't declared war. As you and I both know, that is just a formality. We must protect our countries and carry out our duties, regardless."

He continued, "Accept my apologies for this slight breach of protocol for our attack, although I can offer you the respect and privileges of your rank as an officer. We'll take you to England with your crew and, in time, we shall release you on probation."

"Ah, you are very gracious offering me safe passage. How much will the ransom be?" questioned the plucky French captain.

"Ransom? What? No, you'll be pardoned as is customary for officers," repeated the Admiral.

"No, no. Pirates do not pardon, they ransom. I'll remain with my crew until we're freed by ransom, yet I'm afraid I have no money."

René—tired, wounded, and worn—chuckled to himself at the spunk of the old man. By accepting the Admiral's terms of surrender, Captain de Bouville would have validated their actions as legal. By insisting he must pay a ransom, he condemned their actions to piracy. Insultingly clever and pointedly correct, René thought.

"I see," said the Admiral, twitching. It had been a trying three days, and he had lost too much sleep to lock horns. "You may sort out your status as prisoner or hostage after we return."

René, as they led him to confinement, caught sight of Louis, his clothing soaked with blood. Although this had been a hard lesson for his nephew, at least he was alive.

The *Orford* put into Penlee Sound near Plymouth, where they transferred the prisoners to shore. The French officers, as the norm, could live in private dwellings in England under oath of honor not to escape. Captain de Bouville, who refused any special treatment or to take any oath, remained with his crew on a dreaded prison hulk. René and Louis left with the other officers on long trips to inland English towns, far away from the coasts.

CHAPTER NINE

The Deadly Duel

François returned from patrol and learned that Louis was now a prisoner of war.

In the salon at the manor, Marie was sitting at a table reading a book and looked blankly up at him as he entered. It was the first time she hadn't greeted him at the front entrance after returning from a voyage.

"You've heard," François said.

"First, it was a rumor from my sister and then a letter from your sister in Brest." Marie put the book down on a side table.

"I can't imagine how awful it must have been before you discovered the details. As an officer cadet, he'll be fine."

She spoke without emotion. "Louis could have lost his life and now sits in a prison."

"Well, that's a miracle considering how many crewmen the ship lost before ending up on the seafloor. We should be thankful he's now out of combat."

"Dearest," she paused a moment and continued, "You had said you'd keep him from sailing with René, yet he sailed. You said he'd be safe with René, yet he was in a battle and they wounded him. Now you tell me he's safe in an English prison for the duration of the war. How can I be relieved or believe you?" Kissing him on his cheek, she whispered, "Welcome home." Then she returned to her seat to read her book.

François had never seen her in such a mood. Marie wasn't the hysterical person he had expected to see, just a faded character, devoid of emotion. As he gazed out the window, he caught sight of the crumbling stone turret and walls a short distance from the house. Roofless and missing stones: that was all that remained of the château in which his family defended the king generations ago. Like the lonely turret, he felt abandoned and old.

"Marie, you must forgive me. I thought René could get Louis to change his resolve and sail with me. I didn't understand how much Louis had set his mind. René is innocent of what happened and would die for Louis."

"I know René's not to blame and I don't blame you either, dear. I condemn no one, not even the British." Her eyes went back to her book.

"You're so distant, Marie. I can't help thinking you fault me for Louis getting captured." François hoped she would cry. Anything was better than her detached temperament.

"Perhaps I'm just reflecting on our inability to control events and how random the outcomes of our actions are. They never seem to end as we think they will. I guess there are too many directions events can follow."

"What can I do?"

Marie looked at him and answered, "Nothing, dear. You've done your best."

A month later, François received a letter from the Secretary of State of the Navy. It stated:

> *Monsieur, your son, Garde de la Marine, was so well involved in the battle between ships l'Espérance and Orford that on learning of the account, the King, His Majesty, has made him Enseigne de Vaisseau. He was injured in his head by a gunshot, but the injury is only superficial and I believe you can be calm on his account.*

Another later letter described Louis's imprisonment along with René in Leicester, ninety-three miles north of London:

> *...he is allowed to carry his sword and walk about the town and countryside as long as he returns in the evening.*

Although the conditions of his prisoner status and health were a relief from imagined horrors, François' anxiety over Louis's safety in Britain remained.

* * *

René de Saint-Alouarn and his nephew, Louis, had healed of their wounds. Quartered by the British Navy in different houses in Leicester, they met daily to chat and stroll through the town and countryside. Townspeople were used to seeing French officers in the village and paid them no mind. The French bought things. Their money was as good as an Englishman's.

"Louis, so far you've had luck with your naval career," said René as they walked along a road outside Leicester. "My earlier years in the navy were so dull. Here you've already seen action, been wounded, and captured."

"True, but the action was brief, the wound slight, and this isn't much of a prison," Louis responded, joking.

Around a bend, a cocking cart approached them. As it drew near, the men stepped to the grassy side of the narrow way to allow room, but a partridge, spooked from its hiding place, took flight in front of the horse, which bolted at the flapping and turned up a slight incline next to the road. The wheels angled too far and tipped a passenger onto the ground as the driver pulled at the reins.

"Oh, my God! Please, let me help you, madam," said Louis in French, the first to rush to the woman's aid.

The woman, already rising, glanced at the uniformed man and offered her hand for him to help her.

"I am so sorry," he continued in French.

"I'm fine," she said in English as the cart driver attempted to right the horse.

"Pardon us, mademoiselle. My nephew and I are French officers and he doesn't speak your language," explained René in English.

"Ah, so you're the enemy officers staying in Leicester. Welcome. I hope you're enjoying your confinement," the young woman said.

"The people treat us kindly during our imprisonment," René said, grinning wide. "My name is René de Rosmadec de Saint-Alouarn, *Lieutenant de Vaisseau* and *Chevalier*. This gentleman is my nephew and ensign, Louis François de Saint-Alouarn. Whom did we throw upon the road this day, mademoiselle?"

She giggled. "I am Countess Ferrers, wife to Earl Laurence Ferrers of Staunton Harold Hall. Our manor is nearby, two hours up this road."

"Please accept our apologies. How may we repay such a beautiful countess? An armed escort, perhaps?"

"No, no, you've done quite enough. Pray tell, are all French officers so flattering to English women?" The countess giggled again.

"Of course not, Countess. Only if the English women are as lovely as you and if the Frenchman speaks English as well as I," René quipped. Her eyes, he noticed, often drifted to Louis. "Louis is trying to learn English, although seldom practices. Maybe the Countess is acquainted with someone fluent in English and French to teach him?"

Louis, hearing his name, tried to make sense of their conversation but failed as they were speaking too fast. The woman was close to his age, very attractive, and had a pleasant smile.

"Aha, my Captain, you sound as if you speak English well enough to teach him. If an English professor comes to Leicester or our manor, I will tell him there's a Frenchman in the village who needs his services. Now I must be going. I have shopping in the village and afterward a long ride back to our manor." With one final glance at Louis, she took the driver's hand and stepped back up onto the tall cart.

"Once more, *ma chére Comtesse,* you have our apologies and our hearts," René said, bowing low. Louis copied.

The carriage pulled away and the two officers stood watching until René broke the silence.

"Well, the countess found you interesting!"

"Huh? No, she's married and is a countess. What attraction could she see in a foreign prisoner? Your sight is failing, Uncle," Louis answered.

"Marriage means little and titles less, believe me. She stole glances at you from the moment you offered your hand. Youth! It lets your head blind your heart and your heart blind your head, both always at the wrong time. There was a day, not long ago, when she'd steal glances at me. Those days are passing as surely as seasons turn." René laughed, reminiscing.

They parted and Louis walked along the village's main street toward his quarters.

"Good day again, Louis the ensign." It startled him, spoken in French. Louis turned to discover the countess and her driver walking behind him. The driver carried a bundle tied with twine for his mistress.

"Oh, good day," stammered Louis, surprised. "I was not aware that you spoke French."

"A learned governess taught me. French was a mandatory part of our day. Where's your uncle?"

"He's on his way back to his room. Did you recover from the fall?"

"No bones were broken and the blacksmith is fixing a loosened wheel." The countess enjoyed talking in French, although the earl, also speaking it well, forbade its use at the manor. She found the young Frenchman pleasant. She was twenty, although he looked younger to her.

Louis had missed hearing a French female's voice. Pretty, he studied her as often as he could without chancing to appear rude.

The countess asked him how the navy had captured him and an unguarded conversation ensued. They chatted in a relaxed manner while meandering along the twisting streets. An affinity developed: for Louis from a lack of feminine company, and for the countess from a lack of anyone her age at the manor.

Neither watched where they walked, engrossed in their talk, and soon found themselves on a street neither recognized.

"Gracious, I believe we're lost! Let's stop before we get further from Market Street," she exclaimed, laughing.

"The roofs are so high I can't see any landmarks or steeples. Maybe I should run off and find a street I recognize. You wait until I come back," Louis offered.

"Stay. I'll send my driver to discover where we are. Perhaps he can ask someone."

As she sent the driver off, Louis asked, "Do you enjoy living in a manor rather than in a city?"

"Leicester is a pleasant change from the manor. I come as often as I can."

"I see. Life at the manor can be boring, I suppose, without the interesting shops and activities in a village."

"No, it's not that," she said with momentary sadness. Stopped, they now rested against a hip-high stone wall.

"Why? Don't you enjoy living at your manor, Countess?"

The young woman remained silent for a moment, her eyes dropping.

"I'm sorry and didn't mean to intrude on your privacy," apologized Louis.

"That's all right, I brought things onto myself. The manor is beautiful and spacious. The servants are wonderful. The earl is another matter. Everyone is aware of it, even here in Leicester. Someone might describe only his mannerisms and anyone could name him."

"That must be very difficult for you. Did your family arrange the wedding?"

"Well, once my family learned of his interest in me, the pressure was enormous. The marriage was my duty to the family;

it was a wise financial decision; he could increase our social status; and on and on—never-ending. In the end, I agreed. It was a most tragic mistake." The countess, her head turned downward, stared at the cobblestone walk.

"I understand the pressures as I'm expected to marry well, too."

"Are you titled?" she asked.

"Someday I'll inherit our estates and a knighthood. My father is François Marie Aleno de Saint-Alouarn, the Seigneur de Kersallic. Our manor is in Brittany. Father is a navy captain. They captured him in the last war."

"Who are you expected to marry?"

"No one, I'm not betrothed yet. It'll be my decision whether to marry her when the time comes, but I'd have to get permission from the navy. I just hope she'll be compatible with me," Louis added.

"Compatible? I'd consider myself fortunate if the earl treated me better than one of his horses."

"What do you mean? The earl doesn't strike you, does he?" Louis asked, shocked.

"Look," she said, pulling back a sleeve of her blouse. Upon her forearm, dark bruises discolored her fair skin.

"God! Does the earl do that to you often?"

The countess covered her arm again and nodded, adding, "He's done much worse. The first month after we married, he broke two of my ribs. Laurence loses control of his temper and isn't aware of what he's doing."

She continued. "Last year he was angry with my brother, Sir Meredith, for not dealing with a matter in London fast enough to suit him. To avenge the tardiness, the earl beat and kicked me around the parlor in front of our servants. His brutishness extends beyond me as well, beating and injuring servants severely."

"Such actions are too extreme. I can't imagine how you live expecting beatings at any time. Countess, you have my deepest concern."

"Now that you're privy to more about me than anyone else in Leicester, Louis, do be discreet. Please, call me Mary when alone. The title countess reminds me of my husband. For a few moments, I want to remember life before our wedding."

The countess felt a weight lifted from her shoulders; she had needed to confide in someone. This Frenchman from another world allowed her to express long-repressed emotions.

"There must be something you can do to stop it."

"No, not really. I try to stay away from him. The earl seldom needs me...ah...physically, if you understand. He has his mistress at the estate."

"What? The mistress lives in the same home with you?" It dumbfounded Louis.

"Not in the manor house but in another house. Just imagine my life with her and her children there while he beats me in my bedroom and makes love to her in hers."

She was crying now. Louis put his hand to her shoulder but the countess turned her face away and sighed. After wiping tears, she forced a smile.

They talked about her problem until the driver returned, pointing toward Market Street. The pace was still slow, each wanting time to tell the other of deeper feelings. The driver, not speaking French or caring what they discussed, wanted to return to his cart to inspect the wheel repair and get back to the manor before nightfall.

When they arrived at the blacksmith's shop, she turned to Louis and told him they'd probably see one another again in the village. While heading back to his quarters, he reviewed all she'd told him. A smoldering rage built inside him as he thought about the earl and his unforgivable treatment of the young lady.

That evening, he met with René and revealed some, not all, of what the countess had told him. René agreed the man was despicable but advised Louis not to involve himself in her hopeless mess. They were in a foreign land. One might expect a romantic relationship, but entangling himself in a marriage dispute between nobles was unwise.

Louis spent more and more time haunting the markets in Leicester hoping to encounter the countess. His vigilance was rewarded when she appeared one afternoon with a servant woman, browsing the shops.

"Good afternoon, Countess," Louis said, approaching her.

"Louis, good to see you again. How is your English coming along? Have you practiced with René?"

"Ah, no. My tongue gets all twisted up in my teeth. I sound foolish trying to pronounce the language. How have you been?" He wondered whether she had received any abuse from the earl.

"Just fine. Care to go for a walk again? I can send my servant on a task and we can talk in private."

"That will be fine. I so enjoyed our last."

The countess sent the servant on a shopping errand and the two began a long ramble. He learned things hadn't gotten better. The earl had become so enraged with a servant he'd stabbed the man in the chest with a knife and hit him in the head with a candlestick. Then he'd kicked the servant so hard between the legs he became incontinent. But no one would file charges against the earl, fearing to lose their jobs. He, thankfully, hadn't beaten or abused her since the last time they'd met.

"Uncle and I have heard nothing about parole, but my father and René are both well-thought of at the French Admiralty. I'm sure my father is doing whatever is necessary to obtain a pardon and release," Louis told her. He wondered if his return to France might sadden the countess; he wanted to leave, yet he also wanted to explore the possibilities of his relationship with her.

The countess felt the same. "Louis, I ordered a new ball gown at the dressmaker's shop on Market Street and will return for fittings. If you wish, we'll meet afterward and continue our conversations."

"That's wonderful, I'll look forward to them."

From then on, they met twice a week for three weeks until, one day, he met not the countess outside the dress shop but a gentleman.

In French, the gentleman said, "You're the French officer waiting to see the countess?"

"Yes, I was to meet with her here," Louis said.

"Then you're the scoundrel," the gentleman replied, pulling a court sword from beneath his coat.

Louis backed away and cried, "Sir, what are you doing? Who are you?"

"I am Earl Ferrers. I am righting a wrong," said Laurence as he posed with his sword *en garde*. "Unsheathe your sword and fight."

"For what wrong do we fight? I have done nothing to deserve your indignation."

"I discovered my wife met you here. The countess verified it. I will have my requital!" Laurence shouted, red in the face.

"Sir, the middle of a street is no location for challenges. Dueling is a private matter. If you wish to talk about slighting your honor, fine. Gentlemen, however, do not fight on a public street."

"Are you denying you've been seeing her every week? You are a liar and a scoundrel. You'll not cuckold me." He waved his sword back and forth.

"Put down your blade, sir. Nothing dishonorable has happened. The Countess Ferrers and I are just friends. She practices her French with me since you forbid it at Staunton Harold. We've only been together in public," Louis explained.

"You refuse me my rights? You are a scoundrel, liar, and *coward*," Laurence replied. He would not listen to an explanation.

"Come, let us discuss this matter somewhere in private. If you wish a duel, so it will be, but not here," Louis demanded.

"A grove of trees grows by the river near the church. I will see you there within the hour if you are an honorable gentleman," Laurence huffed.

Louis found his uncle and, together, they headed toward the steeple of the church by the river. René, though concerned about the confrontation, didn't fear the duel might injure Louis. He had shown himself to be both exceptional in swordplay and brave in the face of danger. René worried over what might happen if Louis wounded the earl, or did worse.

On arriving at the designated clump of giant oaks, the earl stood with his coat off and sleeves rolled up, an opened bottle of wine on the ground. Laurence waved and slashed his sword at an imaginary foe in clumsy motions, betraying little expertise in the art. René whispered into Louis's ear, "If you must fight the fool, a few pricks of your blade will be enough. If not, run him through the leg or someplace not vital. I'd hate to see you go from a prisoner of war to a prisoner of murder. It may not be legal to duel in Leicester."

Louis approached Laurence and again explained his position.

"As I've told you, sir, the countess and I are friends and nothing has occurred which should offend you. There has been no dishonor. If you demand a duel, however, I will appease your request."

"To first-drawn blood. Come feel my sword's bite!" barked Laurence.

The gentlemen met between the trees, saluted, and began the duel. Laurence thrust first. Louis could have drawn blood at that moment but realized he best let the lout thrash about with his toy. Perhaps he'd tire or get it out of his system. Louis parried the amateurish attacks without *ripostes*. After a few minutes of watching, René laughed out loud at the charade.

This angered Laurence. He now used the thin court sword as a saber to slash, making whistling sounds as Louis sidestepped and parried the attempts.

"Fight me!" shouted Laurence now, with eyes bulging and veins protruding. The earl was sweating, his blouse soaked.

Louis had not even begun to perspire. It was obvious the earl intended to give Louis more than just a scar for the imagined offense. Bored, Louis decided enough energy and time had passed. He parried an awkward thrust, used body leverage against the earl's shoulder and arm, and pulled the sword by the hilt out of the earl's hand. In one graceful motion, he threw the sword into the river.

"If you intend to duel, you must first learn to use your body as well as the weapon," Louis said, like a swordmaster scolding a student. Louis placed his blade upon the neck of the dumb-founded Laurence and told him, "Why your wife is faithful to you, I cannot understand." He flicked his blade on Laurence's neck and produced a half-inch-long scratch. "First blood," Louis declared and walked away.

"Humph," he said to René as they walked up the hill. "Such a waste of time. My first duel with a nobleman and it culminated in embarrassment for both."

The countess never appeared again on the streets of Leicester. Louis stopped looking for her after a few weeks.

* * *

Halfway through the year, Abraham received news expected but unwanted.

"Abraham, it's not official yet, however, Versailles plans to expel English workers again from France. We owe it to you to prepare in case it should be true," Caffieri told him with a grimace.

Two days later, the navy posted a notice making it official. The government then issued passports to all English workers, who had to leave within the month.

"Things were going so well for us. If we must leave, can we put the house in your hands until the war ends?" asked Yvette.

Anton responded, "I'll take care of the house. André will help me."

"While you're taking care of the house, what shall I do in England to make a living? The navy could press me again. I don't want to return to sea," Abraham said, recalling earlier fears.

"Don't think about that," said Yvette. "Let's plan for the good possibilities. I can search for a job in a bookstore in London again, or you might get your old job back at Woolwich. There are a thousand directions this might take us. It's exciting."

"You may be right, but this change is most unwelcome. I'd prefer working here now that I've been getting more responsibility."

On the last day at work, the men gathered around Abraham to express their wishes for his success. Caffieri, too, joined the crowd and gave him his final pay with a wink. "You're welcome anytime, Abraham," he said in parting, "however, in the future, we'll hire you back under a French alias."

After their merchant ship arrived at Sheerness, the couple took a quick coach ride to London. With enough money for a decent inn, they stayed near St. Paul's Churchyard, the center for the book trade, hoping Mister Willocks had restarted his business.

Yvette inquired about positions and information on Mr. Willocks. Only one shop owner remembered the man, whom he hadn't seen in years. Yvette regretted that she hadn't sent him a letter to see how he was doing or whether he had opened a new shop.

Abraham worked at various small shipyards from the end of summer until January of the next year, until he found temporary work at the Blackwall Yard, a private shipyard near Deptford. The pay was meager, but it sufficed while Yvette continued looking for a position. And better, the yard gave him a letter of protection from impressment. Sadly, they discovered Mr. Willocks had died less than a year after the Cornhill fire. No booksellers had positions open, and no one was hiring a woman for anything but menial work.

"Abraham, I speak English too poorly. My accent makes people afraid of me."

"Your English is good enough. And your French accent is like pepper on beef, it seasons you. We must look at this honestly. Your clerking at the bookstore was a rarity. It's being a woman that limits your prospects. That said, if anyone can convince a shopkeeper to hire a woman, it's you."

"You're sweet, dear. Still, I don't have a job after a year living in London and with little hope of finding one. As long as this war goes on, people also see me as the enemy." Yvette frowned, looking away.

"So don't search for work. We're getting by on my salary. If an interesting position comes along, try to get it," Abraham answered.

"Don't work? What would I do then? Sit around doing nothing? At least in Brest, I was making lace." She paused, and he knew her old depression over being childless was returning.

"My, I could use a break right now," Abraham said. "Let's go for a walk along the river."

"Certainly, but why there? It smells so bad when the air is warm."

"Would a chocolate house smell better?" he suggested, hoping to cheer her.

She smiled at the idea. "Ah-ha, great idea!"

They paid the admission fee of a few pennies at the chocolate house and took a seat away from the raucous crowd around a dice table. In the far corner, two musicians playing a violin and viol stopped to take a break. Yvette ordered her chocolate while Abraham asked for wine, and they sat watching the crowd. Soon the music, chocolate, and throng had healed her worries.

Though it was a lovely moment for them, Abraham felt a prick of unfairness. All he wanted was to work as a shipwright, but France didn't want him. All Yvette wanted was to raise children near her parents, but they were childless in London. He'd have to think of a solution. At least, for now, they were safe from the war and getting by with the little he made. Someday, he hoped, they'd return to France and their cottage by the river.

* * *

Washington Shirley now commanded the captured *Duc D'Aquitaine,* a 3rd rate 64-gun, and patrolled the Channel. She handled smartly with good speed after a repair and careening. Washington felt comfortable on her.

"Lieutenant, I like this ship. I haven't been on one that sails right since the *Renown.* Guess that says something about our shipbuilding establishments, don't you think?"

"Sir. I noticed the *Renown* at Portsmouth. Looked like they repaired and refitted her for duty," said the lieutenant.

"Aye, Captain Mackenzie is commanding her. He was on patrol with me years ago when I captained the *Renown* in Jamaica. He always coveted her and now he has her. I spoke to him not long ago after the repairs and he told me the *Renown* lost much speed. Such a shame. She flew when I sailed her."

"Where is she now?" the lieutenant asked.

"Last year, Mackenzie had her in the descents on Saint-Malo and Cherbourg. Now she's at the Port Royal station in the West Indies." Washington was flooded with memories of brilliant blue skies and tropical islands. "The *Renown* did great there against the smugglers, but they hobbled her speed and now she'll have a rough time of it with the fast Jamaican sloops. It'll depend on how well Mackenzie takes to her handling."

The *Duc D'Aquitaine* headed back to port after a quiet cruise in the Channel. In port, the navy informed him he'd be changing ships yet again, commanding his fourth ship in only two years.

After arriving home, he expressed his exasperation to Anne. "Lord, now they have me going to the *Temple,* a new 70-gun ship of the line. Not that I mind it so much because she's a new ship and bigger. Still, I got used to *Duc D'Aquitaine* and enjoyed her handling. I prefer the French-designed ships."

"Washington, the switch is because they find you're capable of the duty. You're one of their better commanders," Anne said.

"They trust me with the *Temple*. Although I'd have loved to test the *Duc D'Aquitaine* in action."

Anne continued, "Then to cheer you up, I'll tell you wonderful news."

"Wonderful? Then let me hear it."

"Mary is divorcing your brother!"

"What? That's not wonderful—that's phenomenal news!" Washington howled.

"The court accepted the petitions. If all goes as expected, the House of Lords should decide in Countess Mary's favor. She'll finally be rid of Laurence," Anne said.

"So, the countess did it. Good for her! When Mary approached me last year about a divorce, I knew I couldn't see her locked up at the manor for the rest of her life. Laurence didn't allow her to go anywhere or do anything, not even to shop in Leicester. I was glad to sign the petition for her. Did she write when the Lords will review it?"

"The letter stated by June, if she survives until then. That's not all. Your mother and cousin also signed petitions supporting the divorce."

"I was afraid I'd be the only one of our family claiming cruelty. So, they signed? With the three of us backing Mary's divorce plea, it'll make the decision obvious to the Lords. Although I feel sorry for Laurence, he caused it himself."

In June, while Washington sailed the new *Temple,* Anne received word Parliament approved the divorce. The countess left the manor that very day to live free. Laurence had opposed the divorce and explained before the House of Lords he was plagued by brief periods of lunacy. The Lords rejected his claim outright. If they had agreed insanity was the reason for his abusiveness to Mary, by English law they couldn't have approved the divorce.

After the divorce decree, an arrogant Laurence threatened the court. "I am sorry that you were able to bring such ample proof of my not being a lunatic. Perhaps I will appear before you again for a worse crime!" Another hit to his ego, as part of the settlement, Parliament ordered Laurence to support Mary. His long-time steward was to oversee the endowments to her.

* * *

François had sailed from Brest over a year earlier on board *l'Aigle* for a posting in Saint-Domingue. After François received new orders to return to Brest, he headed for his French home port. His thoughts turned to Louis as the winds whistled in the lines and the waves beat against the sides of the hull. The duel Louis had fought over a countess in Leicester bothered him; he hoped René's influence hadn't caused it. At least the two had been returned to France.

Britain's war strategy was making it impossible for France to divert or prevent blockades of Louisbourg, still a target of the enemy; the fortress was on borrowed time. But François' worries were with his family, learning of a terrible typhus epidemic. François sped for his manor to discover how his family had fared.

"Marie!" he called. No one had greeted him. "Marie!"

Footsteps answered his call and two girls appeared before him: Marie Renée, sixteen years old, who ran fastest, followed by Marie Charlotte, only nine years old.

"Father!" they both exclaimed.

"Where's your mother?" he asked, hugging them. "Is she home?"

"Mama's coming," said Marie Renée, pointing to the staircase. Marie appeared at the top, smiling.

"You missed Louis by a week," she said. "He's on his way to Martinique."

"Damn. It's been two years since we were together last. Is he with René again?" asked François.

"No, Louis said he's on *le Défenseur*. I don't know if that's good or not. I've decided to give up on trying to figure out which ships are best. Seems no matter the size, things happen anyway."

"You're right, *le Défenseur* is big, a 74-gun. Louis should be safe on her, especially in Martinique during the hurricanes," replied François. "How are you, dear?"

"We're fine," she answered. "You saw how Brest looks, didn't you? It was horrible."

"Everyone in the West Indies learned of the quarantine. Tragic news travels on wings. It'll be a decade before they restore everything to normal."

Marie led them into the salon. "Father, you should have seen Louis. He looks like a man now," commented his older daughter, Marie Renée.

"As opposed to what—the goat he resembled?" he joked. "At his age, every year will bring out more and more masculinity. Just like you. Not long ago you looked like a skinny girl. Now, look at you, a fine, shapely young woman."

Marie Renée blushed and answered, "Oh, you wait until you see him, Father. He's grown up now. He's not the boy who left with Uncle René."

"And he fought a duel over a countess," added little Marie Charlotte.

"I read that in your letter." François looked to his wife. "Marie, tell me the details of this duel."

"Nothing much. Louis's friendship with the countess offended her husband, an earl. It seems, he's a rash fellow and challenged Louis to a sword fight. Naturally, Louis won the duel with no harm done. He said he never met the countess after that."

"Although he's a smart boy, I guess he's not yet smart enough to avoid a predicament like that. I take it the friendship didn't get too involved?" His brow rose.

Marie smiled at the question. "Not involved to any extent, at least from what Louis confided. They became friends and nothing more. No, he's not taking up his Uncle René's favorite pastime."

"Pastime? What pastime does Uncle René have?" asked Marie Charlotte.

"Marie Charlotte," spoke up Marie Renée, "You're so naive. Uncle René likes to..."

"Enough, Marie Renée. Your sister is not old enough to understand," scolded her mother.

"Right, let's change the topic. How's the manor doing?" asked François.

"Planting is done and we've had good rain so far. I finished a few books on agriculture. I think we should follow their recommendations. We can grow turnips this year to feed the cattle. They do it elsewhere, why not here?" Marie replied.

"Turnips? I don't know if they'd grow well here. You handle things as you think best though. You've managed the manor fine so far."

"Also, a stone fell from the old château tower last week and nearly killed one of our horses. When will you tear down that old ruin?"

"Marie, that's something I'd never demolish. I've loved that old tower since a child. Besides, it stands as a great monument to my ancestors."

"It'll stand as a tombstone if it falls and kills someone someday," she laughed. "And speaking of great monuments, will the fortress at Louisbourg stay French?"

"It doesn't look good. The enemy will probably take it by the end of the summer. We can't relieve it. If Louisbourg falls a second time, we have nothing to bargain with to get it back as we did in the last war. I think the British won't stop until they have all of Canada."

As François foresaw, in June of 1758, the British arrived in New Breton with a massive flotilla of twenty-three ships under Admiral Boscawen. In addition, an army of over twelve thousand men waited on transports. The enemy outnumbered the French defenses by four to one. They destroyed the few French warships in the harbor and forced Louisbourg again to surrender.

To force an end to the war they were losing, France planned a decisive victory. By January 1759, François commanded *le Juste,* carrying 70 guns and 600 men. François's brother, René, took over as his second in command on the same ship.

"With all the flat-bottomed transports being built, it's obvious we'll invade somewhere," laughed René. "I think we're going back to Louisbourg to retake it." René had paused his circuit of the young ladies at the ball to chat with his brother and nephew.

"I doubt we're headed for Louisbourg. That's saddling a dead horse. The king wants the war over and will strike where he can gain the most. By hitting Louisbourg, we'd just prolong the struggles over Cape Breton and New France again. We could be headed anywhere," replied François. "Every time I venture to guess, I'm wrong. The Brest fleet is the last Atlantic fleet left of any strength. I'd say something closer, something more in line with ending the war. I'm hoping something bold."

"Louis," asked René, "what are your feelings on the troops gathering in the ports? Do you agree with me or your father?"

"Well, Uncle René, I have to side with him," Louis said. "My father has a keen insight into naval matters."

Louis's reply made François proud. It seemed Louis's return from Britain and Martinique had changed him into a young gentlemen. The fears François bore over René's influence vanished; Louis now thought for himself, more in tune with the feelings of others, more like what his sister had claimed, and more thoughtful of his parents' desires. The change pleased François.

They talked until almost the end of the ball.

* * *

Washington Shirley on the *Temple* patrolled the coast of France off Brest with the Blue Fleet, led by Admiral Hawke, blockading the French. The winter gales blew. When spies reported movement near French harbors, they shipped out to prevent old Admiral de Conflans's fleet from slipping out of Brest.

The *Temple* was one of twenty-three ships of the line and five frigates, making a formidable force. By the time the British fleet had returned to Brest, however, most of the enemy ships had departed, now heading south. Admiral Hawke pursued and sighted the French fleet in late November. Admiral de Conflans's fleet held twenty-one ships of the line, plus frigates on orders to escort transports northwest for a brazen invasion of Ireland. After his first diversion, another fleet would invade Scotland. Then in a pincer movement, a third fleet would attack the great English naval port at Portsmouth. When he realized the pursuing British ships outnumbered his fleet, de Conflans sought refuge in the shoal-and-rock-guarded Quiberon Bay along the French coast.

"It's red. Hawke has signaled a chase," Washington, spying the signal flag, said to his first lieutenant. "Ready her for battle and hang topgallants so we don't lag. Keep her helm steady."

Regulations normally required a line of battle formation, but the poor weather and uncharted bay dangers forced the ships into a disorderly, rushing herd with the *Temple* in the van.

"What's seen above?" Washington called upward.

"Sails, sir—off the port bow!" came back.

"Mind the distance to keep from running afoul, one point to larboard."

The sound of gunfire exploded as other leading ships exchanged fire with the French rearguard. It'd be just minutes before Washington engaged the enemy 70-gun ahead of him.

* * *

The French Admiral de Conflans ordered his fleet into line, anticipating the English fleet might catch up to them. His local pilots knew the rocky coastline well as they headed for safety in the bay. The English captains were ignorant of the shoals and reefs. De Conflans hoped the dangerous pinnacles might keep the English vessels from following. But Admiral Hawke's fleet had overtaken his rearguard ships. In mid-afternoon, they exchanged fire. Worse for the French fleet, the gale now blew from the northwest, making sailing their ships windward into Quiberon Bay impractical while under attack.

Eventually, the main bodies of both fleets clashed. François and René's ship, *le Juste,* fought hard against the *Temple,* commanded by Washington. Neither captain was aware they had met a dozen years earlier in a similarly heated fray over *la Renommée.* A British 60-gun ship blasted at *le Juste's* starboard side, assisting Washington's *Temple.* The French ship, putting up a valiant defense, took iron from both sides with another enemy coming on fast to join.

"A hell of a voyage!" shouted René over the thundering cannons.

"René, you should have stayed a prisoner in England," François laughed. "Best if we make for a river—the Loire or the Vilaine. We might sail free of this."

"Ready about!" François told the helmsman to steer southeast for the Loire River.

Both Saint-Alouarns made their way to the poop deck and assumed command from there. Metal buzzed around them, splintering the deck, masts, and rails as cannons spewed and British marines fired their muskets upon *le Juste.* Although outnumbered, the ship persevered as she returned damaging fire at her opponents.

"We seem to be making progress," François told René as their ship pulled away from the fight. Only the *Temple* was near them now.

Washington, seeing their withdrawal, pointed his sword first to his marine snipers above and then to the enemy's poop deck, signaling a concentrated fire on the officers. As the fusillade of musket balls and canister shots rained upon the French officers on deck, one clutched himself and fell.

"François!" yelled René as he held his brother, now stricken and bleeding from the shoulder. René feared the worst until his brother moaned. The crew hurried François belowdecks and René, now in command of *le Juste,* ordered canister shot against the decks of the British warship.

The first blast wounded crew the entire length of the *Temple.* René ordered chain shot to take down the *Temple's* masts, lines, and shrouds. This he concentrated on the waist, damaging the main mast.

He fought on against the *Temple* until the early November night darkened the battle scene. Not having time to inquire about his wounded brother, René ordered the ship to disengage and head for the Loire River, hoping to make it up the river in the dwindling daylight. As the ship pulled away from the *Temple,* the British warship loosened a broadside of canister shot and René dropped to the deck.

Through the intense pain, René struggled to stay conscious as blood poured from his mouth and nose. Soon, his pain lessened and he went light-headed.

Crewmen carried him to the ship's surgeon. Within minutes, he lay beside his brother. René looked over, saw François's labored breathing, and prayed for him. Never before had his older brother been in such a perilous condition, and René feared more for François's life than his own. He wondered for a few brief seconds if this might be their end. A horrible pain suddenly stabbed at him and René gave into an overpowering need for sleep and closed his eyes—never to open them again.

By the next morning, *le Juste* had eluded the English in the dark and struggled to the mouth of the Loire River. As the rising sun lightened the sea and sky, François, never regaining consciousness, passed to join his beloved brother. *Le Juste* became grounded on the rocks at the mouth of the river and the crushing waves destroyed the ship. Over five hundred of the six hundred fifty crewmen perished.

Aboard the *Temple,* Washington began repairs on the damage and dropped anchor as he saw the other scattered vessels do. He heard distress signals throughout the night and knew the losses on both sides to be great.

The storm continued into the morning, with enemy ships still within sight. Admiral Hawke signaled ships to weigh anchor and attack; however, the ferocity of the high seas prohibited most ships from obeying. Many of the craft became grounded, others needed repair, and several the winds dismasted. The best that could be done was to wait out the storm. Washington ordered his topgallants struck and anchors dropped.

The captain of the British *Essex,* disregarding the dangers of the tempest, attempted to carry out the admiral's orders and sailed to do battle with *le Héros*. The storm ran the *Essex* aground on a shoal and the waves destroyed her.

As the high seas passed, so did the Battle of Quiberon Bay. Admiral Hawke ordered the *Temple* and eleven other warships southeast to reconnoiter Basque Road, a bay near La Rochelle, for any French stragglers of the battle.

The losses were great for the British, as the *Essex* and the *Resolution* shattered on the rocks. The combined losses for the French fleet were staggering. Besides *le Juste,* they also lost *le Superbe,* unbelievably sunk with all hands after just two broadsides from the *Royal George*.

Le Thésée sank with all hands along with her captain, the famed de Kersaint, after waves flooded her lower gun deck ports. Admiral de Conflans's flagship, *le Soleil Royal,* ran aground, and the admiral burned her, also the fate of *le Héros. L'Inflexible* broke her back on shoals and wrecked when trying to enter the Vilaine River. The enemy captured *le Formidable.* The French fleet lost seven ships of the line while the British lost but two. Tragically, although four hundred English crewmen lost their lives, the French appallingly lost over two thousand five hundred men.

The outcome ended French plans to invade Ireland, England, Scotland, or anywhere else. The British had soundly decimated the Brest fleet, their last remaining sea power in the Atlantic. News of the climactic defeat brought great criticism upon de Conflans, eliminating the last lingering shred of confidence the French had in their navy. The Battle of Quiberon Bay would diminish France's sea power for decades.

Louis de Saint-Alouarn and his sisters comforted their mother upon hearing of the sacrifices of their father and uncle. Although Marie had always feared for François's safety, his passing now ended that dread. She grieved deeply, but years of being a seaman's wife had prepared her emotionally for the tragedy. His frequent absences had strengthened her self-reliance; she recovered. The king granted the widow a pension of twelve hundred livres for her losses.

The nation's people, from Paris to the remotest hamlet, despaired. France had lost many of their best sea captains, best ships, and their sea war in a single battle.

* * *

Abraham and Yvette learned about the great British victory at Quiberon Bay with mixed emotions. For Yvette, the disastrous conclusion to Brest's fleet dismayed her and would later prove both a source of profound grief and contemplative joy. Abraham had long decided that war was a waste and the French defeat illustrated with men's lives the errors of their leaders. Even so, he realized the practical possibilities of new employment opportunities.

The couple sympathized with the victims' families while struggling to overcome their own challenges. His job insecurity and her childlessness continued unresolved.

* * *

Washington returned home to commendations on his gallantry. Anne, now accustomed to the long absences of a warrior husband, started to drink chocolate to enhance the chances of having a child—just as women in France, she'd heard.

Washington was finally achieving the recognition his family expected. These were the beginning of glory days for Washington Shirley and for Great Britain. The empire had finally vanquished their long-time foe's best fleet. Its people, waiting for a similar victory on the continent to end the war, now ruled the seas.

END OF BOOK I

LIST OF CHARACTERS, TERMS AND GLOSSARY

MAIN CHARACTERS

Unless noted as fictional, the main characters mentioned in the book were drawn from historical sources. Fictional license, however, was taken for story development, dialog, and literary effect on all characters.

Burston, British ship lieutenant on the *Lark* (Fictional)

Caffieri [kah-fehr-yee´], French master sculptor at the Brest shipyard and designer of ship decorations

Cheap, British captain of the *Lark*

d'Aché [dah´-shee], Madame, French noblewoman (Fictional)

de Bouville [duh • boo-vee´], French captain and admiral

de Conflans, Marquis [deh • kohn-flons´ • mahr´-kee], French naval officer, governor of Saint-Domingue, and admiral at the Battle of Quiberon Bay

de Kersaint, Guy [deh • kehr-sahn´ • ghee´], French captain

de Saint-Alouarn, François Marie Aleno [deh • san´ • tah-lew-arn´ • fran- swah´ • mah-ree´ • ahl´-ehno], French naval captain

de Saint-Alouarn, Louis François [deh • san´ • tah-lew-arn´ • lew-ee ´• fran- swah´], son of François

de Saint-Alouarn, Marie [deh • san´ • tah-lew-arn´ • mah-ree´], wife of François

de Saint-Alouarn, Chevalier de Rosmadec, René Louis Aleno [deh • san´ • tah-lew-arn´ • sheh´-vah-lyeh´ • deh • rows-mah-dek´ • ruh-nay´ • lew-ee´ • ahl´-ehno], French naval captain, brother of François

Du Guay [dew-gay´], French commandant of the navy in Brest

Elliott, Anne, wife of Washington Shirley, daughter of John Elliott, Esquire

Façonneur, André [fah´-seh-nehr • ahn´-dree], ship pilot in Brest, brother of Yvette (Fictional)

Façonneur, Anton [fah´-seh-nehr • ahn´-tohn], carpenter in Brest, father of Yvette (Fictional)

Façonneur, Gaëlle [fah-seh-nyehr´ • gah-el´], wife of André (Fictional)

Façonneur, Louise [fah´-seh-nehr • lew-eez´], wife of Anton, mother of Yvette (Fictional)

Façonneur, Yvette [fah´ seh-nehr • ee-veht´], daughter of Anton and Louise, sister to André (Fictional)

George, I, King of Great Britain (1714–1727), born 1660

Goubert [goo-bayr´], Madame, Bretton woman in London, friend of Yvette (Fictional)

Hastings, Selina, Lady (nee Shirley) wife of the Earl of Huntingdon

Louis XIV [lew-ee´], King of France (1643–1715), born 1638

Louis XV [lew-e´], King of France (1715–1774), born 1710

LaBrouche, Pierre [lah • broh-ush´ • pee-ehr´], police inspector in Brest (Fictional)

Maurepas [moh´-reh-pah], French Secretary of State of the Navy

Meredith, Mary, Countess, wife to Laurence Shirley, 4th Earl Ferrers

Robinson, Abraham, British shipwright (Fictional)

Shirley, Laurence, 4th Earl Ferrers

Shirley, Washington, British naval officer, 5th Earl Ferrers

Smelt, British captain of the *Viper* and *Renown*

Townsend, British commodore of the Port Royal station, in Jamaica Warren, British commander of blockade fleet at Louisbourg

Watson, Thomas, British captain of *Northumberland*

Wickham, British commander of the *Lark*

Willocks, English bookseller in London during the Cornhill Fire

Glossary of Terms & Pronunciation Guide

This list of terms found in the story may have other definitions.

abaft: Behind

above-water: The part of a hull that is not in the water

"Absolument": [ahb´-sew-leh-mohn], "Absolutely"; Fr.

adze: A long-handled axe-like tool with a single blade perpendicular to the handle for dressing wood

Aix-la-Chapelle: [iks´-lah-sha-pel´], A former Imperial Free City in the Germanic States (now Aachen, Germany)

aloft: In the ship's rigging; overhead

apostasy: The renunciation of a political or religious belief

astern: Toward the rear of a ship

armed *en flute:* [ahn´-floo], Armed with a reduced number of cannons; Fr.

bar shot: Dismantling ammunition for a cannon consisting of two cannonballs connected by an iron bar

basket-hilt: A protective, dome-shaped sword handle

battery: A fortified cannon emplacement

beam: The widest measurement of a ship or the side of a ship; the perpendicular midpoint of a ship's length

beat to quarters: To beat a drum as a signal to prepare for battle

Bertheaume Bay: [behr´-thewm], A northern bay outside the Road of Brest

bitts: The posts on the bow for fastening lines and cables

boatswain: [boh´ • suhn], A ship officer in charge of the deck crew, rigging, blocks, cables, anchors, and chains

bow: The front of the ship

bowsprit: The spar projecting from the bow

broadside: To fire all the cannons on one side of a ship; also a newspaper

by the board: To go over the side of the ship; also overboard or gone

bulwark: The part of a ship's side above the upper deck level

Camaret Bay: [kah ́-mehr-reh] A southern bay outside the Road of Brest

canister shot: An anti-personnel ammunition for cannons consisting of a canister filled with small iron balls

capstan: An upright revolving wood cylinder used to haul cable to hoist anchors, etc.

careen: To clean off underwater growths from a ship's hull bottom

cathead: The overhanging beam at a ship's bow, to support a raised anchor

"C'est la guerre": [say • lah • gehr], "This is war"; Fr.

chain shot: The dismantling ammunition for cannons consisting of two cannonballs attached by a chain or linked bar used against rigging and sails

chase gun: A cannon located in the bow or stern for attacking ships ahead or behind

château: [shah-toh ́], A fortress, castle, or stately building such as a manor; Fr.

chevalier: [sheh-vahl-yay ́], A knighted person; Fr.

chivaree: [sheh-vah-ree ́], A surprise celebration of friends or neighbors on a couple's wedding night or day

cocking cart: A small two-wheeled carriage pulled by one to three horses usually with one seat for two to three people

colors: The ship's flags, pennants, and ensigns

corvette: A warship smaller than a frigate with one deck of guns

course: The lowest sail on a mast

crank: When a ship tends to roll easily

crosstree: The horizontal timbers at the top of a mast to support the top, higher mast, lines, and shrouds

Crozon Peninsula: [krow´-zohn], The southern peninsula between the Road of Brest and the Atlantic; Fr.

cutter: A small single-masted, square-rigged ship with a spanker sail

denier: [deh´-nyee], A French coin approximately 1/240 the value of a livre; Fr.

"Deux ancres sont bons au navire": [dew • zahn´-krehs • sohn • bohn´ • oh • neh-vehr´], "Two anchors are better for a ship"; Fr.

draft: The water depth needed to float a vessel

écu: [eh´-kyew], A French silver coin worth 3 French livres; Fr.

en flute: [ohn-flyewt´], To be armed with a reduced number of cannons; Fr.

enseigne de vaisseau: [ahn-sayn´ • deh • vay-soh´], A lieutenant; Fr.

ensign: The main flag on a ship indicating nationality

fieldpiece: A portable cannon mounted on large wheels

fish: A temporary repair using long staves lashed in place

footings: A wedge-shaped wood supporting the mast base on a deck

fore: Toward or at the front

fore-and-aft ship: A ship with sails running lengthwise to the hull

forecastle: [fohk´-sahl], The raised fore-deck at the bow of a ship.

foremast: The mast nearest the bow of a ship on a ship having numerous masts

forestay: A line or cable from the bow supporting the foremast

Fort *Beausejour:* [boh´-zeh-zhyoor], A small French fortification along the Missaguash River in northern Acadia; Fr.

Fort *Duquesne:* [dew-kayn´], A French fort near present-day Pittsburgh in the Ohio River Valley; Fr.

Fort *Gaspereau:* [geh´-speh-row], A small French fortification east of Fort Beausejour in northern Acadia (current day Nova Scotia); Fr.

founder: To fill with water and sink

frame: The "rib" of a ship holding the hull planks

freeboard: The sides of a vessel above the waterline; also height above a ship's waterline

frigate: A smaller warship built with one full gun deck

Garde de la Marine: [gahrd • duh • lah • mar-in´], A naval academy or its cadet; Fr.

gig: A small ship's boat, usually reserved for use by the ship's captain

go to hull: To furl the sails and bring the ship to a standstill

Goulet: [goo-lay´], The channel between the Atlantic Ocean and Road of Brest; Fr.

grapeshot: The packaged small iron balls for cannons to shoot at enemy personnel

gundeck: The deck that contains the most cannons or the highest deck that is completely covered by an above-deck

gunwale: The upper edge of the hull above the deck

hardtack: A dried, hard wheat flour biscuit

haul to: To steer toward; to turn the ship toward something

haut monde: [oh • mond´], The high society; Fr.

hawsehole: The hole in the bow of a ship through which the anchor cable or hawser passes

hawser: A thick cable holding the anchor; to moor a ship to a dock

heading: The direction a ship is pointing

heel: To roll sideways; also to keel over

helm: The ship's steering mechanism; ship's wheel

helmsman: The person steering the ship

hulk: A ship with no masts used as a prison ship, storage ship, or abandoned

hull-down: A nautical term meaning only sails and masts are visible

Île d'Aix: [eel • dehks´], A small island near Rochfort, France; Fr.

Jacobites: The restoration of the Stuart line supporters, Scottish rebels

Janissaries: The sultan's elite personal household guards.

jib: A triangular staysail on the bowsprit or mainmast running fore to aft; any triangular sail set before the foremast to the bowsprit or the bow

jibboom: A spar used to extend the bowsprit

jury rig: To make temporary repairs to a mast or rigging

keel: The main timber or "spine" running the length of a hull's bottom to which all the ship's frames or "ribs" are attached; also to heel, to roll

keelson: The timbers lying atop the keel to provide structural strength

knot: The nautical speed of 1.15 miles per hour

la Fine: [lah • feen´], A French warship meaning the *Fine One;* Fr.

l'Aigle: [lay´-gleh], A French warship meaning the *Eagle;* Fr.

l'Alcide: [lahl´-ceed], A French warship named for the Roman hero Hercules; Fr.

l'Amphion: [lahm´-fyewn] A French warship named for Zeus' son, Amphion; Fr.

la Panthére: [lah • pahn´-thehr], A French warship meaning the Panther and renamed the *Amazon* after capture; Fr.

la Proté: [lah • proh´-tee], A French warship named for the Greek sea god Proteus; Fr.

l'Aquilon: [lah´-kee-lohn], A French frigate meaning the *North Wind;* Fr.

larboard: The port side or left side of a ship while facing forward.

la Renommée: [lah • reh´-noh-may], A French frigate meaning the *Renown;* Fr.

launch: A ship's largest boat propelled by oars or sail (pre-modern era); also to put into motion on water

league: A nautical measurement equal to about 3.45 miles (5.56 kilometers)

le Blonde: [luh • blohnd´], A French warship meaning the *Blond;* Fr.

le Castor: [luh • kas´-tohr], A French frigate meaning the *Beaver;* Fr.

le Défenseur: [luh • day´-fahn-suhr´], A French warship meaning the *Defender;* Fr.

leeward: The opposite direction from where the wind is coming

le Florissant: [luh • floh-ree-sahnt´], A French warship meaning the *Flourishing;* Fr.

le Fort de Nantz: A Spanish treasure ship renamed for the fort in Nantes, France; Sp.

le Griffon: [luh • greh-fohn´], A French warship meaning the *Griffon;* Fr.

le Héro: [luh • eh-roh´], A French warship meaning the *Hero;* Fr.

Leicester: [leh´-ster], The English town in Leicestershire, Midlands; Br. Eng.

le Juste: [luh • zhew´-steh], A French warship meaning the *Righteous;* Fr.

le Lys: [luh • lees´], A French warship named for the river Lys; Fr.

le Mars: [luh • mahrs´], A French warship named for the Roman war god Mars; Fr.

l'Emeraude: [leh´-meh-rohd´], A French frigate meaning the *Emerald;* Fr.

le Royal Louis: [luh • roh-yehl´ • lewee], A French warship named for Royal Louis; Fr.

le Soleil Royal: [luh • soh-leh´ • roh-yahl´], A French warship meaning the *Royal Sun;* Fr.

l'Esperance: [leh´-speh-rahns´], A French warship meaning the *Hope;* Fr.

le Superbe: [luh • sew-pehr´-beh], A French warship meaning the *Superb;* Fr.

le Thésée: [luh • tay-zeh´], A French warship named for the Greek hero Theseus; Fr.

lieutenant de vaisseau: [lew-tehn-ahnt´ • deh • vay-soh´], A naval captain; Fr.

lignum vitae: The "tree of life" from the Bahamas used as a cure for syphilis

l'Inflexible: [lahn´-fex-eeb´-leh], A French warship meaning the *Inflexible;* Fr.

livre: [leev´-r], A currency closely equal to a pound sterling or $450 today; Fr.

longboat: A launch or longer boat with 8–10 men rowing

lubber: A landsman or inexperienced sailor

lying to: To configure the sails to keep the ship still in the water

"ma chére Comtesse": [mah • shehr • cohn´-tehs], "my dear countess"; Fr

magazine: An area or room where gunpowder is stored

mainmast: The central or tallest mast on a ship

mainsail: The first sail at the bottom of a mainmast

make fast: To tie something tightly

merchantman: A non-military ship carrying passengers or cargo

mess: A nautical term meaning an area to eat; food or meal.

messieurs: [meh-syewrs´], Gentlemen; Fr.

midship: The middle section of a ship, between fore and aft

midshipman: A commissioned officer candidate or cadet

mizzenmast (or mizzen): The stern-most mast on a ship having many masts; the third mast or a mast aft the mainmast

oakum: The tarred rope fibers used to caulk wood planks on ship seams

ordinance: To be out of service for repair, or maintenance; also, in reserve

ordinary: A reserve status for ships, or mothballed and out of use

ordinary seaman: A sailor apprenticed to become an able-bodied seaman

orlop deck: The lowest deck on a ship that has four or more decks

"Oui—la frégate est le vôtre": [whee´ • lah • free´-gaht • eh • lah • voh´-treh], "Yes—the frigate is yours"; Fr.

parral: A wooden ring that slides along a mast vertically

parry: In swordplay, to block an attack with one's sword

Penfeld River: [pin´-fehld], The major river running through Brest to the Road of Brest and the Atlantic Ocean; Fr.

pieces of eight: The old Spanish silver coins, each equivalent to $380 today

plaçage: [plah´-sazh], An extralegal or common-law marriage between a European man and a Native American, African, or Creole woman; Fr.

plaçée: [plah-see´] A woman married by plaçage but not legally recognized as a wife; Fr.

point: A ship's course in relation to movement, wind, or compass

poop deck: The highest deck at the stern of large sail ships above the quarterdeck

port (or portside): The left side of a ship (also larboard) when facing the bow; direction to the left of a ship

powder monkeys: Young boys who carried powder canisters to the guns and did other jobs aboard ship

pressed: To force into naval service

preventer chains: The heavy chains attaching the rudder to the stern of a ship

privateer: A civilian ship granted by a country to prey on enemy ships

prize: A captured enemy ship, its cargo, and crew

prow: The portion of the bow of a ship above the waterline and most in front

purser: [puhr´-ser], A commissioned financial and supplies manager aboard a ship

quarterdeck: The raised deck behind the mainmast at the stern where officers command

quarter gallery: The enclosed balconies on a ship's stern corners for officers

Quimper: [kehm-pehr´], A town in southern Brittany, France; Fr.

ratlines: The rope rungs between the shrouds used as ladders in climbing the masts

Raz de Sein: [rah´ • duh • sah´], A sea passageway to Brest; Fr.

reaching: To sail across the wind's direction between 60–160°

Recouvrance: [ruh´-kew-vrahns´], A section of Brest; Fr.

Royal Écossois: [roy-ehl´ • eh´-kew-swah], expatriated Scottish troops in France; Fr.

redoubt: An entrenched or temporary fortification

reef: To shorten a sail or the strips used to do it; also shallow rocks or coral

renommée: [reh´-noh-may], Fame or renown; Fr.

rigging: The system of masts, spars, lines, and cables, to support sails

riposte: [ree´-post], In swordplay, a counter-attack after a parry; Fr.

running: To sail with the wind at more than 160° or directly away

Saint-Domingue: [sahn´ • doh-mahn´-geh], A French colony and port in the West Indies (present-day Santo Domingo, Dominican Republic); Fr.

scantling: The dimensions of the timbers used in a ship

scarf: The staggered cut used in joining timbers in ship construction

scupper: A hole in the hull to drain water off a ship's deck scuttle: A barrel of fresh water; or to purposely sink your ship

scuttlebutt: Rumors

seigneur: [sayn-yewr´], The landowner of a royal land grant; Fr.

ship of the line: The largest naval warships with two or more decks of guns

short-haul: To shorten by pulling; also, the shortest distance allowed

shroud: The heavy ropes or cables used to hold up the masts and attached to the sides of the ship

sloop: A smaller ship with one mast

snow: A ship with two masts, square-rigged, and with a spanker

sou: [sew´], A French copper coin worth 1/20th the value of a livre; Fr.

spanker: A fore-to-aft sail attached to a spar with an end attached to the rear-most mast

spar: The long wood timber used to hold sails or rigging

spontoon: A short pike carried by and indicating an officer's or sergeant's rank

square-rigged: A mast rigged with sails perpendicular to the ship's length

starboard: The right side of a ship when facing the bow; the right side direction

stay: A rope or cable used to hold up a mast or spar permanently

staysail: A sail attached to a stay and running fore to aft

stern: The rear or aft part of a ship

storeship: A ship used to store supplies or goods

strike: To haul down the flag; to surrender by taking down the flag

stunsails: The smaller extra sails attached to spar ends

tack: To turn the ship windward in a zigzag pattern to advance against the wind

taffrail: The stern rail of a ship or boat; the carved panel above the galleries at the stern tender: A smaller vessel for transporting people or supplies to a ship

topgallant: The mast or sails above the topsail or topmast

topgallant sail: The sail attached to the topgallant mast that is higher than the topmast

topman: A crew member working in the tops or tending sails aloft

topmast: The second mast section above the deck

tops: The upper parts of a ship's masts

topsail: The second sail up a mast

topsail ship: A ship with a topsail mast, usually a larger ship

treenail: [treh´-nahl], A long wooden peg about 11/2 to 2 inches in diameter, used to attach planks and to join timbers

two-decker: A warship with two complete decks of cannons

van: The forward part, head, or vanguard of a fleet of ships

Versailles: [vehr-sahy´], The royal château outside of Paris, France; Fr.

waist: The middle section of a ship

wear: To turn a ship by moving its head away from the wind

weather side: The side facing the wind

weigh: To raise the anchor

yard: A spar hung from a mast to hold the sail

About the Author

D.E. Stockman

D. E. Stockman served in the military and upon college graduation he turned to the graphic arts. His profession carried him from publication printing of periodicals such as *National Geographic* and *Playboy* magazines, to book illustration and cover design for the imprints of Simon & Schuster, Harcourt Brace & Co., and Pearson Education. After writing articles for an e-magazine and trade journals, he began his series of historical novels. David currently lives in the Chicago suburbs with his wife Valerie.

His award-winning three-book series, *Tween Sea and Shore,* originally released by FireShip Press and republished by Penmore Press, follows the adventures of noted historical and fictional characters linked to a frigate, *la Renommée.* The French ship's story, researched by the author for over a decade, uncovered remarkable connections among people in the mid-1700s. David unveiled their story beginning with his debut novel, *The Ship's Carpenter,* which continues in his second book, *Captains of the Renown,* and in the third, *Waves of Glory.*

IF YOU ENJOYED THIS BOOK

Please write a review.
This is important to the author and helps to get the word out
to others
Visit

PENMORE PRESS
www.penmorepress.com

All Penmore Press books are available directly through our website, amazon.com, Barnes and Noble and Nook, Sony Reader, Apple iTunes, Kobo books and via leading bookshops across the United States, Canada, the UK, Australia and Europe.

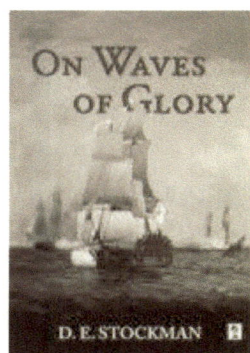

On Waves of Glory

By

D. E. Stockman

On Waves of Glory places the reader beside Count Guy de Kersaint, one of France's greatest ship commanders during the mid-1700s, as he pursues a courtship with Marie on shore and learns the mariners' lore at sea. Clashing in sea battles, surviving Chickasaw raids, and rescuing Barbary Coast slaves portray just a few of the dramatic exploits in his adventurous life. Guy strives for elusive fame and an unrequited love...which will destiny grant?This is the third book of the award-winning Tween Sea & Shore Series. All are based on historical records of those "iron men" who sailed the fastest frigate of its day, la Renommée—the Renown.

PENMORE PRESS
www.penmorepress.com

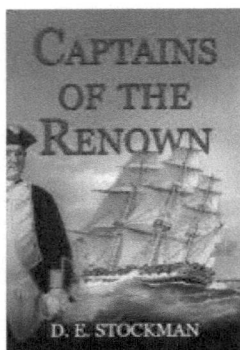

CAPTAINS OF THE RENOWN

BY

DAVID E STOCKMAN

"*Captains of the Renown* intricately weaves history with gripping drama—piercing the veil of history to affect the modern reader...Stockman bulds the tension so expertly I had to flip a few pages ahead to diffuse my anxiety...I can assure any lover of the genre—you will find this an informative and gripping read. I recommend you pick up a copy."—Ryan Armstrong, USA Today Bestselling Author

The Seven Years War rages and the British frigate *Renown* returns to sea and the many lives she's ferried turn upside down in this second book of the award-winning series. Abraham, an English shipwright, and his wife Yvette confront childlessness and poverty in mid-1700s London until help comes from his old friend, Captain Shirley. Unspeakable acts change Shirley's life and transform Abraham, at a dear cost.

PENMORE PRESS
www.penmorepress.com

Brewer's Private War

By

James Keffer

A chance meeting in a tavern on Martinique brings a man from Brewer's past back into his life. Brewer discovers this man - a mentor of his when he was a raw midshipman - has turned to piracy, and Brewer is determined to track him down and end his reign of terror over British shipping in the Caribbean. Captain Brewer soon discovers that still waters run deep when he is kidnapped by his former mentor and warned to stop while he still can. With the help of the US Navy, Brewer finds his quarry in the Bahamas, only to chase him to Washington City and find himself staring down the wrong end of a pirate's pistol!

PENMORE PRESS
www.penmorepress.com

Penmore Press

Challenging, Intriguing, Adventurous, Historical and Imaginative

www.penmorepress.com

Printed by Libri Plureos GmbH in Hamburg,
Germany